DARK HARVEST
Arlington Hts., Illinois · 1991

Night Visions

9

Introduction by F. Paul Wilson

· all original stories by ·

Thomas Tessier

James Kisner

Rick Hautala

illustrated by

Phil Parks

Table of Contents

The publishers would like to express their gratitude to the following people. Thank you: Ann Cameron Mikol, Kathy Jo Camacho, Stan and Phyllis Mikol, Dr. Stan Gurnick PhD, Raymond, Teresa and Mark Stadalsky, Greg Manchess, Tony Hodes, Tom Pas; and to the world's greatest "therapists": Ron Gutman, Dave Hopkins, Tom Carter, Matt Goetz, Dan Murphy, Mitch Haubert, Kathy Zundell, Cheryl McCarty, and Laura Scaglione.

And, of course, special thanks go to the most important people to this book. Without them NIGHT VISIONS 9 would not exist; Thomas Tessier, James Kisner, Rick Hautala, F. Paul Wilson, and Phil Parks.

Introduction

Horror is dead.

Or if not dead, at the very least moribund and teetering on the edge of forever.

Or so we're told. We hear it from some editors, some publishers, and even some book sellers. We hear it from fanzine and prozine columnists and pundits, from self-proclaimed experts on the entire scope of publishing.

Horror is dead.

Sorry, no. Horror, like rock and roll, will never die. (Wait . . . maybe that's not such a good analogy. Judging by what's coming out of my radio speakers these days, rock may be deeper into a coma than horror fiction.)

No, not dead. But horror has been having some serious health problems lately, most of them related to its rapid (rapid, hell— *phenomenal*) growth during the 1980s. The problems have been mostly logistical.

Logistics. That's a military term most of us heard *ad nauseam* during Operation Desert Storm. It refers to procuring, maintaining, and transporting material, personnel, and facilities. In a nutshell: making sure the frontlines don't run out of the supplies they need to keep on fighting.

This is what Hussein couldn't do in Kuwait and southern Iraq.

11

This is what the publishers couldn't do in the bookstores in regard to the horror genre.

Horror got too big, too fast.

Think about it. In the Fifties, who was writing horror? Matheson, Bloch, and Wheatley, and that was about it. In the Sixties—Matheson, Bloch, and Wheatley, plus that bestseller by Ira Levin. The Seventies were launched with THE EXORCIST, followed by the movie, followed in mid-decade by somebody named King. In those three decades you could read everything—new and reprint—that was published in horror. *Everything.* I know. I did it. It got a little hairy by the end of the late Seventies with all those gerund titles, but I managed.

By the Eighties we were off to the races. I had to give up my omnivorish ways and become more selective.

And there's the rub. As I was becoming more restrictive in my choices (due to constraints on my reading time), the mass reading public was getting into the horror groove in a big way. And Stephen King's novel a year in those days was only whetting their appetites. More, more, more. Give us more. And when publishers see a demand, they rush to satisfy it. Nothing wrong with that. That's what a free market is all about: You want it? I'll see if I can get it for you.

Publishers started horror lines, horror imprints with neato horror logos. The market was booming, everything was selling like crazy. Trouble was, there wasn't enough good horror fiction to meet the demand. Publishers projected three horror slots a month—lead, middle, bottom. And when they didn't have the inventory to fill them, they went hunting. Hang around the bar at some of the more writer-intensive conventions and you'll hear some amazing stories: Writers getting calls from editors saying, "I've got this horror slot in April and it's gonna go begging if I can't find something to fill it. Can you get me a seventy-thousand-word giant-bug/evil-child/haunted-house/disturbed-burial-mound/vampire novel by the end of next week?"

Not a few damn fine writers took those offers. Why not? If they didn't fill the slot, somebody else would. The money might as well be in their pocket as in somebody's else's. And what the hell, they weren't going to use their own name anyway.

And that's okay. There are bills to pay and the bank doesn't care if the mortgage payment originated in royalties from a thousand-page treatise on the significance of porridge in the works of Charles Dickens

INTRODUCTION

or from *The Jellyfish That Plopped on San Diego.*
The important thing here is the publishing/editorial mind-set that was operating.

Filling slots.

That's not the way to develop a loyal audience.

Yes, I know all the arguments about the realities of modern bookselling, how the chain-store tail is wagging the publishing dog. Keep talking. The polls are closed and the results are in: too many second- and third-rate horror novels were shoved into the racks to fill the slots in the programs; those novels, a number of which should never have been published, were packaged to look like every other novel that had achieved a modicum of success in the preceding few months. The horror-fiction racks became a choice between Tweedledum and Tweedledummer. The readers get fed up with cloned covers outside and cloned fiction inside.

Horror fiction became fast food. Some of the publishers should have had golden arches over their doors. Predictably, the readers became tired of the assembly-line product. Cries of "Where's the beef?" arose. But even when the publishers managed to acquire some of the filet mignon we all know is out there, they plopped it into their regular hamburger boxes, dooming it to molder on the shelves.

Their logistics failed: they weren't getting the right stuff to the right people.

Boom became bust.

Which brings us to the NIGHT VISIONS series.

NIGHT VISIONS doesn't follow a schedule, doesn't worry about filling a slot. This is the ninth volume since 1984. The process is simple. Take two well-known writers and another talented but not-quite-as-well-known writer and turn them loose. Thirty-thousand words each, no holds barred.

If the purpose of horror fiction is to disturb and unsettle, then Thomas Tessier is certainly one of the all-time masters. I know of six novels he's done. There may be others. The ones I've read have been profoundly disturbing. His novella here, "The Dreams of Dr. Ladybank," is no exception. It probably should be labeled with one of those *Warning: Contains explicit scenes of sex and violence* stickers. And it is indeed disturbing—so deeply disturbing in some scenes that you are tempted to laugh to keep from screaming. (*Not* a happy sound.) His three characters, drawn from both extremes of the socioeconomic strata, are all sociopaths in one manner or another. As you breeze

13

through his effortless prose you will come to loathe the upper-echeloner, a professional man of education, taste, and means; a natural response to the ultimate user: a very unique sort of psychic vampire. You will find your sympathies falling resolutely in step with the two low-lifes. Each is a hustler and a ne'er-do-well and a user in his own way, caring nothing for his fellow man, possessing nothing of value to offer human society. This is no little accomplishment for an author. Tessier makes it look easy. In less skillful hands the result easily might have been disastrous.

But Tessier is working on a deeper level here, exploring what is perhaps the ultimate horror—loss of control over your actions, your decisions, your everyday life. No matter who you are, you have a right to your own life. This is something so fundamental that we often take it for granted. And I believe it is at the heart of our fascination with the vampire. The vampire's victims find that not only have their lives been stolen, but of their deaths as well. They walk the night eternally, ruthlessly sating an appetite they'd find repugnant in life. The two low-lifes in "Dr. Ladybank" do not rise from the dead, but they do have control of their lives siphoned away from them.

You will not soon forget this story.

James M. Kisner plays in another key entirely. Many keys, in fact. He can be grim, he can be touching, he can put you on with tongue firmly in cheek. After reading his five short contributions here, one can almost envision him sitting by a campfire, grinning wickedly and rubbing his hands together as he dreams up new tales to elicit laughter and raised hackles from his listeners.

Kisner is not as well known as Tessier or Hautala, but that's destined to change soon. He's not a new kid. He's the author of nine novels, has regular columns in *Mystery Scene* and *Pulphouse* magazines, has had stories in SCARE CARE, STALKERS, HOTTER BLOOD, PHANTOMS, a number of the MASQUES anthologies, and many more, and has even taken up comic book scripting for titles like LEATHERFACE. His current novel is THE QUAGMIRE. He's due for overnight world recognition any day now.

Kisner is a good choice to hold up the middle of this volume. Makes me think back to my involvement in NIGHT VISIONS 6. Paul Mikol called early in 1987 and said he wanted Sherri Tepper and me for that particular number. Did I know of a relative newcomer I could recommend that I'd be comfortable sharing the volume with? A name immediately came to mind. I'd read his first three novels and knew

INTRODUCTION

he had something.

I said, "Ray Garton."

Paul said, "Who?"

"His latest novel is LIVE GIRLS," I said. "Pick it up and see if you want to publish him."

Paul called back a week later and said, "We've got to get this Garton guy. How do I get ahold of him?"

Well, finding Ray is a whole other story. But the point is, you've got to have a certain something to get into NIGHT VISIONS. They don't take just anybody. They're interested in quality. I didn't have to sell Ray to Paul. Ray, pretty much an unknown then (his first publisher, Pinnacle, was going down the tubes just as he was getting up to speed), sold himself with his work. He's anything but an unknown now.

The same with James Kisner. You may not know his name now, may not have read anything by him before, but I have a feeling these stories will whet your appetite for more. The man is a born storyteller.

Finally we come to Rick Hautala who likes to refer to himself as That Other Writer From Maine or That Other Writer Who Answers to "Rick", but he's overly modest. As the bestselling author of NIGHTSTONE—over a million-and-a-half copies in print at last count—and many other popular novels, he's about as close as you can get to a household name with a name no one can pronounce. Hautala apparently couldn't decide between writing a number of short stories or a single novella, so he chose the middle path. What we've got here is a series of four interconnected stories bridged by folk tales, all coalescing into a sequel of sorts to his novel, LITTLE BROTHERS.

Quite frankly, "Untcigahunk" is a delight. I don't know anything about Micmac folklore, but if the Little Brothers aren't a part of it, they should be. And the three bridging folk tales, with their touching descriptions of the Old One and the creation of man and the Little Brothers, give Hautala's contribution a spiritual scope, a sense of breadth and depth too rare in horror fiction—hell, in *all* fiction— these days.

NIGHT VISIONS 9 is proof that horror isn't dead. It's only taking a breather, recharging its batteries. It will be back full strength before you know it. Meanwhile, it's alive and well in the following pages.

F. Paul Wilson
April, 1991

15

Thomas
Tessier

A Divine Image

Cruelty has a Human Heart
And Jealousy a Human Face
Terror, the Human Form Divine
And Secrecy, the Human Dress

The Human Dress, is forged Iron
The Human Form, a fiery Forge.
The Human Face, a Furnace seal'd
The Human Heart, its hungry Gorge.

—William Blake

PROLOGUE

"It's an amusing thought, Ian, but . . ."

"Impossible."

"Well, yes."

"Science fiction."

"And weak on the science," Jack said.

"But doesn't the idea itself excite you?"

"Not really. I mean, what's the point? Everyone knows it's a dead end. Besides, even if it were possible, and I'm not for a moment admitting that it is, but if it were, you'd probably wind up with a raving psychotic on your hands, and that's not my idea of fun. Psychotics are very boring people."

"Psychosis is by no means inevitable."

"This is a splendid malt, by the way."

"Help yourself to more."

"Thanks, I will."

"The point you're refusing to acknowledge is the simple fact of communication, establishing once and for all that it really is possible. My God, Jack, that's a huge leap and you know it. You can't deny it."

"And you can't prove it."

"Perhaps I can."

"Well, I'd love to see it."

"What would you say if I told you I've found a suitable mind for the experiment?"

"I'd say she's probably young, impressionable, quite pretty, very malleable, and a great piece of ass."

"Jack."

"But I'm afraid that your getting her in bed and fucking her brains out will not be widely accepted as scientific proof."

"All right, I give up."

"Ah, don't stop now, Ian. I'm enjoying this. I haven't had such a good mix of booze and bullshit since college, when we used to sit up late at night, trying to figure out what the hell an ethic was, and how to get around it. We called those sessions the Utica Club, because that's all we could afford to drink."

20

"But I'm serious."

"Okay, you're serious, and you've got this, uh . . ."

"Subject."

"Right, subject."

"Two of them, actually," Ian said with a hint of smugness in his tight smile. "Two young men."

"Men, huh? You must be serious."

"Yes, and the fact that there are two of them should provide proof enough to justify continuing the research, don't you think? One might be a fluke, but two different people, who are strangers to each other, who respond and meet and interact *by design*—you would take that seriously, wouldn't you?"

"Sure, but come on, Ian. You can't do that with people. If you could, somebody would have discovered it by now. It's not as if we're completely ignorant of how the brain works. What it can and can't do—and I'll tell you one thing, it can't do that."

"The human brain does generate extremely low frequency radio waves, ELF signals. That's a well-known fact."

"Yes, but you can't do anything with them."

"If you say so."

"Not like you're talking about."

"We'll see."

"So, are these guys patients of yours?"

"No, they're just a couple of losers I met."

"And they agreed to go along with whatever it is you plan to try out on them, this experiment?"

"They don't know anything about it."

"What?"

"That would ruin everything, Jack. If they knew, they would expect, and expectation would contaminate their minds. Of course I haven't told them anything."

"Uh, have *you* ever heard of ethics, Ian?"

"Which one did you have in mind?"

"Oh, the one about not experimenting on people without their knowledge and consent. Seems to me there might even be some kind of a law about that."

"Tsk, tsk."

"What exactly is it you intend to do?"

"Nothing. That's the beauty of it."

"I don't understand."

21

"I'll just be thinking, Jack. That's all. Thinking of them and perhaps even for them."

"Ah, that's all right. Thinking isn't against the law, not yet anyway. But how will you know if it works?"

"I'm not sure, but I imagine it will become apparent one way or another."

"Well, if it does work, let me handle the legal side of it. Maybe we can sell it to Sony, ha-ha."

"That's a thought."

"I can see it now. Everybody will go around wearing a smart little beanie on their head, with an antenna sticking up. They'd sell like Walkmans — or should it be Walk*men*?"

By the time Jack finally left, after sopping up a good deal more single malt scotch, Doctor Ian Ladybank was almost sorry he had mentioned his little secret. But he had to tell someone, and Jack was the closest thing to a friend he had. You can't stumble across something like that and then not want to shout about it.

Nor was it really a little secret; it was serious, major, an awesome challenge. He was sure it had in fact been discovered by others, in the past, although they might not have understood what it was the way he did. It was a skill, it had limits, and it was suitable only for personal purposes.

Amazing, how it had happened. Doctor Ladybank had given the matter a lot of thought over the years. The brain was his hobby, as well as his vocation. He read everything that came out and he even made a special study of radio science. His obsession wasn't his alone — there were other people active in the field. He was aware, for instance, of the theory that some UFO sightings may be triggered by localized disturbances in the earth's magnetic field that interfered with the wave cycles in the observer's brain. It was a matter of some significance to Doctor Ladybank — although few others seemed to consider it important — that the earth, the planet itself, was constantly broadcasting its own ELF waves, and that they were remarkably similar to those generated by the human brain. He devised his own mental exercises, instructing his mind to do what it had never done before.

All of this led nowhere until a young woman named Shelly had come to see him, not long ago. She thought she was stigmatic and she had the wounds to prove it. Her case was not as interesting as it had seemed at first glance but she was an attractive little creature. In his waiting room, as he was showing her out, Doctor Ladybank

22

suddenly found himself wishing, or willing, that Shelly would reach up and touch her breast. A silly but typical erotic fancy, borne no doubt of mid-afternoon tedium. The girl did not respond, but her boyfriend, who had accompanied her to the office and was standing nearby, absently rubbed his Megadeath T-shirt at the spot where it covered his left nipple. The young man's blank expression indicated complete ignorance.

Stunned, Doctor Ladybank at first could not bring himself to believe what had apparently just taken place. It was too easy to be true. But yes, he had felt a tiny mental spasm at the instant the thought—wish, command, whatever—formed within his mind. Doctor Ladybank was flushed with a sense of accomplishment, happy as a boy who suddenly flicks his wrist in precisely the right way and at last manages to skip a rock across water.

He stood by the window in his office a few minutes later and watched Shelly and her boyfriend walk away down the street. When they were almost out of sight, Doctor Ladybank had a parting idea for them—and sure enough, the boyfriend's hand swung around to pat Shelly's ass. That evening Doctor Ladybank thought about the boyfriend again. *You need to talk to me. Urgently.* Less than a minute later, the telephone rang. He was Alvin Doolittle, but he preferred the nickname Snake.

The other one was sent to Doctor Ladybank, like many of his cases, by the juvenile court. Tony Delgado was only sixteen, but he had his own apartment, a trick pad near the river in the south end of the city. It was a decrepit neighborhood, full of rotting old tenements and abandoned factories, a tidal basin of foundered lives, but it provided all the tolerance and anonymity needed for Tony to practice his trade.

Doctor Ladybank quickly sized the boy up as innately Machian in affect. What Tony possessed was not quite a mind, but more of a constantly shifting panorama of received images and sensations. He learned little but survived, thanks to an underlying canniness that for nearly three years had helped him dodge both the law and the retribution of the streets. A minor stupidity had led him to juvenile court, which promply fobbed him off on Doctor Ladybank, who within a quarter of an hour had the youth uttering numbers in German while tugging at his earlobes.

It was a discovery that should be important. It should give Doctor Ladybank power, fame, wealth—all the usual prizes. The only trouble

23

was, he didn't know how to take the next step. What to do with this fantastic skill. How could he present it in such a way that would satisfy the scientific community? He could make videotapes of sessions with Snake and Tony, inducing all kinds of bizarre and unlikely behavior, but that would prove nothing. Not the least of Doctor Ladybank's problems was the painful fact that this skill of his simply didn't work with most people. He tried it with everyone he met now, but the original poor fools were the only two in the plus column. In spite of the odds against it, he was dogged by a fear that both of them really were flukes. Maybe it was just a freak of nature, devoid of any principle or broader application. But even if that were so, there was still a measure of personal satisfaction in what he was doing.

And it was early days yet. Doctor Ladybank was sure that he would learn much more as he pursued his experiment, and sooner or later the ultimate answers would come to him.

− 1 −

Tony Delgado thought he understood the problem. This Pied Piper, to give him a name, had a special kind of radio that he used to beam his infernal messages into Tony's brain. It had been going on for a couple of weeks now, and the situation was only getting worse. Tony had tried to catch the Pied Piper several times before he realized that it was impossible. The Pied Piper was only about six inches tall, and could appear or disappear at will. Many times he was heard, not seen. There was no way Tony could get a hold of the little demon.

Tony was running out of possibilities. He had gone to Dom's Connection, the largest electronics store in the city, but they told him they didn't have any kind of jamming device that would do what he wanted. They suggested that he consider buying a good radio or stereo system, and just play loud music whenever he was bothered. But Tony had already tried that with the boombox he owned, and it didn't work. Static-ridden, distorted perhaps, the Pied Piper still got into Tony's head.

THE DREAMS OF DR. LADYBANK

Now Tony had another idea. He rooted through the underwear in the top drawer of his bureau, and came up with the stiletto he had acquired somewhere along the line. It was his best weapon in the awkward moments that occasionally arose, not so much for use as for display. In Tony's chosen line of work it was sometimes necessary to introduce a deterrent factor, that slight touch of intimidation that prevents serious trouble, and the stiletto had never failed to chill a tricky customer. He was pleased to find that it hadn't lost any of its sharpness, though for the task he had in mind now all he would require was the very fine tip of the gleaming blade.

Tony Delgado lived in a small apartment in the heart of the south end. He was sixteen, and had been on his own for the best part of a year now. He had a perfect body, which he took care of religiously because it was his bread and butter. At five-ten, he was neither too tall nor too short. His physique was slender and boyish, and he avoided the muscular look, but he exercised enough to maintain a body texture that was both supple and firm.

He had one good room, the large one where he entertained his customers. Tony had invested a lot in that room, setting it up for the fantasy scenarios that were his trademark. He sometimes had to discourage mushy johns who wanted to use his personal bed or to stay all night. He preferred it that way, keeping the rest of his place, and life, off-limits. Tony's bedroom was small and cluttered, the kitchen bug-infested. The bathroom was modest but clean, and one way or another it saw a lot of use.

The trouble started more than a month ago. Tony had always been successful at avoiding the police until then. He had picked up a john at a bar in the neighborhood, but when they got outside the asshole lost his nerve. A patrol car happened to pass by as Tony was kicking in the rocker panel on the man's shiny new car. It should have come to nothing. The asshole naturally refused to press charges. However, Tony then made the unfortunate mistake of giving the cop a hard time, even shoving him away once. Since he was still a minor, Tony was sent to juvenile court, where some drip of a judge gave him a boring lecture and then ordered him to see a psychiatrist.

What a joke that turned out to be. For one thing, the guy had a funny name, Lady-something. Ladybug would be right, Tony thought, because the shrink was the crazy one. He was straight, and even beautiful, but as the interview went on Tony began to feel like he was stuck with a creep. It was no one thing the guy did that bothered him, just a very uncomfortable feeling that got stronger all the time. Tony had never experienced anything like that, and he had met some strange people.

In the end, the shrink talked pure nonsense. He told Tony to watch out for the bright lights, bright colors, and, most of all, bright flowers. What kind of shit was that? Tony decided Doctor Ladybug was in bigger trouble than he was, and he nodded his head politely, agreeing with everything the shrink said.

It must have been the smart thing to do, because he was sent home to his mother, no additional sessions required. He was free of any legal obligations. Tony was back at work in his apartment that same night.

Tony's mother understood nothing. For thirty years she had worked at a dry-cleaning shop, and still did. Some people argued that the fumes were dangerous, and Mrs. Delgado did get headaches regularly, but it was steady work and there was a lot to be said for seniority.

She believed anything Tony told her. He was her youngest child, born when she thought her body was past all that. And he was the best when it came to calling her, visiting and giving her little gifts. So kind and considerate. She didn't like the fact that he lived away from her when he was still so young, but there was nothing she could do about it. Kids grow up quicker today, they do what they want, and Tony didn't have a father around to lay down the law. But at least the boy was good to her, and he lived less than a mile away.

So his first brush with the law had come to nothing, and his mother still lived in happy ignorance of his activities, but Tony faced other problems. AIDS had claimed or scared off some of his top customers, and to keep his income up he was forced to cruise the bars more often. That multiplied both his legal and medical risks. So far he remained clean, but business was tough, and getting tougher every week.

He had also developed a taste for coke. The good stuff, not that crack shit. But it cost money, and Tony was also convinced that it was one of the reasons he was so jumpy of late. However, these drawbacks were not enough to curb his appetite. They were simply new factors to bear in mind.

Worst of all, the Pied Piper had entered his life. At first Tony thought he was imagining things, or that it was some kind of weird side-effect of the drug. He would glimpse a trick of light or a play of shadows, but it was always on the other side of the room, and he

THE DREAMS OF DR. LADYBANK

always caught it out of the corner of his eye. When he turned to look carefully, there was nothing to see.

Then there were the sounds. Tony began to think of them as messages of some kind, though he never really understood them at all. They were like bubbles of noise that burst open deep inside his head. There was always a lot of static with it, which is how Tony finally cottoned on to the possibility that the Pied Piper was broadcasting to him. It was possible to pick out a few words now and then, sometimes a phrase or two, but none of it ever made any sense. Tony did get a certain feeling of urgency, and that only aggravated his distress.

Soon enough, the little man emerged tauntingly, letting Tony see him clearly—if only for a brief instant at a time. Now, a day never passed without one appearance, usually more. He never actually said anything, and his expression was always blank. The little fucker was a constant torment, even when he wasn't there. The only positive thing was that so far he hadn't turned up when there was a customer present.

Tony went into the bathroom and turned on the light around the mirror. He stood close to it, opened his mouth and found his targets. Tony's teeth were not perfect. Over the years he had accumulated a few plastic or composite fillings. They were okay, he figured. He wanted the two larger ones that were made of lead or silver, some kind of metal. It seemed obvious to him that the Pied Piper was using those fillings as built-in receivers for his transmissions. The metal picked up the beam and relayed it along the nerves in Tony's jawbone on to the center of his brain. So, if he could just get rid of those two fillings he might solve his problem. He had called three different dentists, but they seemed to think it was a set-up for a lawsuit, and turned him down cold. The only alternative was to do it himself.

It wasn't easy. At least he could get at the two fillings and still see what he was doing, but for the longest time the tip of the blade found no hold. Tony grew frustrated, then angry as the knife slipped off the tooth and jabbed his gums. He tasted a little of his own blood when he swallowed. His open mouth filled with saliva too fast, and some of it trickled down his windpipe, setting off a violent but useless coughing jag. Tony's eyes were bleary as he tried to refocus on the tooth. He was beginning to think it was an impossible chore, but then the point of the blade finally lodged in some tiny crevice for a second. It slipped off almost at once, but he was encouraged, and several tries later he found the spot again. Tony worked it carefully, digging the

27

tip into the gap and trying to expand it. As long as the metal blade touched the metal filling it jangled the nerves in his tooth like a constant electrical charge, but he would endure that to get rid of the Pied Piper. Any pain would be worth suffering if it would end the daily nightmare visitations.

Tony's eyes continued to blur with tears and his jaw ached, but he was making progress. Now he had gouged enough of a crack to be able to use the knife as a lever. But whenever he relaxed or became careless, the knife would pop loose again and stab Tony in the gum or on the roof of the mouth. The saliva that spilled out on his chin was distinctly pink. Worst of all, the goddamn metal filling seemed to be welded to the goddamn tooth. No matter how hard he pried at it, there was barely any movement.

"Come on, you fuck," Tony whined. "You're killing me."

Then he screamed and dropped the knife as he reached for the wall to hold himself against as a blast of pain shot through his entire body. The knife clattered in the sink. This is too much, he thought as he reached for it with trembling fingers. But then he discovered that the filling was loose. Yeah, he could move it with his tongue. It was still hooked in there, but when he poked it repeatedly it felt like it was rattling in place. Gasping for breath, Tony forced himself to re-insert the knife.

"*Ein, zwei, drei . . .*"

He increased the pressure, and the pain blossomed, weakening him so much that all the strength in his body seemed to be flying out of his pores. One last shove—the filling was at last torn free, but the knife blade scraped a bloody furrow across the roof of Tony's mouth at the same time. He nearly swallowed the jagged filling but managed to spit it into the sink. It bounced around like a deformed marble before coming to rest. Tony was dizzy and drained, and the hole in his tooth felt enormous, but he had done it. One down, one to go. He washed his mouth out, and then sat on the toilet lid for a few minutes to rest.

The second filling seemed to take longer, probably because he had little patience left. His arms and neck ached, along with his jaw, but somehow the pain bothered him less. Tony pushed on, desperate to finish the job, and eventually he was rewarded when the second filling slid off his tongue and joined the first one in the sink. He felt an enormous sense of satisfaction, freedom and accomplishment. He took the two lumps of twisted metal into the kitchen, opened the window, and threw them as far as he could out in the weed-choked, trash-strewn backyard.

Tony rinsed his mouth again, this time with warm salty water to stop the bleeding. Then he poured a large scotch, to remove the bad taste and soothe his nerves. He sat down in his one good room and sipped the drink carefully. God, he was still shaking. His arms and legs felt so weak. He let his tongue dance over the two holes in his teeth. They were huge. The edges were so sharp he would have to be careful not to cut his tongue on them.

But no dentist could refuse him now. Two fillings fell out when he was eating. Tough pizza crust, say. Or peanuts, or when he bit into a steak. It didn't matter what. That kind of thing happened all the time. Tony would insist they be replaced with plastic or porcelain fillings, anything but metal.

He smiled faintly as he sloshed the whiskey around in his mouth. It stung his exposed nerves, but he knew that it was also beginning to deaden them. The pain was fading deliciously.

Zzzzt.

Oh no, no.

Zzzzt.

Tony put the drink down on the table because he was afraid he might drop it. This can't be happening. He looked around the room nervously. A glimmer of movement, then gone. A shadow that passed in an instant, as if a bird had flown by the window. Then the static cleared up beautifully.

—Ah, that's much better.

The words blared inside Tony's trapped mind.

—You can really hear me now, can't you!

— 2 —

"*Hic, haec, hoc.*"

"Say what?" The bartender looked puzzled, wary. "What?"

THOMAS TESSIER

"You said something to me?"

"No," Snake replied. "I didn't say nothing to nobody."

"You want another beer?"

"Yeah, I want another beer," Snake said, his voice brimming with defiance. "And a clean glass."

The bartender brought the drink and the glass, withdrew some money from the small pile of cash in front of Snake, and muttered to himself in Spanish as he turned away. Lousy greaseball, Snake thought as he inspected the new glass. I'm sitting here, minding my own business, having a quiet beer, and this asshole has to get on my case. Say what? Say, fuck you, bro.

At least tonight Snake knew what he was doing in this place. He was waiting for the whore, Toni. Last night he had no idea at all why he had come there. The El Greco was a pisshole of a bar, buried in the unfriendly depths of the south end. But Snake went out last night, leaving Shelly behind alone and cursing, and he'd come straight across the river to this dump. He hated the place. It had the terrible smell of food you'd never want to eat, and it was full of jabbering spics. They all had the same look on their faces too, mean and vaguely pissed off, as if every damned one of them had to go through life with a splinter up his dick.

They wouldn't bother him, though, because Snake was wearing the colors. Sure, they could beat the living shit out of him if they wanted to, but they knew he'd be back sooner or later with thirty of the hardest fuckers around who would trash the El Greco, along with every spic they could get their hands on. Nor did it matter that Snake was no longer exactly in good standing as a member of the Legion of the Lost; he wore the colors, and that was all that counted in a situation like this. The colors commanded respect, or at least fear—which wasn't very different.

Last night he sat in the same place at the bar for nearly an hour, wondering what the hell he was doing there and why he could not bring himself to leave. It was odd, but then some odd things had been happening to Snake lately. Headaches, for one, the kind that ordinary painkillers didn't cure. And, according to Shelly, he was talking to himself more and more. But that was crazy. It stood to reason that a man can't go around talking to himself and not know it. Could he? What about that latest incident, the one with the bartender a few minutes ago? No, it was impossible. In a noisy place like this, the bartender made a mistake.

30

Besides, Shelly had her own problems. She'd gone quite pale and spotty in recent weeks. She also scratched herself a lot, so much so in fact that it had reached the point where she had these ugly open wounds in her hands and feet and on her body. Then, as if that weren't enough, she decided they were the marks of Christ on the Cross. Snake had to take her to the doctor, who sent them along to a shrink. Dumb fucking bitch. He ought to sell her off to an out-of-state gang, but the way she was now, her sales value was scraping along the bottom. Shelly was so bad that he didn't even want to touch her anymore—unless he had to hit her.

Maybe that was why Snake had come to the El Greco, to meet a new piece of ass. He had accomplished that much last night, when Toni sat down beside him and they got to talking. She was a fine item, all right. Cute fanny, long legs, pretty face. She could be a bit fuller up front, but Snake had never been all that keen on big tits. He liked women lean and—snaky.

It didn't bother him that she was a spic. Somehow, that was okay in a woman. Toni's creamy skin was such a pleasant contrast to Shelly's newsprint surface. And the eyes—deep, round, warm and brown, with flecks of gold. Snake couldn't remember the last time he'd looked closely at Shelly's eyes, but now he thought of them as washed-out blue peas adrift in a pinkish-white glaze. No question, Toni was an exotic gem in comparison.

It did bother him, however, that she was a whore. He didn't care how many men she fucked. The problem was that he lacked the money to buy her talents. Even if he had it, it would go against the grain for Snake to spend it on something he'd always managed to get for free.

He and Toni were eventually able to work out a deal based on non-cash considerations. She liked coke, and she needed Demerol. Snake had experience and helpful contacts in the field. He was strictly minor league, but he did know how to cut himself an edge in such transactions. It was one of the many ways in which he cobbled together an erratic income.

"Darling."

"Hey, babe." Snake smiled as Toni edged close to him at the bar. "You look great."

"Buy me a drink."

"Sure. What'll you have?"

"You forgot already. Tsk, tsk."

31

"Yeah, well . . . What was it again?"

"Red Death on the rocks."

"Right."

As there were no other barstools free, Snake gave Toni his. He signalled the bartender. Toni looked fantastic in a clinging black mini-dress. Snake could hardly take his eyes off her legs, but he did turn away long enough to watch the bartender carefully when he took the money for Toni's drink.

"You can take your sunglasses off."

"I like the dark," she replied.

"It's dark enough in this dump."

Toni sipped her drink. "Do you have something for me?"

"I told you I would."

"I know what you told me, but do you have it?"

"Of course I do."

"You're a darling. What is it?"

Snake leaned close to her. "God, you smell great."

"What do you have?" Toni repeated with an edge in her voice. "What do you have for me?"

"Demerol."

"Beautiful." Toni relaxed and smiled at him. "There is one thing I have to tell you."

"Yeah? What's that?"

"It's the wrong time to use my little pussy."

"That don't bother me, babe," Snake declared proudly. "In the Legion of the Lost we don't just poke bloody cunts, we hunker right down and eat 'em."

"Really?" Toni gave a dramatic shudder. "Sounds icky. And it would bother me, darling. But you know, I really have a great ass, and I'm sure you'd love it."

"Yeah, it looks good, and I bet it feels like velvet," Snake said. "But I ain't no butt-fucker."

"So there are some things the Legion of the Lost won't do," Toni said sarcastically.

"Damn right."

"Oh well. I guess—"

"Read my mind," Snake told her.

"I give great head."

"Right. You better, babe."

"How many pills do you have?"

"Put it this way. You owe me five blow jobs."

Toni looked rather disappointed. "But darling, you will be able to get more, won't you?"

"What do you do, eat 'em like candy?"

"I'm in pain," Toni said resentfully.

"You need somebody to look after you," Snake pointed out, a clever idea forming in his mind. Blow jobs every night. A great source of income. He would move her out of the south end and put her to work making real money, no more of this back alley boffing for bucks. "Yeah, somebody who'll take good care of you."

"I take care of myself."

"I mean a regular guy."

"I've got a hundred regular guys, darling."

"To protect you," Snake clarified firmly.

"I've never needed protection."

"That just means you're overdue for trouble."

"Oh." Toni didn't seem to care for what Snake had in mind, but then her face moved slightly as if she had just felt a twinge of pain, and then she smiled up at him. "Oh dear."

"Yeah, but don't worry about it, babe," Snake told her with a wide grin. "Now that I'm here you'll be all right. I'll take care of you and you'll take care of me, right?"

"You might decide you don't want me," Toni said. She had a peculiar smile on her face. "When you get to know me."

Snake laughed. "Oh, I'll want you, babe, you can be sure of that. Matter of fact, I want you right now."

Toni discreetly slipped her hand between Snake's legs.

"Mmm, so you do."

"Come on, let's go."

"Your old lady must not be treating you right."

"What old lady?"

"I can tell, darling."

"Yeah, well, she's on the way out," Snake said. "She just don't know it yet."

"No one ever does."

"Come on," Snake said anxiously.

"Let me finish my drink," Toni insisted calmly. "Besides, I can see that you like standing in the middle of a crowd of people and having me touch you this way. It's nice, isn't it?"

"Jesus, babe."
But she was right.

— 3 —

—Greetings, plasmodium.
"Hey, I've been looking for you."
—Stand by.
"Where are you?"
—Here.
"I can't see you."
—You can hear me.
"Come on out, man. Let me see you."

Tony had a large mayonnaise jar. If he could just get his hands on the Pied Piper long enough to shove him into the jar and screw the cap on . . . Into the trash . . . Into the landfill . . . But, only after Tony hammered a few nail holes in the cap and then steamed the brain-eating son of a bitch alive over a pot of boiling water for a couple of hours.

But maybe Tony wouldn't throw him away. Maybe he'd put the jar on a shelf in the living room and let his johns goggle at it. What the hell is that, they'd ask. Souvenir from the Caribbean, he'd tell them with a straight face. My voodoo chile.

—Slime.
"Where the hell are you?"
—Everywhere.
"Yeah? Where's that?"
—In your head.

"That's what I have to talk to you about," Tony said. "You have to let me call a dentist and get an appointment, because my jaw is killing me all the time now."

—No.
"I can't take it anymore."
—No.

34

"Fuck, man, why the fuck not?"

— He'll see what you did to your teeth and he'll think that you're crazy.

"I *am* crazy."

— He'll get them to lock you up.

"I'm locked up here most of the time, talking to myself."

— I am always with you.

"Then come on out and let me see you."

— See!

Suddenly Tony couldn't see anything but the Pied Piper. It was as if he were inside Tony's eyeballs, peering into his brain. He had an evil grin on his twisted face, and now his filthy hands came up and started scratching at the inner lining of Tony's eyes in an effort to shred through the membrane. Scarping, ripping, peeling the cells away with ridged fingernails that were as sharp as razorblades.

The pain was excruciating. Tony slid off the chair and fell to his knees on the floor, holding his head in his hands. He was too weak to scream, it felt like the breath had been sucked from his lungs. One hand groped blindly toward the small brown bottle on the coffee table. Tony had tried all the regular store-bought painkillers, but none of them helped. Finally he had scored some Demerol from a beautiful idiot named Snake, his new friend. The Demerol was fantastic, although it never really lasted quite long enough. Now Tony had just a few left.

— No.

The muscles in Tony's arm went dead. His fingers fumbled at the brown bottle but could not grip it. *Please,* came the whimper from the back of his skull. *Please let me*— but a shrill racket overwhelmed his feeble thought.

— Sorry.

Tony began to beat his head against the floor.

— So you want the people downstairs to come up and find you like this? They'll call a doctor and he'll decide you're crazy. He'll have them lock you away forever.

Tony continued to bang his head on the hardwood floor in an effort to knock himself unconscious.

— Listen.

Tony could no longer lift his head; it rested face down in a smear of blood. But the pain had let up, and his brain began the laborious

35

process of forming clear thoughts again. His breathing came back
in short, shallow gasps.

—You can have your pill.

Tony tried to reach for the bottle, but couldn't.

—Not yet. Only when you have listened to what you must do
for me.

"Yes."

—And accept.

The air was thin and liquid. It had a raw, unpleasant edge that
reminded Tony of grain alcohol.

"What is it?"

—You must bring someone here.

"Who?"

—Someone you trust.

"I don't trust anybody, man."

—Nevertheless.

"How can I, with you hanging around?"

Business had fallen right off the table ever since the Pied Piper
had taken over Tony's life. He couldn't dare bring anyone home when
he no longer had control of the situation. He had to go out at night
all the time now, hustling quick tricks in toilets and alleys for prices
he would have laughed at a couple of months ago. Tony's whole world
had shriveled around him like the skin on a rotten corpse.

—You can.

"Can I take money from him?"

—Yes.

"And do my job?"

—That is what you must do.

"I get it," Tony said, smiling faintly. "You can't see me when I'm
outside, and you want to watch. Right?" For once the Pied Piper was
silent. Tony chuckled. "That's okay, man, that's cool. But you have
to understand." His voice took on a pleading tone again as he pushed
himself over onto his side. "I can't go on living like this. It just won't
work."

—Leave the living to me, plasmodium.

"I mean it, man. I'm dying in my socks. People will come to see
what's the matter, why I'm not in touch. My family, like that, you
know what I mean."

—Then deal with them.

"I can't handle it."

—Why not?

"I just can't. I'm afraid."

—Of what?

"You . . ."

—But, I'm you.

"The fuck you are," Tony protested. "I'm sick. I hurt all the time now. The only way I can face people is in the dark, and it's all because of you. Not me, I'm the one you're doing it to, and maybe I should be locked away somewhere. Maybe that'd be the best thing."

—Nonsense.

"You're killing me. Day by day, you're killing me."

—Ingrate.

"Come here, you little shit."

Tony had regained a slight measure of strength by now, so he lunged in the direction of where he thought the Pied Piper might be, but his fingers grasped empty air. The demon was gone. Tony knew it at once from the sudden lightness he felt, the release of his mind.

It was the worst attack yet. Tony's heart banged inside his chest, weak but frantic, and his skin was slick with sweat. His arms trembled, nearly buckling, as he made an effort to sit up on the floor. He looked at the thin patch of blood on the hardwood and felt a terrible anticipation of his own doom. This is how he would die, like an animal. Like trash, like slime, unseen, all but invisible, stepped on, rubbed away, a smear, a tiny stain on the street.

Tony crawled up into the chair. He saw the brown bottle of Demerol, but he no longer felt the need for any. Save them. The ache in his jaw was dull and distant. If only he could manage to grab the Demerol and get it down his throat in the minute before the Pied Piper got a hold of him. It was the only thing that did seem to keep the demon from getting through, at least for a short while. But he would have to carry a loose pill all the time, or else have one installed in a special socket in his teeth, like some of the Nazis. Come to think of it, the holes were already there, waiting to be custom-fitted.

He needed more Demerol, that was the main thing. Enough to keep him safe day and night. It was so damn good, so much better than coke or weed or anything else he'd ever tried. Better even than sex. So what if it turned him into a placid addict, lolling about like a zombie? Anything was better than having that fucker inside his brain.

37

Tonight he would see Snake again, and he would make sure the guy was sufficiently motivated to get more Demerol. There was no way Tony could live without it now.

He noticed the mayonnaise jar on the floor, and it puzzled him for a moment. He picked it up and looked at it. The strands of mayonnaise left inside had turned into a greenish-black slime. Slime, the Pied Piper had called him.

Plasmodium. That was a word Tony knew for certain he didn't know and had never heard before. Until today. Where did it come from? Impossible. Unless the Pied Piper was real.

The pain began to swell like an infernal orchestra in Tony's head, and he reached for the brown bottle.

– 4 –

"Where y'goin'?"

Snake looked over his shoulder. Shelly was still on the old couch, which sagged nearly to the floor. She looked like she was sampling coffins and had found one that suited her. She had been lying there most of the day. She was out of it, brain-blitzed on those pills the shrink had prescribed for her. Shelly discovered happiness when she doubled the original dosage and now she didn't scratch herself so much. She was also a lot easier for Snake to handle, although his feelings for her did not improve. Snake was hooked on Toni.

"Out," he replied curtly.

"Out where?"

"Fuck you."

Shelly struggled to push herself up on one elbow. It wasn't a pretty sight. Scrawny arms and legs. A whining, watery voice that came from a face resembling a tombstone. She also broadcast an odor that would pit steel. He looked away from her and put on his Legion of the Lost leather jacket.

"Snake . . ."

"Don't wait up."

THE DREAMS OF DR. LADYBANK

Twenty minutes later Snake parked his beat-up Dodge Colt on South Freedom, hurried around the corner and entered the El Greco bar. The usual do-nothing crowd was on hand, drinking, yammering over the soccer table and sticking their chests out at each other like animals. Snake hated them all. They seemed to smirk at him and laugh to themselves whenever he came in, but not one of them had the balls to take him on because they knew he'd kick the shit out of them. Snake knew about spic fighting abilities—they were game little roosters, but hit them in the body and they all break up like a sack of sticks.

Toni was there too, as she knew she damn well better be. It hadn't taken him long to straighten her out on that score. Snake was not to be kept waiting, not for one minute. You have to make sure a whore knows her place and toes the line, otherwise she'll piss all over you. Snake was pleased, but didn't show it, though he did tell her she looked sexy when she came and wrapped her arm around his waist. They got drinks and sat down at the far end of the bar, away from the crowd. Unfortunately, the El Greco didn't run to booths or tables.

Toni smiled, gave him little kisses, murmured in his ear and touched him secretly, but for all that she seemed tense and edgy. Her face was drawn and she toyed with her drink nervously.

"What's the matter, babe?"

"I'm in pain," she said.

"Drink your drink, and have another."

"You know what I mean."

"Relax."

"You got more?"

"Sure," Snake said.

"How much?"

"Jesus, you are jumpy tonight. Enough, okay? I have enough for you."

Toni settled down a little and stroked his thigh gratefully. Nice. Snake was pleased, but not entirely happy. His efforts to advance the situation in the last ten days had so far failed. He loved the blow jobs in his car, parked in a dark lot, and he knew he had a hold on Toni, but his control over her was only partial. She had agreed to consider working exclusively for him, but still would not commit to it. Snake's dream of free sex *and* free money hovered just beyond his reach. For the moment.

"But," he said quietly.

"What?" Toni's face tensed immediately. "But what?"

"I'm not happy."

"Why?"

"Take those sunglasses off."

"Pretend I'm a stranger, hot for you, and—"

"Take 'em off," Snake demanded. "It's dark enough here."

"Okay." Toni removed the shades and blinked, wincing. Then she smiled at him. "Whatever you want, darling."

"That's better."

"Besides, I'm hot for you anyway, you know."

"Yeah, well." Snake tried to look cool, but it wasn't easy to ignore her hand between his legs. "Listen to me."

"What's the matter?"

"I want you working for me."

"I know, but—"

"You don't belong down in this part of town. I can take you to better places, fix you up with guys that have more money. You can pull a ton, and I'll take care of everything. Everything you need, I'll get it for you."

"Sounds good," Toni said in a neutral tone of voice. "Maybe we could do that, but I'm not ready for it yet."

"No? We could leave right now, head on up to the Green Door and bag a half-dozen yuppies in no time."

"But not tonight, darling. I don't feel too good."

Snake shrugged his shoulders as if it didn't bother him one way or the other, but the expression on his face tightened.

"There's something else."

"What?"

"I'm getting kind of tired of doing it in the car."

"Oh."

"Don't worry, babe. You're great. But I'd like to go back to your place, where we can take a little more time and really do it right. Slow and sweet, you know?"

Toni looked unhappy. Snake knew he was walking a fine line. She had already made it clear to him that she didn't bring anyone home, that it "wasn't convenient" for some reason which she would not specify. If he pushed her too hard, she might decide to drop him and take her chances with somebody else. Whores know so many people. It might take her a few days, but sooner or later she'd find another source of coke and Demerol, and Snake would be left out in the cold

THE DREAMS OF DR. LADYBANK

Toni was too valuable to lose. It wasn't often that you found such a hot young thing, such an unusual beauty who really could perform. Toni was a sizzler.

But damn it, if Snake was going to be her one supplier, then he was entitled to more than he was getting. She didn't even let him touch her hardly at all, aside from a little ass-grabbing and an occasional brush with her nubby tits. Snake wanted more, much more. He wanted to roll around naked with her on a bed, to watch her strip, to splash around together in a bubble bath—the kind of things he did with Shelly, when she was human. Toni was great when she put her nose to the grindstone, but Snake was determined to strike a better deal.

"Darling, I will take you back to my place, and we'll have a wonderful time—many wonderful times."

"All right."

"But," Toni said, holding her hand up, "I have to get myself organized first."

"What the fuck does that mean?"

"I told you, I'm suffering the most monumental pain, from my dental problems. That's why I need the medicine."

"Right," Snake said wearily. He knew better than to ask why she didn't just get her dentist to write a prescription. She was a no-hope junkie whore, and it wasn't hard to figure out what the future had in store for her, but at least he had found her while she was young and still had a lot of tread. She was worth taking a certain amount of bullshit to keep. "How long will that be?"

"Next week."

"Really?"

Her eyes danced vaguely, avoiding him. "I hope."

"Jesus, babe."

"You poor darling," she said soothingly, caressing him again discreetly. "I'll make it up to you, just wait and see. I will, I really will. We'll have the most fantastic time together. And in the meantime, I'll suck your brains out, I'll drink you dry."

Talk like that dazed Snake. "God, you make me hot," he told her. "Let's get out of here."

"First."

Business first, was what she meant. Snake expected that and had prepared for it. In his pockets he had two packets of pills, a larger quantity in case Toni met either or both of his demands, and a smaller

41

number if she turned him down. It was time to yank the leash. Snake slipped her the packet containing half a dozen Demerols. Without looking at it, her eyes widened in alarm.

"That's all?"

"'Fraid so, babe."

"Why?"

"Recession. Supply and demand. Things are tight. Remember when I told you it'd be a lot easier if we worked together?"

Toni was trying to look stern, but it didn't suit her. "You know I can find other sources," she said.

"It isn't wise to take business away from the Legion," Snake countered, falling back on his last serious threat. Not that the Legion gave a damn about him. However, Toni didn't know that, so the threat was as good as real. "It makes 'em want to go out and kick somebody's face in, that kind of thing."

"All I want is a little time," Toni said pleadingly.

"What I just gave you is a little time."

Toni sighed unhappily. "All right."

"Now, let's go out to the car."

— 5 —

Tony couldn't stand it anymore. The pain was too much for him to bear. Three days ago he had finally gone to a dentist and had his teeth filled with some kind of plastic. It was a hideous session, lasting hours. The dentist obviously thought that Tony was crazy because of what he had done to his teeth, and for not removing his sunglasses. It cost a lot, and since Tony was not a regular patient and had no dental coverage he was obliged to fork over the money in advance. That was smart on the dentist's part, as Tony never would have bothered if he knew the fillings weren't going to work. They didn't.

At first he thought it was just a matter of time before the pain wore off for good, but after three days it was clearly there to stay. Perhaps he should have had new metal fillings installed to interfere

42

with the Pied Piper's broadcasts, but the originals hadn't really done the job, and it now seemed likely that Tony's teeth had little if anything to do with the strength or weakness of the torment he experienced.

He hadn't actually seen the Pied Piper in some time now, but the messages still came through several times a day. They meant little to Tony, aside from the sheer pain and terror they caused him. It had reached the point where he spent most of his time in bed or on the couch, weak from the last onslaught, trembling with dread in anticipation of the next one.

The pain usually subsided at night, and Tony would go out to eat and then hustle up some work. He tried to do what the demon voice wanted. He brought several customers back to his place and performed magnificently. They were cheap bums who didn't deserve such royal treatment but Tony would do whatever it took to please the Pied Piper. When the voice returned, however, it was always dissatisfied, and the agony continued.

Worse, Tony hadn't seen Snake since the night before he went to the dentist. He needed more Demerol, huge amounts, to get him through each day and make life somewhat bearable. Tony stabbed a glossy fingernail at the ice in his drink. It looked as if Snake would not appear at the El Greco tonight. That was bad, because Tony was completely out of Demerol. It had occurred to him that unless he got some he might kill himself tomorrow—assuming the Pied Piper would let him. Tony didn't know what to do. He left the bar, planning to return later. In the meantime, he would hit a few other places and see if he could find Snake.

The bastard was jerking his chain, that's what it was. Tony wouldn't work for him, wouldn't take him home for a long night of sex. Well, there was a problem. Somehow, Snake had yet to grasp the fact that Tony was at least nominally male. Tony could work the straight side of the street, but that was nerve-wracking, and he had no appetite for it. Nor could he bring Snake home, as it wouldn't be long before the Lost Legionnaire noticed some little something taped flat between Tony's legs.

Tony pulled a couple of quick tricks in his wanderings, but he didn't find Snake. He eventually found himself crossing the bridge into Riverside. It was a poor working-class neighborhood, virtually identical to the south end but for the fact that there were very few blacks or Hispanics in Riverside. It was for the most part unknown territory to Tony, but for some reason he felt he was heading in the right direction.

He tried a few bars along the way, looking in, then turning to leave immediately. Tony had long ago developed an ability to recognize places where he was sure to get beaten up.

He had to work out something with Snake. He could tell him the truth, and probably get beaten up for that, but at least it would clear the air. The charade couldn't go on much longer, and it might be better to get it over with sooner than later. But he had to have something to appease Snake. A share of Tony's income from gays—that might do it. Why not? It was the same kind of deal Snake wanted, except that Tony would be working his regular beat, not the cash-laden yuppie straights at the Green Door. The money might be less but it was still money for nothing. And Tony would have his steady supply of coke and Demerol. Yeah, it might just work out.

Nonetheless, Tony shuddered at the prospect of confronting Snake with the truth. Was it really necessary? Tony had enough cash on him now to buy a few days' worth of pills. Do that, just pay for the medicine, take it and go. No sex, no promises. Keep it strictly on a business footing. And if Snake insists on more? Tell him it's that time of the month. No, Tony remembered he had done that only a week or two ago. Vaginal fungus? Snake might want to eat it. Tell him you've got the clap, and you're out of action for a while. Head, yes; anything else, no.

The rattletrap Dodge Colt—there it was. Tony was amazed. He had found Snake. Almost. The car was parked in front of an aged triple-decker. On one side of the house there was a vacant lot, then a bakery and some more shops. On the other side, there was a diner, now closed, and a bar that Tony had already checked. Across the street, nothing likely. It had to be this apartment house. But which of the three apartments?

Tony started on the ground floor. He pushed the doorbell, but it didn't ring. He was about to knock when, through the side window, he caught sight of an elderly man sitting in an armchair in the front room. Doubtful. Tony went up the battered stairs. The light was mercifully dim, a single hanging bulb nearly burned out, and the air was permeated with the compressed smell of stale cooking—decades of it. The apartment on the second floor was dark and the screen door was locked. Tony caught his breath, and then continued on to the top floor. Lights, a dull noise inside. Tony knocked. Nothing. He knocked again, louder. Still no sign of a response. He knocked hard enough to hurt his knuckles.

THE DREAMS OF DR. LADYBANK

"Yeah."

The voice was faint and distant, but Tony was certain he had heard it. He tried the door, and it opened. He entered a narrow hallway. It was dark, but light came through an archway ahead on the right. Tony took a few steps and stood, looking into a drab living room. There was a girl on the couch.

"You must be the little woman."

"Who're you?"

"I'm looking for Snake."

"He's out."

"Where?"

"I don't know."

"His car is out front," Tony said. "Would he be somewhere in the neighborhood?"

"He went with Crabs."

"What?"

"Crabs. His friend."

"Oh." Tony felt uncomfortable talking across the room. He moved closer to the pathetic girl, who made no effort to get up. She was squeezing her fingers strangely. "Are you okay?"

"No. I'm out of medicine and I'm all fucked up."

"So am I."

Without thinking about it, Tony went to the couch and sat on the edge of it beside the girl. She looked awful.

"That's a pretty dress."

"Thank you." Tony glanced at the girl's hands again and was shocked to see that she was digging her nails into the palms, and blood was oozing between her fingers. She was gouging out a hole in the center of each hand. "What're you doing?" Tony cried in a voice strangled with alarm.

"It's Jesus," the girl said. "Jesus is in me."

"Jesus?"

"These are His wounds." The girl's eyes were brighter now, lit with enthusiasm. "Look at my feet."

Tony turned his head and glanced back. "Oh my God."

"Yes, yes."

"Honey, let me—"

"And look here."

Before Tony could do or say anything, the girl yanked up her T-shirt, revealing a pancake breast. *That's not much bigger than mine,*

45

Tony thought. Then he noticed the running sore in the side of the girl's body, about the size of a silver dollar. The skin around it was streaked with dried blood. She must have picked at it for hours, days. It was terrible to see, but also fascinating and even exciting. Tony felt as if he'd walked into this girl's dream.

"Nobody believes me," she said sadly.

"I do," Tony found himself saying.

"You do?"

"Yes. I do."

The girl smiled. "You're so pretty."

"When is Snake coming home?"

"I never know."

Tony's eyes drifted helplessly back to the bloody wound near the girl's breast. The skin had not been allowed to form a scab. The wound has the wet, puckered look of a vagina, Tony thought in a fog of wonder. You have two of them and I don't even have one. He couldn't keep from smiling.

"Put your hand in," the girl said. "Just like they did with the Lord Jesus. Go on. Please."

"My hand won't fit."

"Your finger then."

Tony hesitated, but then was astonished to see his hand move toward the girl's body. His middle finger slid effortlessly into the moist wound. It terrified him to picture the long artificial nail, hard and sharp, pushing deeper into the girl's body, but he didn't stop until the finger was in all the way.

"Tell me your name."

"Shelly." Then, "No. *Jesus.*"

Tony felt as if he had plugged into a chaos of heat, turmoil and liquid. Shelly's body quaked violently, her eyes shining, an unfathomable expression on her face. Pain and peace, maybe. Her hands clutched Tony's arm, pressing it harder to her body.

The next thing he knew, he was in a squalid kitchen, washing his hands in a stream of tepid tap-water. Roaches huddled in the gap between the backsplash and the crumbling plaster wall, but he ignored them. Tony's mind couldn't seem to focus on anything for more than a second or two, and now the pain was starting to seep back in at the edges.

Where was Snake? But that didn't matter. Go away. Get out of here. Now. You can always kill yourself tomorrow, but if you stay here

46

they'll come, and they'll think you're crazy. And then they'll lock you up, and it'll be too late to do anything.

In the living room, Shelly was still. Her eyes followed him as he approached. He imagined the faintest smile on her face, or maybe it was actually there. At the edge of his vision, where he could not quite look, he knew that Shelly had inserted her finger into the wound. Her hand twisted and poked. There was a lot of bright red, and it was spreading, but Tony looked away. Then he left as quickly as he could.

ENTR'ACTE

Doctor Ladybank chatted with Jack and his wife, Gloria, for a few minutes, and then took his drink out onto the terrace. The party was in full swing, and it was a little too hot and crowded inside for him. The evening air was pleasantly cool, sweet with a mix of fragrances from Gloria's flower garden. Nice woman, was Gloria. A bit too nice for a rogue like Jack, but they seemed to get along and had been together for years.

Doctor Ladybank normally didn't care for social gatherings, mingling with a lot of strangers, making forced conversation, but every now and then Jack threw a good old-fashioned cocktail party that simply couldn't be missed. This one came at a particularly good time. Doctor Ladybank needed a break. He'd been giving too much of himself to his experiment lately.

It didn't tire him, it wasn't stressful, there were no nasty side effects at all as far as he could tell. But it was utterly irresistible! In just a few short weeks he had become thoroughly caught up in the lives of his two subjects. He resented any time spent away from them. Work, eating, sleeping—the bulk of his normal activities had faded into dullness.

There were many problems yet to be resolved. First, was the lack of quality time with Tony and Snake. It was often difficult to get through to them, especially at night. When Tony went out, Doctor

Ladybank almost always lost contact. The same applied to Snake. It was not an absolute rule, however. There were several times when he did reach them at night, including a few important moments. Doctor Ladybank had no idea whether that was because of the intensity of his concentration or merely the configuration of their surroundings.

By now he had a rough idea of the range of his effect on the two young men. It went from basically annoying them to generally influencing their behavior, and peaked at substantial control of their thoughts and emotions. It was dazzling, but also somewhat perplexing. He could hurt them, to the point of unconsciousness, but he had not yet learned how to make them laugh or feel sudden moments of spontaneous pleasure. Doctor Ladybank regretted that, as both Tony and Snake were doing so much for him, and they lived such unrewarding lives. But he didn't regret it very much; there was no place for sentiment in science.

Feedback was bliss. That was perhaps the most exciting part of Doctor Ladybank's discovery. How would he know if his efforts were really working? In practice, he found that he just knew, he sensed it somehow, without knowing quite how he knew. It was not as if he "heard" Delgado answering him, for instance. But Doctor Ladybank's thoughts and directives flowed intuitively, as if they were in fact conversing on some new level, and thus, when he held either of them in the strongest contact he was aware of what they were doing, how they responded and what his own next words should be. To Doctor Ladybank it didn't qualify as vicarious experience but there was certainly an intellectual thrill in it.

It was a bitter disappointment to him that in the four weeks since he had happened on the technique, as he thought of it, he had not found anyone else receptive to it. That was definitely a puzzle, apparently defying the laws of chance and probability.

The greatest mystery, though, was at the heart of the whole experiment. To what degree did he affect their behavior? Was it mostly his doing, or was he just providing an added mental shove, urging them along paths they would have taken anyway? So far, it was impossible to know for sure.

A mosquito buzzed close to his eye. Doctor Ladybank went in and got another drink. He was buttonholed by Margaret Zuvella, a lawyer with the Public Defender's office. She didn't fit in with Jack's corporate law crowd but she was young and very attractive, which

48

made her an ideal party guest. Doctor Ladybank had met her on one of his court-appointed cases, and they'd encountered each other a few times since. What a subject she'd make, he couldn't help thinking. But when he tried the technique, it had no effect whatsoever on her. Sad. They chatted about a nineteen-year-old pyromaniac they had both tried, and failed, to keep out of prison a few months ago.

"He set a fire in the library," Margaret said with obvious delight. "Then he got the prison laundry."

"Splendid. Troy's a determined lad."

At that moment Jack horned in, looking loose and well-oiled, but not at all tipsy.

"Maggie," he said, smirking like someone about to explain an inside joke. "I have to warn you."

"About what?"

"Ian here. You better watch out. He can make you take your clothes off right here, in a room full of people."

A tendril of dismay uncoiled in Doctor Ladybank's mind.

"Really," Margaret said, smiling. "How can he do that?"

Jack tapped his forehead. "Brain waves. He beams them over to your brain and makes you do whatever he wants."

"Jack." Doctor Ladybank forced himself to chuckle and shake his head dismissively.

"I'd love to see it," Margaret said.

"Honestly," Jack continued. "Ian is conducting experiments on a couple of people, doing just that. How's it going, by the way, Ian? Got them jumping through hoops yet?"

"You're not," Margaret said.

"Of course not," Doctor Ladybank replied. "Jack and I were laying waste to a bottle of malt last month, and we were talking about clairvoyance, telepathy, that kind of thing. It was just a load of idle speculation, that's all."

"Ah." Margaret nodded.

"Oh, Ian, come on now," Jack protested. "You were damn well serious about it. I wasn't, but you were."

The silly crock was pushing it. Doctor Ladybank was shaken, but he maintained an expression of placid indulgence.

"It was the whiskey talking," he told Margaret. "Then, and now, in Jack's case, I'm afraid."

"I see."

Jack gave up, and the three of them laughed politely.

"I still think it's a good idea," Jack said as he started to leave in search of others on whom he could shower bonhomie.

"What is?" Margaret asked.

"If Ian gets you to take your clothes off."

"Jack, go away," she told him, trying to suppress a giggle. "Go away and behave yourself."

Yes, Doctor Ladybank thought. Go away, Jack.

– 6 –

For once in his life something had gone right. If he hadn't been in the right place at the right time the cops would have put the collar on him in a flash. They knew him, they'd busted him a couple of times in the last few years, though never for anything too serious. Yeah, they'd love to hang some hard time on his ass if they could, but Snake was covered.

It was a minor miracle, looking back. Half of his life, it sometimes seemed, was spent in transit, scraping around, looking for this guy or that, hanging out—unaccountable time witnessed by nobody who would ever remember. But on the night Shelly died, Snake fortunately had been with or seen by other people for every minute of the hours in question. More amazing, they all stood up for him when it counted.

He and Crabs had gone to Rudy's early that evening. The two of them teamed up to monopolize the pool table for several hours, winning drinks until nearly midnight. Then they decided to go to a nightclub called Ravens, on the other side of town. They were turned away at the door and exchanged mean stares with—of all people—a cop moonlighting as a bouncer. Snake and Crabs were both known to the cop; he'd thrown them out of Ravens a couple of months earlier. Retreating across the road to Cher's Plus Two, a titty bar favored by area bikers, Snake and Crabs met a number of other people they knew. They stayed until closing time, two a.m. By then they were in such good spirits that they decided to drink a nightcap or two at Snake's

50

place. Instead, they found the dead body and promptly called the police.

What a way to go, Snake thought as he drove aimlessly around town. Shelly. She had her good side, a while back. But to die like that, to carve a hole in yourself with your own fingernails, and bleed to death . . . Jesus. It was enough to make Snake wonder how he had put up with her for so long. She must have been stone cold loco, so far off the wall that she couldn't even see it. To tell the truth, however, he had never imagined she was that sick. Weird, sure, and the laziest damn thing on earth. But not sicko sick. Maybe Snake should have paid more attention to that shrink who saw Shelly. Maybe they all missed something then.

Oh well. It was over now. Any residual feelings that Snake might have had for Shelly disappeared when he learned that he, as her common-law husband, had to pay to dispose of her remains. If she had any relatives, he didn't know who or where they might be, and she didn't leave much more than a pile of dirty clothes. She lived light and went fast, amen. Snake didn't hesitate to choose the cheapest available cremation (the "Bake 'n Shake," according to Crabs). Shelly's ashes were in the jar on the seat beside him now. It was time to find somewhere nice for her.

The ocean was too far away. A babbling brook would be nice, but then Snake considered the fact that any moving waters in this old mill city were bound to be thoroughly polluted. What about a park? Open air, a quiet setting, flowers—shit, he could strew her ashes right in a flowerbed. That would be perfect. But then again, it wasn't so easy. The two or three city parks Snake knew of had pretty much gone to seed, neglected, overgrown, dangerous. The best one was adjacent to the public library, and it wasn't so bad, but even there the winos used the flowerbeds as a toilet and a parade of fags stalked the shrubbery.

It wasn't as if Shelly deserved a spot in Arlington National Cemetery, but Snake felt obliged to do the best he could. He hadn't been much help to Shelly in what turned out to be her last weeks alive. Plus, she had spared him the aggravation of throwing her out, so he figured that he owed her something.

There it was! Snake knew he'd found the ideal place for her as soon as he drove around the bend in the road and saw the green expanse of a fairway in the distance. The city golf course. She would like it, he had no doubt. All he had to do now was find an attractive little spot off to the side somewhere, maybe beneath a birch tree in the rough. Hell, there might even be a clear brook in a place like this.

Snake parked the car along an open stretch of the road, took the container of ashes and walked quickly through the weedy grass toward the fairway. It was the tail-end of dusk, so if he didn't find a place soon he'd end up dumping her in the dark.

There was a foursome a hundred yards away, but they were on the way in, their backs to Snake. He jogged across the fairway. The woods on the other side looked promising, but when he reached them he found the ground unsuitable. More tall grass, rocks, and bare dirt where paths had been worn. At least at the library she would have had flowers. Damn it all anyway. He was looking for the kind of scene they put on greeting cards and in Disney films, but this was just a bunch of useless country-type land.

Snake pushed on. A few minutes later he came out on the far side of the woods, and he was startled by the sudden change. He was in someone's backyard. Nice looking house, must have cost an awful lot. Beautiful grounds, too. Snake hadn't tried burglary, but this would be the kind of place to start with if he ever felt like having a go.

He had other business now. His eyes had settled on a lovely rock garden just a few yards away. Snake hurried across the lawn to it. Oh yes, the perfect resting place for Shelly. There were cascades of delicate flowers, clusters of blue, purple and white, not much pink or red. Just the colors you saw at funerals, Snake thought as he bent over and started to scoop out a hollow in the rich soil. You'll love it here, kid. The kind of folks who live in a place like this will take real good care of you, or at least the garden around you.

"What do you think you're doing?"

Snake jumped upright. He had been about to unscrew the cap of the jar containing Shelly's ashes, but now he froze, gaping at the middle-aged man who stood ten feet away, hands on hips. Must have seen me from the house, Snake thought uselessly. He wasn't worried about having been discovered by the homeowner, but he was puzzled. The guy was a stranger, and yet seemed familiar. Snake could turn and run, and he knew he'd get away easily, but somehow the urge to flee had been transformed into curiosity.

"Who are you," the man demanded, his voice more threatening, "and what do you want?"

"Hey, Jack." Snake was surprised to hear himself say that. "How the hell are you, Jack?"

52

The man's head clicked back a notch. Then he stepped closer and peered at Snake.

"I don't know you."

"Sure you do, Jack. We used to hang out at the Utica Club, remember? *Agricola, agricolae, agricolorum.* Right? *Hic, haec, hoc, ad hoc,* in hock around the clock with bock beer."

Even in the gathering darkness, Snake could see the man's eyes widen as he tried to digest what he'd heard. Snake couldn't help him. He had no idea.

"Get out of here this instant."

"Jack, lighten up."

"I'll call the police."

"Why don't you crack open a bottle of Glen Grant? We can sit down and talk twat, just like the old days."

The man tottered, then turned stiffly toward the house.

"Jack, Jack . . ."

Snake scooped up a rock and caught the man easily. The rock crushed the back of his skull, creating a wreath of pinkish-grey jelly around the edges of the impact. The man grunted once, the last of his breath forced out of him. He hit the lawn and didn't move again.

Snake pulled the body over onto its back. Now the wife will have to sell this place, he thought. Who knows what'll happen to the rock garden? The new owners might well dig it up and plow it under. That wouldn't be right. You're going to get a real fancy burial, Shelly. Elegant casket, expensive plot. Can't beat it.

He unscrewed the jar, forced the man's mouth open, and began to pour the ashes down the throat. It soon filled. Snake tamped the coarse powder down with his fingertips. Believe me, Jack, if you saw Shelly at her best you *would* want to eat her. That would have been when she was about fifteen.

The cheeks bulged, Snake noticed when he was finished. Jack the Chipmunk. Best I could do. Time to take a *haec.*

So long, kid.

− 7 −

Tony washed down the Demerol with a gulp of Red Death on the rocks. Behind the shades, his eyes watered slightly, but he felt his body steadying. That was mental, since he knew it would take a good five minutes before serenity began to kick in and all was right with the world again . . . for a while.

"You look happy, darling."

"I buried Shelly."

"Maybe that's it. Where did you put her?"

"Somewhere out in the countryside," Snake said with a vague wave of the hand, as if he'd suddenly lost interest in the topic. "It's a pretty place."

"I'm sure it is."

Tony had heard about it only last night around this time, as they were sitting on the very same two barstools at the El Greco. It was boring. Tony didn't want to listen to another word about the stupid cunt who'd bled herself to death, but Snake was having a hard time putting it behind him. He kept pulling away from it, and then sinking back, like a car stuck in a rut. It was morbid, as well as incredibly tiresome.

Tony had his own uneasy feelings about Shelly. He imagined he had met her—or was it a dream? Anyhow, he had this picture of her in his mind, like he could see her dying. It was probably because Snake had given such a graphic description of what Shelly looked like when he found her. And it had stayed in Tony's head, making him feel very uncomfortable.

Part of the problem was that Snake kept him jangled up in a state of constant uncertainty, dishing out the pills in ones and twos like candy. Wouldn't sell a quantity, even though Tony had the cash. Snake wanted other things, and so he was making a move for absolute control. It was clear and simple, but Tony had yet to figure out a worthwhile response to it. Shelly's death was a minor week-long distraction that didn't really change anything in Tony's life.

The easiest thing, of course, would be to stop using Demerol or coke, period. Then Tony would be able to kiss Snake goodbye, and how sweet that would be. The big clod had lost any semblance of attractiveness he might have possessed. Not that he was ever anything but a trick and a supplier as far as Tony was concerned. The game was fun at first, but now Snake's mean and demanding way of treating Tony most of the time was simply unbearable.

And how could he get off the drugs? That was impossible, at least in Tony's present condition. They weren't drugs, they were medicine. They kept him alive. Whether that was a good idea was another matter, but as long as he wanted to survive all the pain and mental interference, he had to have his medicine.

Zzzzt.

Oh God, no. Not now, not here. Tony had a terrible fear of the Pied Piper getting through to him in a public place. Even if it was only the El Greco, where some pretty weird things happened from time to time.

Zzzzt.

Fucker. Get lost. Ignore him. But that never worked. The demon had continued to haunt and hurt Tony everyday over the past week, never letting up for long. The Demerol helped, but it was by no means a perfect immunity. All it did was keep the agony in moderate check for a while, so that Tony remained just this side of suicidal. The Pied Piper still got through.

—Plasmodium. Found you.

"Be right back, darling," Tony said to Snake. "I've got to make a trip to the little girl's room."

"Yeah," Snake muttered.

Tony slid off the barstool, wobbled for a second on his high heels, and then clattered quickly across the linoleum. Thank God the pisser was vacant. Tony shut the door and leaned against it, pressing his head to the blotchy particleboard.

—I want him.

"Fuck off."

—You heard me.

"For what?"

—Bring him home.

"It won't work with him. He's straight."

—Do it, slime.

"Listen, when he sees my *cojones* he'll go crazy. He'll tear them off and shove 'em down—"

Tony went blind and sagged to the damp floor, too stunned to make a sound as pain exploded throughout his body, abrading every cell in his nervous system. It felt as if sonic booms were being triggered inside his brain and the plates of his skull were about to crack open at the seams.

Yes, yes, okay. He couldn't even get the words out, but the torture died down immediately. Tony found that he could breathe again, he could think, he could see the slick of scummy water his face rested in on the floor. He was theoretically still alive, a fact of dubious value. Why is this happening? Why are you doing this to me?

—Because you are slime.

You got that right. "But you're me, right? That's what you said a while back, fucker. If I'm slime, so are you."

Silence. Relief. Goddamn, Tony thought as he struggled to his feet, I shut him up. I shut the Pied Piper up. At least for a minute or two. Turned him right off. Tony gripped the sink to steady himself and then looked in the mirror. His face was grimy and wet from the floor. He washed himself and applied some fresh make-up, regaining a little composure in the process.

It was no good. The Pied Piper was gone for now, but he had delivered his message. Tony had to bring Snake home tonight, and whatever happened from that point on—would happen. Might even be better if Snake did go beserk and kill him. That would put a stop to all this misery. He could see the newspaper stories. An anguished biker tricked by a transvestite—Snake might have to transfer to the Foreign Legion to live that one down. Meanwhile, Tony's tearful mother wouldn't believe a word they said about him and his queer life. She'd hand out pictures of him as a choirboy and talk about the perfume he gave her last Mother's Day (because she was still young and pretty).

Why the fuck not? Who the fuck cares anyway? When you live in the shadow of the curb, where else do you expect to die? Grab the best chance that has come along in years. If you don't, that little demon fucker will just come back and eat at you, rip away at you, until you do what he wants. Get it over.

Besides, Tony knew that the column inches, however lurid and distasteful, would be a kind of comfort to his mother. Maybe not right away, but in the long term. A front-page murder story was better than no obituary at all.

– 8 –

The place was a dump on the outside, but the living room was nice enough. In a spooky kind of way. The shades were drawn and the only light came from a large floor lamp with a fringed shade that cast the room in a soft golden glow. The air was humid and warm, but it had a sweet scent that added an exotic, mysterious touch, and the furniture was comfortable. It wasn't the way he'd fix up a room, but Snake decided that he liked it as he sat back in a big armchair.

Toni was on edge, nervous as a high school girl on her first date. What a riot. Snake wasn't going to make it any easier for her. Why should he? This was his payoff. He was going to enjoy every minute of it. On the way there from the bar Snake gave her explicit instructions. He was to be treated like a king, she was to wait on him, pamper him, baby him, indulge him, humor him, and above all, she was to tease him to the max. He couldn't wait for that to start. This was going to be the greatest damn fuck Snake had ever had, the one he'd dreamed of for years.

The whore looked good, real good. Her hair was quite short, and it was brushed and slicked back in a striking fashion, and it looked so wet you'd think she had just this minute stepped out of the shower. Tonight her dress was almost elegant, not at all the usual trashy glitter.

She wore a white blouse that hung loosely on her flattish upper body, and a long wrap-around skirt that had a nice way of parting to flash her terrific legs when she walked. Toni was somewhat on the tall side, a sort of slum-pussy version of Jamie Lee Curtis without the front porch.

"What would you like to drink?"

Better already, Snake thought. Just being there had changed her tone of voice. Gone was the bar room hustle, replaced by such a sweet desire to please—God, he loved it. Toni was standing beside the chair, close to him. Snake liked that too. He placed a hand on her leg, just behind the knee, savoring the firm flesh beneath the fabric of her skirt. It was one of his favorite sexy spots on a woman's body. You could feel those wires—no, what the hell are they called, tendons, sinews?—that run all up and down the leg. Neat.

"Do you want a drink, darling, or . . . not?"

"Mmmm."

Snake's hand slid higher, taking the skirt with it, but Toni stepped aside gracefully, escaping his reach. As she did so, she contrived to flap the front of her skirt open briefly. Very nice little move, Snake thought appreciatively.

"Well?"

"Got any bourbon?" he asked.

"Of course."

"Okay, let's have a large glass of bourbon, on the rocks and with a splash of water."

"*Ein, zwei, drei.*"

"Huh?"

"What?"

"What'd you say?"

"I said it's on the way."

"Okay. Fine."

A little weird, but what the hell. Snake already had a good buzz on, so nothing was going to bother him. As long as Toni did her part. From where he was sitting he could see her in the tiny kitchen, pouring the drinks. At that moment, she put the bottle down and bent over. She opened her skirt and fiddled around with the catch on her garter. It took a moment for the significance of the navy blue ribbon and the bare skin to register. Oh Jesus, she's wearing stockings, Snake realized with joy. And now she's showing me. Man, this is just like being in the foreplay part of a porn movie. Scenes like this were the best—the teasing, the slow seduction—even better than the wild sex that would follow soon enough. But now Snake wasn't just another jerk-off watching the picture; he was starring in it.

The bourbon was good and there was plenty of it in the heavy crystal tumbler Toni brought him. She sipped a pale liquid from a glass about the size and shape of a lipstick holder.

"What's that?"

"Cointreau," she told him.

"Oh yeah." None of that Red Death shit here. She was doing it all right, no question. "Nice stuff."

"Snake?"

"Yeah?"

"Do you have any metal fillings?"

"Metal—what?"

"Metal fillings in your teeth. Lead, silver, like that."

58

"Oh, sure. Lots. I've got a regular scrapyard in my mouth, everything but gold. Why?"

"Do you get much static?"

"Just from people who don't know better," he replied with a quick laugh. "But I soon straighten them out."

"So . . . You don't hear anything?"

"Like what?" Like, what the hell is this all about?

"A voice."

"Just yours and mine, babe." Snake sounded calm, but he was beginning to worry. She looked nervous, close to panic, in spite of the fact that she was sitting on the couch, drink in hand, her thigh tantalyzingly visible. "Hey, relax."

As if on cue, Toni said, "Whatever they want."

"What?"

"Whatever they want."

"Who?"

"Men."

"Oh." This was an abrupt shift, but it was definitely a lot more promising, so he went with it. "Such as?"

"Come on my face. Come in my mouth."

Her voice was stiff, and her eyes seemed to be fixed on some remote inner point. However, Snake now thought he understood the game. She was going to tell him about the things she did. Dirty talk to turn him on. It was a little more open and blunt than he would have liked, but he was prepared to cut her some slack if it had the desired effect.

"That's pretty normal," he told her.

"Ride my ass."

"Some do like that. Not me, but some do."

"Tie me up. Blindfold me."

"Uh-hunh."

"Hurt me."

"Not too bad, I hope."

"Piss on me. Shit on me."

"Aw, Jeez." That was exactly the kind of stuff Snake didn't want to hear. How the hell could he lick her body now, with that stuck in his mind? "Where? On your back or stomach," Snake said hopefully. "Right?"

"And my chest. And face. And mouth."

"That really drags me down, babe." The script had gone into some other movie. Snake was not happy. The only thing that kept him from clocking her on the jaw was the fact that he didn't want to give up yet. There was still a chance Toni would snap out of her robot stare and get back on track. "I wouldn't treat you bad like that," he said. "I'd treat you like a queen."

Toni suddenly began laughing. Snake didn't understand, but he smiled at the improvement in her manner. She appeared to be much more relaxed again. He also liked that foxy look in her eye as she tuned in to him.

"Darling, would you really be a good boy?"

"Sure."

"I want you to do something for me."

"What?"

"Promise not to peek? Promise not to touch where you're not supposed to?"

"Well, I don't get it."

"Put your drink on the floor and sit forward on your seat."

"Okay."

When Snake did what she told him, Toni got off the couch and carefully stepped up onto the coffee table, inches from his face. Hey, hey, hey, Snake thought. This is more like it.

"Here," Toni said, handing him her glass of Cointreau. "I'd like you to rub it into my skin. Just the bare skin now, and you must behave yourself."

"O-kay."

Snake splashed the liqueur on his hand and then placed the small glass on the table. Toni pulled her skirt open, and cupped one hand modestly over her panties. The sight of that navy blue underwear against her golden skin was fantastic. Snake lovingly stroked her upper thighs, above the stocking tops.

"Mmmm . . ."

"Your hand is in the way," he dared.

"You don't touch there. Understand?"

"Yes."

"That's good. You're a good boy, aren't you?"

"Yes."

"And you're doing a good job. What does it smell like? You can put your face closer."

Snake went so far as to put his face between her thighs, his cheeks

60

touching her. His forehead bumped against her hand. Toni didn't stop him.

"Oranges."

"Right." Now her fingers gently pushed his face away. "The back, too. Don't forget the back."

Snake poured the last of the Cointreau in his hand, and Toni turned slightly on the table. She pulled the skirt higher, so he had a clear view of the flimsy blue fabric stretched tightly over her ass. He rubbed the back of her legs gently and slowly, while his eyes were locked on target just above. Toni's other hand was still planted on her crotch, so deeply that her fingers curved up in sight from behind. Odd, but Snake barely gave it a thought as he had other things on his mind. His hand inevitably slid up and grazed her firm round bottom. She let him do that until he began to squeeze it energetically, insinuating his fingers beneath her panties, and then she spun around.

"I told you to behave."

"Oops."

"Never mind, you did a good job."

Toni stepped down from the coffee table and took her spot on the couch again. Snake took his drink from the floor and slurped a major mouthful. He smiled at her and let his eyes drift slowly along the length of her body, stretched out on the couch. As if responding to his gaze, one of her knees pushed up so the flap of her skirt fell away.

"Did you hear that?" she asked.

"What?"

"The voice."

"No." She was still a little crazy, he thought. "You hear voices, you better see the Doc."

"Which doctor?"

"The witch doctor, yeah," Snake said with a laugh. "Hell, I don't know. Go to a shrink, babe."

His eyes were on her legs and he didn't feel like discussing anything else. Toni's arm had fallen casually across her crotch, another peekaboo move that tickled Snake, and her thumb rolled in a small arc on her upper thigh. Lightly, back and forth. It was mildly hypnotic, very arousing.

"Tell me about him," she said.

"Who?"

"Your doctor."

"I don't have one."

"But you know one."

"No, I—"

Snake hesitated. Well, he did know one. Technically. He'd met Shelly's shrink, back a month or two ago. But he didn't know the man, in fact he couldn't even remember the guy's name.

"Go on."

As if to encourage Snake, Toni now stretched out completely on her back and raised both knees up straight. Then she let them loll open and she rubbed herself in a slowly escalating rhythm as her body squirmed with pleasure. Snake didn't know what he could say, but he didn't want to stop the show. He was caught up in it almost as much as Toni was.

"The Doc is okay."

"Yeah . . ."

"The Doc is good."

"Yeah . . ."

"He'll take care of you, but you have to trust him."

"Yeah . . ."

"And do what he tells you."

"*Yeah.*"

Her knees drove toward her chest, her hands worked in a last frenzied rush.

"I wish I could tell you his name."

"*YEAAAAAAAAHH!*"

Her body rocked convulsively, then turned rigid. She puffed air in short bursts. You momma, Snake thought. He nearly missed his mouth as he tried to take a drink with his eyes frozen on the girl. You hot little whore momma, that was better than a sexpic. The way she had done it with her clothes still on somehow made it that much more real. It was like peeking through the window next door and watching your teen queen neighbor engage in self-service fun. Snake had a hard-on, and he was clean out of words.

Toni rolled over onto her belly, her skirt rumpled and still showing a lot of leg. Her face was pressed to the couch, her one visible eye peering brightly at Snake. There was the faintest of smiles at the corner of her mouth.

"You like to watch."

"Hey." Snake shrugged with a grin.

"You do, and you like to have someone do it for you. That's okay, darling, that's cool."

"Well, not always . . ."

"I'll do it for you. Special, because you're special."

"So are you, babe."

"Come on with me."

Snake followed her into the bathroom. It was dark, and Toni didn't turn on the light. Instead, she pulled the door so it was almost shut, allowing only the slightest illumination to filter in from the living room. She had Snake stand facing the bathtub and told him to unbuckle his belt and unzip his pants. She was right behind him, speaking in a low soft voice, caressing his back.

"Grab hold of the shower bar," she directed. "That's right, that's it. Now close your eyes and imagine you're in a luxurious hotel room somewhere, maybe Paris, or Rio. You're high up, maybe forty floors, and the view is fantastic. You stand at the window and gaze out at the spectacular scene. It's night, and it's like a dream, just being there. The city is far, far below, but it's all lit up like a million shiny jewels. Now, a young woman comes into the room. Women always come to you, so you don't even turn around, you just know she's there. For you. She comes right to you, her hands flowing over your body. You still don't turn, you watch the city below and you let her love you—"

Her hands snaking around him, finding his nipples, squeezing them through his shirt, then planing down, snagging his pants and taking them to the floor. Her face to the small of his back, her hands gliding up the front of his thighs. She takes his cock in one hand, cups his balls with the other, tightening her grip with expert care as her face burrows into his backside. She licks and explores until she finds the puckered rim.

"Ohhh-aaaah . . ."

She tongues it delicately while her hands play him in front, the pace of her movements increasing steadily. Snake heaves with anticipation, his body shaking beyond his control, and she knows he is about to come. Her tongue plunges deeply into him.

"Oooooh-Gaaaaaahd . . ."

He shoots off. Little spattering sounds from the porcelain tub, but they're almost lost in the noisy rush of breath above. Snake can hardly hold himself up by the shower bar, he's so weak and dazed by this onslaught of pleasure. He still can't believe it, what she did to him. So good.

63

"Toni . . ."

She had backed away from him a little. When he glanced over his shoulder at her he caught sight of the swift movement, but he didn't understand it. Then he felt it, and it was the last thing he felt. The stiletto blade punctured his spine, paralyzing him. The tip snapped off, but she kept hammering the broken blade into his body, up and down, between the ribs, into his flabby midriff, blood blossoming in a spray of grey roses, his hands slipping off the shower bar, the slow dizzy fall through hot buzzing air, and still it came at him, that knife, *bam bam bam bam bam bam*, arcing at him, fixing him for all time, his shiny metal transport to the end of the night, *bam bam bam bam bam*, out of the grey, the gloom and the shadows and into the perfect no pain the perfect no night the perfect no light the perfect the

— 9 —

silence was terrifying.

Tony was shaking so violently that he had to hold onto the sink and the wall to keep from falling to the bathroom floor. He hit the switch and the ceiling light went on. It was temporarily blinding, since Tony didn't have his shades, and he whimpered in pain. The floor was covered with blood—such a vibrant red—he could see that much as he squinted through his tears. Tony breathed deeply, sucking air in an effort to hold off panic.

Snake was in the tub. Tony had pushed him into it when he saw that the guy was about to keel over backwards on top of him. Now the only thing he could think to do was to leave him there in peace. He's draining, Tony told himself. Let him drain. It was the best place for him.

But then what? He couldn't move a big body like that on his own, and he certainly couldn't get it out of this building or the neighborhood without being seen. Not even in the middle of the night.

Impossible. This is bad, bad, bad. He hazarded a glance in the mirror. A savage stared back.

"What now?"

Nothing. The little shit. Tony noticed his stiletto on the floor, and saw for the first time that the tip was broken. Where was the other piece? The way his life was going, that would turn out to be the one little thing that landed him on Death Row. The two hundred-plus pounds of incriminatingly dead meat lying in the tub suddenly seemed as vast as a continent, and somewhere in that land mass was a vital scrap of metal. He had to find it and then get rid of it.

Tony edged closer to the bathtub. Jesus, why did he have to stab the guy so many times? But why did he ever have to stab him at all? Dead, Snake looked merely pathetic. A nobody. Just one more poor stiff who wanted to live, and be loved by somebody, but who never quite got a handle on his life. Not all that different from me, Tony thought.

But, on to business. Tony picked up the stiletto and washed it under the tap in the sink. Then he wrapped it tightly in the hand towel, wiping it several times to make sure he didn't leave a fingerprint on it, and carried it into the kitchen. He dug up a plastic supermarket bag and put the knife in it, towel and all. He rolled it into a tidy little parcel, squeezing out as much air as he could, and he used the loop handles to bind it with several knots. He set it aside on the counter.

Tony wasn't ready for the next step yet, so he changed into jeans and a T-shirt, put on his sunglasses and had a large drink to settle his nerves. He didn't feel better, but at least he was somewhat calmer.

The silence was truly awful. Tony thought he could hear the cells beginning to turn rotten in Snake's body. Snake had become a factory, a death mill where billions of tiny forces worked away nonstop at the process of decay. Snake was sliming out, so there was no time to waste.

He mopped up the blood on the bathroom floor, and then began the awkward job of removing Snake's clothes. Why? It seemed the thing to do. In the pockets of Snake's cheap black pants he came across a wallet containing thirty-two dollars, and a medicine jar that held fifty Demerol pills. Fifty of them! To think I almost felt sorry for you, you cheap bastard. I'm in good shape now, he thought gleefully. Tony burned the driver's license along with a few other papers in the kitchen sink, wiped Snake's wallet clean, and buried it in an empty milk carton in his garbage bag. He put Snake's clothes in another bag.

So far, so easy. Three ordinary parcels to throw away. But what about the big parcel in the bathtub? Tony needed help. The Pied Piper had gotten him into this mess, so where was he? Not a peep. The little fucker. I'll bring him here fast. Tony got on his knees and smashed his forehead against the kitchen floor. It worked immediately.

—Slime.

"Jesus, man." He struggled to his feet. The pain wasn't so bad but black spots peppered his vision for a moment. "You can't take me to a certain point and then leave me there alone."

—I can do anything.

"Then get rid of the guy in the bathtub."

—That's your problem.

"I might as well call the cops," Tony said. It was a bluff, and not a very good one, but it had just occurred to him that the Pied Piper needed him, or wanted him, in some way. He reappeared the minute Tony banged his head on the floor. For the moment, at least, it seemed to give Tony a slight amount of leverage. "I'll tell them he was a trick, and he turned nasty and pulled a knife, and I had to defend myself."

—That's the ticket.

The quick mockery worried Tony. "Why not?"

—You defended yourself by stabbing him all those times in the back?

"Well . . ."

—Remove the body, plasmodium.

"How do I do that?"

—Piecework.

"No way, man, no way. I'd rather call the cops, and take my chances that way."

—Yes?

"You bet yes. I'll do it right now."

Tony turned toward the telephone, but froze, and then sagged against the wall. It was as if invisible hands were wringing his liver, and at the same time a tiny neon worm burned like acid in the depths of his ear, eating its way into his brain.

—Yes?

". . . No . . ."

—I own your mind, which means I own your body. Listen and hear, boy. I can make the acid pour into your stomach all day, I can dump adrenalin into your blood till your heart shivers so bad it knots up and can't send oxygen to your brain, I can bleed your eyes and ears. I can make your nose run so much you'll drown in your own snot. I can cover you with sores, I can make your skin itch so much you'll scratch it to bloody shreds, and I can bloat your balls so they're as big and foul as rotten apples, or I can make them as small and hard as orange pips. I can squash them, I can make you piss hot acid and ground glass, I can make your lips peel off like layers of parchment, and your muscles turn to mush. I can make you chew up your tongue and spit out the bits. I can turn the marrow in your bones to lava, I can fill your mouth with fungus and raise hordes of maggots in your arsehole. And believe me, I can keep you ticking along this way forever. Yes?

"... Yes ..."

—Good little plasmodium. Now get to work. Use the Ginsu steak knives you got from that nig-nog limousine driver. They're tacky, but they'll do the job.

"You know everything in my life?"

—Your life is mine.

Then he was gone. Tony obediently got the steak knives and took them, along with every spare plastic bag he could find, into the bathroom. The pasty bulk of flesh was still there.

"Sorry man, but you're already dead."

Tony made a few tentative slices at one elbow, and promptly threw up all over the corpse. Jesus mother's tit, he'd never get through this. He made sure that the drain was fully open, turned on the cold shower and pulled the curtain around the tub. While Snake was being sluiced down, Tony went to the sink to pat water on his own face and rinse his mouth out. Then he took a Demerol, figuring it would help him through the ordeal.

A few minutes later, he hummed as he cut loose Snake's left forearm. The elbows and knees were trouble enough with all those wires to saw, but the shoulders were much worse, far messier. At least the head was easy. By then, however, Tony had filled every plastic bag he had. He would get more tomorrow, but for now the only thing he could find to put Snake's head in was the spaghetti pot his mother had given him. It had a lid. Tony squirted some wash-up liquid in with the head and added water until the pot was nearly full, hoping the detergent would delay the inevitable rot and stench. He placed the covered pot on the stove, where it did not seem too conspicuous.

*　　*　　*

He did as much as he could, eight plastic-wrapped items, the head in the pot and the torso still floating in the tub. When he woke up the next morning, Tony had to have a shower. He couldn't stand the feeling of dried blood on him, dried scum, and the bits of Snake's flesh that had lodged beneath his fingernails. He had fallen asleep as soon as the last package was taped up. The only way he could have his shower was if he had it with the torso too, since there was nowhere to put it. Reluctantly, that's what Tony did, heaving the ghastly thing as far back in the tub as possible and then standing directly under the showerhead. He had to clear the drain a couple of times, as it got clogged with greasy chunks of gristle and meat. Tony showered quickly, then sat on the edge of the tub and cleaned between his toes with running water.

As he had done the night before, he filled the tub until the torso floated, and sprinkled pine-scented kitchen cleanser on it. To be on the safe side, he added two-thirds of a bottle of Canoe, the last of his rubbing alcohol (which was also useful in certain sexual scenarios) and a blue toilet tablet. That should keep the smell down for a while.

Sleep had refreshed him somewhat. Tony didn't need the Pied Piper to tell him what he had to do. Fortunately it was overcast outside. He put on his sunglasses and went to the supermarket to buy the largest and heaviest trash bags they had. He also bought a couple of rolls of sticky packing tape, more detergent, rubber gloves, alcohol and disinfectant. The store's fluorescent lights were getting to him, even with his sunglasses on, so he picked up a pair of mirrored clip-ons that helped considerably.

Tony had a couple of ideas. He now thought he knew the best way to get rid of the torso, and in the back of his mind he had a rough notion of how to escape the torments of the Pied Piper once and for all. But he would have to approach it carefully when the time came, never quite letting his thoughts settle on it, or else the demon might tune in and foil the attempt.

It was a long day, taking four trips in all. A piece of arm and a piece of leg each time. He carried them in a gym bag, and he dropped them in litterbaskets, dumpsters, anywhere reasonably safe, where they were unlikely to be noticed and opened. He even managed to slip one forearm into the trash bin at Burger Billy's, along with the remains of his lunch. By the end of the afternoon Tony was exhausted from all the walking he had done, but he also felt enormously relieved that much of Snake was scattered around the center of the city. Out of my life.

THE DREAMS OF DR. LADYBANK

Tony examined the trunk of Snake's car, to make sure it had enough room for the torso. Some people fill a trunk with garbage and then just leave it there, God only knows why. Snake's trunk had a well-worn spare tire, a jack and some small tools, and the puzzler: a beat-up copy of Elvis's *Blue Hawaii* album. Good place to keep your record collection, Snake. Tony parked the car right in front of his building.

He had a drink, though he didn't need it to relax. He felt serene, almost — *almost* in some kind of control of his life once more. Tony had sailed through this horrible day, popping Demerol whenever the wave seemed to falter.

What day was it anyway? Sunday. Time? A little after six in the evening. Good, perfect. People were eating, and in a few minutes they'd sit back to watch *60 Minutes*. There would not be many cops on patrol at this in-between hour.

Wearing the rubber gloves, Tony somehow got the torso into a large heavy-duty garbage bag. He knotted and taped it, then slid it into another one. Was a third bag necessary? Why not? There was no point in taking chances. Tony wiped a thin streak of scum from the outer plastic when he finished, and dragged the big sack into the living room. He removed the rubber gloves and carefully put bandaids on his fingertips. With the torso, at least, there would be no prints on the bags.

Now. No need to carry it, even if he could. Tony looked up and down the hallway outside his apartment. All clear, nobody in sight, no sounds of activity. Tony tugged the garbage bag by its plastic loop handles, dragging the load into the hall. He locked his apartment, and then pulled the sack to the top of the stairs. Still no one about. Gripping the loop handles firmly, he tipped the torso over the edge and followed behind, letting it bump down the stairs but holding it so that it didn't bounce noisily out of control. It was like walking the dog, Tony thought with a smile. No sweat. When he got to the ground floor he stepped over the bag and was about to drag it to the front door when Leo Jenks emerged from his apartment. He was okay, a middle-aged man who delivered bread for a local bakery, but Tony wasn't at all happy to see him at that moment.

"Hey, Tony."

"Leo, how's it going?"

"Good, and you?"

"Okay. Just cleaning up."

"Yeah? Whaddaya got there?"

"Newspapers and magazines. You want 'em?"

Jesus, don't get cute.

"Not unless it's *Penthouse* or *Playboy*," Leo said with a sly grin. Like everyone in the building, Leo knew Tony was gay.

"'Fraid not."

"The stuff piles up, huh?"

"Sure does."

"Let me give you a hand," Leo said, bending to reach for one end of the garbage bag.

"No, don't bother, Leo. It's too clumsy to handle that way, but no trouble to drag, you know? Just leave the front door open for me, will you?"

"Yeah, sure. See you, Tony."

"Yeah, thanks."

Fuck me pink, Tony thought when Leo was gone. If he had got his hands on it he'd have known right away that it wasn't a bunch of newspapers and magazines. But it was no time to stand around, worrying about a near-miss. Tony hauled the sack outside to the edge of the curb as quickly as he could.

"Jesus," he groaned, heaving it up and into the car. Fucker must have weighed a quarter of a ton. Tony banged the trunk shut and allowed himself a casual glance around. The old geezer next door was sitting on his front stoop, but he was busy playing with his grandson. There were other people on the street, but none of them seemed to be watching Tony. He straightened his sunglasses, got into the car and drove away.

"All *right.*"

With the window rolled down and the radio playing, it wasn't bad at all, especially since the humidity had fallen. Tony liked driving but he seldom got the chance to do any, so it was a treat for him to be out like this—in spite of the load he had in the trunk. He cruised through the neighborhood, then headed into the center of town. He circled The Green, drove out to the east side and checked the action along the commercial strip leading to the mall. Nothing much happening. Well, of course. It was a Sunday night, and that's the way it's supposed to be. Quiet.

By nine o'clock Tony was ready to get it done. Better to do it while there was still some light in the sky. He drifted north into the woody hills near the highway, on the outskirts of town. There were few houses on these side roads that zig-zagged up the steep valley walls. A power company sub-station. A junkyard. A landfill transfer depot. Not much else. Aha, there it was, just what Tony was looking for: a clearing off to the side where folks dumped unwanted items. He stopped the car and got out. -

Nothing, only trees for a hundred yards in either direction. Tony listened carefully, but there was no sound of an approaching car. On the ground: an abandoned sofa, several bald tires, rusty wheel hubs, a corroded hand-wringer washing machine, and the best sight of all, plenty of garbage bags similar to the one Tony had.

People. Makes you wonder, Tony thought with a smile. There was a junkyard down the road, *and* a landfill station. They could bring their rubbish to either place, but no, they've got to throw it here, along this nice woody stretch of land.

Tony opened the trunk and took extra care not to rip the bag as he pulled it out. He dragged it across some of the other bags on the ground. Still no cars coming. He left the package behind a dirty but unscarred vinyl clothes hamper that had no doubt been discarded because of its ugly design.

Sorry, Snake. We had our moments, one or two.

*   *   *

The pot on the stove was a shock. For some reason, Tony had blanked it right out of his mind. But there it was. Okay, so he still had work to do. Tomorrow he would dispose of Snake's head, and then he would deal with the Pied Piper.

— 10 —

The windowshade appeared to be on fire, which meant it was extremely bright outside. The sun has no mercy, he thought. Men have no mercy—not much anyway, and not often. Everything was

71

supposed to be better now, but it wasn't. Tony thought two days had passed, but it might have been three.

Where was his brain? The sun beat him, the moon laughed at him, nothing worked. He found it hard to keep track of anything. So much time, thousands of minutes, had been spent sitting still, trying to think, trying to focus his mind. Trying to find it.

The Pied Piper had got him once—or was it twice? Hard to be sure. The Demerol helped and Tony had found some silence, but the demon voice jarred him from sleep, pried open his brain when his guard was down. No mercy.

—Open a vein.

"Fuck you."

—Get it over with. Best thing.

Like that, juiced with spasms of pain meant to keep Tony in line. But he was learning. The Pied Piper couldn't be there all the time. Even in a fog of Demerol, Tony managed to organize his thoughts into a rough plan. There wasn't much chance it would do any good, but it was worth a try. Anything was better than going along with this shadow-life, twitching between drugs and torture, barely able to function.

He remembered how he had at first been plagued with a lot of static and garbled bits of words. That had been bad enough, but not nearly as bad as the clear reception he had been getting ever since he removed his metal fillings. The metal had not aided the broadcast, as Tony originally believed, but instead had actually interfered with it, at least a little. So, a lot of metal would block out the Pied Piper completely. Maybe.

The spaghetti pot was taken, unfortunately. Tony put on his doubled sunglasses and ventured outside. The glare was so fierce that his eyes were seared with pain from light leaking in at the sides, and he was nearly blind before he even got to the corner. The supermarket was three blocks away, too far to go. Tony dived into the cool, dark interior of the Sparta Mart, a neighborhood shop that carried groceries and a few basic items. Mrs. Bandana, the wife of the owner, sold a lottery ticket to another customer and then directed her indifference to Tony.

"You got any aluminum foil?"

"Bottom left," she replied curtly, pointing toward the rear of the store.

Tony took two overpriced boxes. He also found some rolls of

masking tape, which he figured should not be as harsh on his skin as the sticky packing tape he had at home. He paid, and insisted on being given a plastic bag to carry his purchases. Tony needed it for Snake's head. Steeling himself to face the glare outside, he ran all the way back to his apartment.

He put the pot in the kitchen sink and removed the lid. The smell was horrendous. He turned on the hot water and let it pour over the head, gradually rinsing away most of the muck. At least there were no worms crawling through the eyes and mouth, nor any other nightmare surprises that Tony had feared. When the water finally ran clear, he dumped the head into the sink and put the pot aside on the counter.

You don't look so bad now, he thought. What was your name? Alvin Doolittle, according to the driver's license. How the hell could a person with a name like that ever get into the Legion of the Lost? Snake sounded better. In fact, he looked better dead than alive. A bit rubbery, but the color had washed out nicely. The skin had the bleached look of white marble, Tony thought, or a fish's belly. There was no sign of trauma in Snake's face. He looked calm, an admirable quality.

Something Snake had said. The Doc this, the Doc that, trust the Doc, do what the Doc says. Hard to tell if it meant anything at all, since the whole scene had been mad, sick. But Snake told him to go see a shrink, and that seemed important. Tony had been sent to a shrink by the court, the weird guy with the weird name. All my troubles started after that. Maybe he can help.

—Easy, slime.

Tony shuddered. "Go away."

—Poor little plasmodium.

"The Doc'll take care of you."

—Maybe I am the Doc.

Jesus, that was a thought. "Are you?"

—You've got two heads now. You tell me.

"I'll find out, one way or the other."

—Will you indeed?

"Believe it."

But the demon was gone, his parting shot a raucous laughter that erupted in Tony's head. It took a moment to clear. Oh yes, I'll kill you, he thought bitterly. If he could just get to see that shrink again, he might find an answer.

Tony took a large, empty trash bag and dropped Snake's head into it. Then he rolled the black plastic tightly, taping it to form a rough ball. When he was satisfied with his work, Tony put the head in the Sparta Mart bag and then picked it up by the loop handles. There. He looked like anybody carrying home a nice big cabbage or honeydew melon from the market.

—Die, you slime.

"Oh fuck . . ."

—Lie down and I'll help you die. It'll be easy, it won't hurt at all. Lie down. Now.

"No, no . . ."

But Tony could feel the demon taking hold of him. The blood in his veins felt like broken glass, slashing him apart, churning his insides into a massive hemorrhage. As he started to fall, he grabbed the box of aluminum foil from the counter, ripped it open and fumbled to unroll a length of it. He hit the floor, rapidly losing strength. He couldn't even tear the foil, but he did yank enough of it out of the box to pull over his head—

—and suddenly the Pied Piper was silenced. Not completely gone, for Tony could still sense his presence, but substantially muffled. He pressed the aluminum foil to his skull, adjusting it to fit more tightly, and then he waited anxiously. Was the demon voice merely toying with him, allowing Tony to think he had won, before unleashing the final assault? It would be just like the sadistic bastard to do that.

But nothing happened, and Tony gradually became aware of a distant, very faint static buzz. There you are, little buddy. A minor irritation, nothing more. No pain. No words. No torture. Tony laughed out loud, shocked with relief and joy.

"It works! It works!"

Now you know you can beat the guy, Tony told himself. It's always something simple, easy to overlook or misunderstand. Like the common cold that wiped out the Martians in that old movie.

*　　*　　*

Less than an hour later Tony was ready to go. You look like a crazy, he thought sadly as he checked himself for the last time in the bathroom mirror. But that didn't really matter because he would be walking through the south end, where half the people out on the street looked damaged one way or another. Maybe he should have kept Snake's

74

car, instead of abandoning it in the lot at the train station. No, the car was a major risk. He'd done the best thing he could with it. Now Tony would just have to walk, and if people stared—let them.

Tony had fashioned an aluminum foil skullcap, which he kept in place with an ordinary headband. For extra safety he had tied a couple of dozen thin foil strips to the headband, making a long fringe that hung down as far as his jaw on both sides, and around the back.

It would be better to wait until evening, but he was anxious to get rid of Snake's head. Besides, Doctor Ladybank wouldn't be at his office later. Now that the Pied Piper couldn't reach him, Tony was full of good ideas. He'd looked up psychiatrists in the Yellow Pages, and discovered an Ian Ladybank. His office address was in the center of the city. That was the shrink Tony had been sent to, no doubt about it. He called to make sure that Ladybank would be in all afternoon, but he didn't give his name or ask for an appointment. It seemed a safe bet that when he walked in with this headgear they'd lead him right to the shrink.

Tony's doubled sunglasses did a pretty good job, but all the light leaking in at both sides was enough to wear him down fast, so he taped the shades to his face with masking tape, overlapping the strips until he had built up a thick screen that tapered down across each of his cheeks. That should do it, he thought. Block out most of the unwanted light and you'll be okay. He could hear the Pied Piper still clamoring to get in, but faint and far away. Oddly, it was good to know the demon hadn't vanished.

Tony walked a couple of blocks with no difficulty. The tape worked fine, his eyes were still okay. No sweat. Well, no, that wasn't exactly true. It was a hot day, very humid, and Tony was perspiring already. But that was a minor inconvenience. He felt good for the first time in ages.

Was he the only person on earth being tormented by the Pied Piper, or were there others? Strange, how Tony had felt a sudden urge to ask Snake if he heard the voice. A very strange thing to do—you just don't ask other people if they hear any mysterious voices. It didn't matter, because Snake had so much metal in his head that he most likely wouldn't hear anything even if the Pied Piper did broadcast to him.

That old movie came to mind again. Was it possible that the Pied Piper was really a Martian, or some other alien? Could this be part of a plan to take over human minds, Tony wondered. Drive us crazy,

75

turn us into slaves? *Because,* he thought, if the voice came from me, if it was all just my own craziness, then how could the aluminum foil work? So the voice had to come from someone or something outside. Ordinary people can't do that, but perhaps it was a top-secret government project. Or aliens. Tony had seen a few stories in the newstand rags about this kind of thing, and he had always laughed them in the past. But this was now. He knew a lot more, from bitter experience. Anything was possible.

What about Doctor Ladybank? The Doc. Was he in on it? Why did Tony feel drawn to see the man today? For help. But the Doc hadn't helped him at all last time. Just gave him some bullshit about watching out for—bright lights and colors. Jesus, maybe I was hypnotized, Tony thought. Maybe that's what this is about. If that's it, I'll kill him. Right there in his office.

How good it felt to be able to use his brain again! It had been so long since his thoughts weren't cluttered or twisted with the Pied Piper's invasive tactics. Tony felt human again.

But he was beginning to think he had make a mistake. He was approaching the center of the city and he still hadn't gotten rid of Snake's head. It was partly due to the fact that Tony had not found a suitable place to dispose of it, but even more because he was simply attracting too much attention. People—every rotten one of them— were stopping in their tracks to gawk at him as he walked along the street. How could he dump his parcel with a big audience on hand? Somebody would step up to open the bag at once and then they'd all grab him before he could get away.

To make matters worse, the aluminum foil skullcap and fringe were magnifying the heat and frying his brain. Tony was sweating like a pig now. He stopped abruptly and went into the department store he had almost passed. The air-conditioning came as a great relief. He wandered around for a few minutes, imagining that all the security people in the place were watching him.

Shit! What if they demanded to inspect his bag? He couldn't very well refuse, they'd just hold him until the cops came. Tony began to tremble with fear. Then he saw what he needed. He kept his shopping bag clutched tightly in one hand, and he went to the counter in the sports department. He paid for a New York Yankees baseball cap, which he put on immediately. It sat snugly on the aluminum foil. The clerk appeared to be in shock, but handed him his change and receipt without a word. Tony then strolled out of the store as if he hadn't a care in the world.

Brilliant idea, he thought. The fringe was still hanging in plain view, and there was all that tape on his cheeks, but he now felt somewhat less conspicuous. It would be a lot better if Tony could do away with the fringe, but that was too risky. If he let the Pied Piper back in, he'd never be free again. Maybe he could do without the fringe, maybe the skullcap was sufficient to block out the Pied Piper, but Tony wasn't about to take a chance.

Burger Billy's was crowded. Tony was pleased to see that he was indeed drawing fewer stares, thanks to the baseball cap, but there were still people watching him. He didn't feel comfortable enough to drop Snake's head in the trash bin, so he turned around and left the fast food restaurant.

The public library. That was the place. There was a large litter barrel (disguised as a piece of mod sculpture) in front of the library. Tony had already tossed one of Snake's feet into it and the newspapers had made no mention of its having been found. Best of all, it was located in the middle of a long sidewalk that went from the curb to the library, which sat back a distance from the street. That meant he could time it so that there was no one nearby when he walked past and dropped the dead man's head in the artsy-fartsy opening of the litter barrel. In spite of the heat, he pushed on in a hurry.

One more block, Tony thought. Then the park. He was sticky with sweat, tired but determined. I'm going to treat myself when this is over. A quick warm bath, followed by a long cool shower. Broil a T-bone steak, wash it down with that bottle of bubbly the TWA steward had given him, do a couple of lines and hit the bars. But tonight it would be for fun, not work.

"Hey, fuckhead."

Tony was only a little way into the park when the half dozen or so teenagers descended on him. Assholes, every one. They had nothing better to do with their time than hassle the elderly, the drifters and the gays who lingered in the park. Anyone they felt they could pester without comeback. They closed around Tony like an evil cloak, taunting him, shoving him, flicking fingers at his Yankee cap, snatching at the plastic bag.

"Fuck off, you little shits."

"Eat shit, fuckhead."

Some of them were a year or two older than he was, but that didn't matter. Tony strode on toward the library, poking elbows at anybody who got too close. They answered by bumping him, and then he was tripped. As he fell, cursing them loudly, he was hit on the head and his hat went flying. The aluminum foil skullcap was knocked loose. Oh Jesus, no. He clamped his hands on it and tried to adjust the headband. Somebody was yanking at the strips of foil that hung across Tony's face.

"Nice hair, asshole."

"What's in the bag?"

"Open it."

The kids were already pulling at the tightly wrapped parcel. Tony jumped up and lunged for it, but they pushed him down again. He had been sweating so much that the masking tape wouldn't stick to his cheeks anymore. Light flooded in, burning his eyes. Tony shrieked at them and swung out with his fists, but he didn't make contact. In return, he was pummeled from all sides. The doubled sunglasses were ripped from his face.

Tony fell to his knees, hands clapped tightly over his eyes. I'm okay, I'm okay, he tried to convince himself. But he already knew from the shouts and screams that they had discovered what he had in the bag. Now he was being kicked and punched, and when he tried to ward off the blows he was hit in the stomach so hard his eyes opened briefly. The color purple ravaged him—he was in a flowerbed full of violets.

Tony screamed.

* * *

"No! Don't touch that, not that! Please don't—"

But they did. They were ready to take his mug shot, and one of the cops calmly reached up and pulled off that stupid aluminum foil thing he had on his head.

* * *

Zzzzzt.

78

EPILOGUE

Life isn't disappointing, but people so often are. They may raise your hopes for a while, but sooner or later they'll let you down. People are . . . Doctor Ladybank pondered the matter for a few moments, seeking to find the right word. Yes, he had it.

People are unworthy.

He was not entirely sure what they were unworthy of, but the point seemed irrefutable. It was difficult to follow every train of thought to the end of the line when you were drowning in a sea of disillusionment. The gift—for that was how Doctor Ladybank now regarded it, not as a skill or a technique—was apparently gone. Radio silence. Day and night he tried to tune in someone, anyone, but he found no one.

What happened? Doctor Ladybank wasn't sure. For a few days after Tony Delgado's arrest, the boy could still be reached. But then he began to fade gradually, and after a month he disappeared altogether. It was not the effect of buildings and metalwork and power lines, or Doctor Ladybank never would have managed to reach across the city in the first place. Nor could it be a matter of distance, as he had driven the fifty-plus miles to the Bartholomew Forensic Institute, part of the state hospital for the criminally insane, where Delgado was being held pending trial. He parked in the visitor's lot and sat there for an hour, trying feverishly to regain contact with the boy. Nothing.

Doctor Ladybank wondered if the failure was his. But he did the same things with his mind, he hadn't forgotten how it worked, anymore than you can forget how to ride a bicycle. Of course, it may have been a gigantic fluke, a scientific peculiarity that had its brief moment and then passed. But Doctor Ladybank could not believe that. He still had faith in his gift. All he had to do, he told himself, was persist. It would come back to him. And he would connect. Believe. Persist.

His favorite theory about this temporary failure centered on the inadequacy of his two subjects. Snake had always been tricky to handle, a dim prospect. Doctor Ladybank had never enjoyed the same intimacy of mind with Snake that he had with Tony. To steer him

79

out to Jack's backyard and then get him over the hump—that was like composing the *Gurre-Lieder*. Delgado, on the other hand, was ravishing in his openness and malleability. Great potential, unlimited opportunity. But something had gone wrong, and Doctor Ladybank feared that he had gone too far with the boy. Now parts of Delgado's brain had simply shut down and were incapable of any mental reception. How else to explain it?

Of course, terrible things had happened. But no, don't say that. Terrible is an emotive word that has no meaning. It would be more accurate to say that unfortunate things had happened. He couldn't explain it, but it was hardly all his doing. When minds meet and interact in such a pioneering way the results are almost certain to be unexpected. Two minds adrift in each other, it was like—and here Doctor Ladybank took comfort in the persistence of the musical metaphor—a vast orchestra lost in the aleatoric reaches of the night.

Besides, Snake and Tony were hardly innocents.

Fuck it, as they would say.

Doctor Ladybank stared at the papers in front of him, but he couldn't see the words. It was that time of day, when he usually summarized his notes on the patients he'd seen, but his mind just wouldn't focus. Such boring and squalid lives that people insist on living . . . Doctor Ladybank was glad when the phone warbled.

"Margaret Zuvella on the line for you."

I remember the bristols, but the face escapes me.

"Yes, put her through." Pause, click. "Hello, Maggie?"

"Hi, Ian. How are you?"

"Fine, thanks, and you?"

"Busy as usual, but bearing up."

Doctor Ladybank gave the obligatory chuckle. "Now, what can I do for you on this rainy Tuesday?"

"I was hoping you'd agree to examine a client of mine. He's indigent, of course, so it'll be at the usual lousy state rates. But he's convinced you can help."

"Oh? What case is it?"

"State versus Anthony Delgado."

"Ah."

"You know him, you saw him a while back on another case. He seems like a major league fuck-up, but what do I know? The state experts are picking his brain now, which is why we need you."

"Yes."

"Yes, you remember him? Or yes, you'll examine him?"

"Both."

"Ian, you're a doll."

Not really—but Doctor Ladybank didn't say that. The tide had come in, his boat was lifted off the sand, and he was sailing again. The time would come, he knew beyond the slightest doubt, when he would make contact, and *connect*, with some other person. When that happened, Doctor Ladybank would progress with the gift, exploring new territory, achieving the unimaginable.

But for now, thanks be to the void, he had a chance to learn more from one of his mistakes. Perhaps even to save it.

*   *   *

Tony smiled when he saw Doctor Ladybank's fountain pen, one of those fat expensive jobs. In happier times he'd had a couple of well-off tricks who used that kind of pen. Check-writers with skinny dicks.

They were in a small consulting room at Bartholomew. It was painted the mandatory institutional shade of pastel green, and it was stuffy from a lack of air-conditioning, but it was as good as heaven —compared to the ward in which Tony was kept. The guard stood outside the door, keeping an eye on them through the sturdy wire-and-glass window. Doctor Ladybank had brought Tony a carton of cigarettes from Maggie. Tony had never smoked before, but in a ward full of wackos it seemed a perfectly natural, even healthy thing to do.

The questions were stupid and boring, but Tony tried to give polite answers. There was something eerie and unreal about this. After so much time, he was still unsure of Doctor Ladybank's true role in what had gone down. Had he been directly involved in all of Tony's suffering? Was he partially responsible for the bleak future Tony faced? It seemed unlikely, because the same man was now trying to construct a "demon voice" insanity defense so that Tony would be spared hard prison time. Not that he relished the prospect of an indefinite committal to the nuthouse.

"One problem," Doctor Ladybank said, "is your assertion that the voice stopped communicating with you."

"Yeah, it did."

"When did that happen?"

81

"When I was still in the city jail," Tony said. "It took me a couple of weeks, maybe more, to get rid of it."

"You stopped the voice?"

"That's right."

"And how did you accomplish that?"

"By banging my head on the bars and the cement floor," Tony explained proudly. "See, it really bothered him when I banged my head on the floor at my apartment. He said the people downstairs would put the cops on me. But I figured, maybe he was afraid I'd shake up the works." Tony tapped the side of his head. "So that he couldn't get to me anymore. In jail, I had the time to try it out, to do it everyday, as much as I could take. And it actually worked. I could feel him getting weaker, and finally I couldn't hear him at all anymore. If I'd only done that at the beginning, I'd have saved myself—my life."

"I see." Doctor Ladybank put his pen down. "Do you have to continue this behavior, banging your head, in order to—"

"Hell, no," Tony cut in. "It did the job, and that's it. I never got a kick out of knocking myself senseless, you know. I'm not crazy. I just . . . went through *something* crazy. And I'll tell you this too: he's still out there, man. I know he is."

"Yes. Now, tell me—"

"Doc, I have a question for you."

"Yes?"

"Why did you tell me about bright lights and colors?"

"Pardon?"

"The first time you saw me," Tony said, leaning forward, his arms on the table. "You gave me some line about watching out for bright lights and bright colors."

"I'm sure I didn't," Doctor Ladybank insisted.

"Yeah, you did. It sounded weird at the time, and I didn't give it much thought. But later, when the voice came and all the trouble really started, lights and colors began to hurt me. They got so bad I had to wear sunglasses and dark clip-ons. But I was still in agony." Tony paused. "Why did you do that?"

"I can assure you I did no such—"

"What was it, some kind of test? Or were you just having a little fun with me?"

"Anthony, you won't help your case this way."

Doctor Ladybank was trying to sound calm, but he was clearly flustered. His cheeks had more color now and his eyes cast about evasively as he droned on about Tony's "willful and naive attempt to embellish the delusion," and other uptown bullshit.

"Doc," Tony interrupted. "I'm a whore. Maybe that's why I can always tell when I'm being jived. I thought it was the CIA, or aliens from space, or that I was just crazy. I doubted it was you, I really did. Until now."

"I'll speak with your attorney."

Doctor Ladybank was trying to look annoyed. He shuffled the papers on the table, picked up his pen and began to write. As if Tony were no longer there, and had indeed ceased to exist.

Writing about me. The subject. That's what you were doing. You weren't trying to read my mind, Tony thought, you were trying to write it, to script my life like a dream or some kind of movie in your mind.

"Plasmodium."

Doctor Ladybank looked up sharply when Tony spoke the word. A ghost of a smile formed around the psychiatrist's eyes, seeming to say *I cannot be hurt by you.*

The baleful, haunting expression on the man's face triggered a profound claustrophobia in Tony. It felt as if the world, the universe itself, and every cell in his brain, was shutting down, blinking off, closing forever, and all that would be left was his sense of awareness— perpetual awareness of the dark around him. The room itself was being blotted out.

Write this!

Tony snatched the fat pen from Doctor Ladybank's fingers and in a single swift motion rammed it nib-first through the shrink's right eye. He pushed it as far into the demon brain as he could, and then sat back, experiencing a remarkable sense of clarity and peace of mind.

Doctor Ladybank's mouth opened slightly. Otherwise, he did not move. His left eye was still open, glistening sightlessly. He appeared to be considering the matter.

James Kisner

Jack's Demon

The sparkling spurt of blood dulled the sheen of the knife as it first pierced the flesh. It plunged again into the victim's throat, muting her screams effectively.

Once his victim's silence was assured, the man with the knife cut across her throat again and again, until the woman's head was barely attached to her body.

He paid no attention to the ragged streams of hot blood that jetted across his face and chest.

He eased the body down in the dark cobblestoned alley and continued cutting the woman, working not with desperation as he should be, but at an urgent, steady pace. He always took his time at a task in order that it be well-done. He had no fear of being caught in the midst of his work, either. He expected never to be apprehended.

When he was finished at last, the woman no longer resembled anything that might have been human. She was a mangle of viscera, blood, glistening coils of intestines, and splattered gore, like something that had dropped off a slaughterhouse wagon.

The man stood erect. Even in the darkness of the alley, he could see what he had done, and it temporarily stunned and immobilized him. Then he examined the deed in the abstract portion of his mind.

It was nothing; it was easy; it was meaningless, yet significant Meaningless in that he could do it again if he wished, five minutes from this moment, or never; significant in that he had proven once

87

again that flesh was not obdurate, that being was not in itself enough, that he could kill and not be involved in the killing.

But was he proving it to himself? Or to another entity that served a greater cause?

He was not really certain. He had difficulty separating his higher self from the inner self, the dark one, the beast that inhabited his soul. The demon.

His memory circled back to an evening a few months earlier when he was walking home from a private club where he had overindulged himself in wine.

Suddenly, without knowing why, he turned a corner and strode purposely towards the Whitechapel district. He had been there only once before, perhaps five years previous, and had paid for the favors of a young whore. He had been filled with loathing for himself for some time after that, but it had passed, and he had assumed a normal life.

This night, however, he had no reason to visit that notorious section of London. It was dangerous for a gentleman to be roaming its narrow streets. He could be robbed or killed. He might be lured again into the arms of a disgusting prostitute and contract a venereal disease. It was easy to succumb to the temptations that festered in an immoral environment where everything was for sale. He definitely did not want to go there.

Except that he was compelled to go.

He felt like something was riding on his shoulder, whispering into his ear, goading him on. He attempted to swat it away as if it were a pesky fly, but it kept murmuring.

It stopped abruptly, and the man did too.

His desire to visit Whitechapel vanished. He spun around and made his way back to the street he had turned off from, hailed a passing hansom cab, climbed inside and directed the driver to take him home.

For a few seconds, he trembled with the thought of what he had almost done. He berated his own weakness; he called himself a fool and an idiot for even considering a foray into Whitechapel.

There were places, after all, where better flesh could be bought if he needed it—places where the fancy women were clean and spoke without guttersnipe accents. Every gentleman knew where those places were, so there was no need to wallow in the mire of Whitechapel.

88

JACK'S DEMON

Presently, he experienced an uncomfortable awareness. His senses were heightened, and the smell of horse dung suddenly stung his nostrils. His eyes watered with the assault of night air. Then, the trotting sound of the horse pulling the cab started to pound inside his head, amplified unnaturally until he became tortured by it—it seemed to be jabbing into his brain with a fork. He clamped his hands over his ears, but the sound could not be shut out. He was about to scream out, when the cab pulled up and stopped in front of his lodgings. He covered his mouth and nose with a kerchief to minimize the smells of the sweaty horse and its dung and descended to the sidewalk.

He paid the driver and went inside the building where he kept a room on the third floor. After letting himself in, he undressed quickly, pulled on his nightshirt, and turned down the gas lamp. His senses had become less acute. He convinced himself he had merely suffered a dizzy spell, perhaps from having drunk too much port that evening.

As soon as he shut his eyes, sleep came. So did a dream: he envisioned himself in a great, empty dark place. Abruptly, he sensed an odd presence rushing toward him. Just as it came up to his face he saw what it was: not a fanciful, elegant demon as his friend Aubrey Beardsley might imagine, but a real demon, a great scaly monster with huge yellow teeth and sharp, blood-stained talons. The demon opened its odious, foul-smelling maw wide and swallowed the man in one gigantic gulp.

He felt himself plummeting into the demon's stomach, sliding down the scaly walls of its esophagus as if he were an oyster. Acid burned away at his flesh. He held his hand before his face and screamed: it had been stripped bare so that only bones remained. With no flesh or cartilage to hold the bones together his hand fragmented, the pieces dropping into the pool of acid.

He opened his mouth wide, expecting to emit an even greater scream. Instead, he awoke, grabbing the bed as if he had fallen.

Panic drained away, and in its wake there came an overwhelming sense of well-being, a calmness such as he had never felt before. He was very much a changed man. The awful vision of the dream had purged something from his soul.

He arose from his bed, turned up the gas lamp and went to study his face in the mirror.

His eyes were not his own!

They were yellowish, blood-shot, almost glowing. The dream had been a lie; he wasn't inside the demon, he realized—the demon was inside him!

Said the demon: *You are mine, now, and I am yours, and together, my friend, we will become one power, a killing force.*

"I want none of you," the man said. "You're merely an alcoholic delusion. Leave me be!"

But we have a mission, you and I, my dear fellow. Our task is simple—the world must be rid of whores.

"No!" the man said. "That is not *my* task."

Yes, it shall be as I have said. You must do as I say, everything I say, in every particular that I say it, or I will consume you from inside; I will devour you as I have countless others who have tried to defy me—whose souls have become part of my flesh. You have no choice, sir!

"I have free will. I can resist you."

The demon chortled, making the man tremble. *What an infantile concept! If there were free will, then there would be no evil in the world, for what man, given the choice, would ever choose evil—when the consequenes are so dire?*

"Your reasoning is specious! You are trying merely to confound me."

I shall reason as I wish. You will do my bidding!

"You are not inside me. This is only a dread vision of some sort, brought on by . . ."

Silence!

To demonstrate its presence the demon made the skin on the man's right hand bubble and pop with blisters until it peeled away, revealing the scaly epidermis of the demon underneath—just as the man had seen it in his dream.

Not dream, he realized now. Not dream, but an awful reality.

You are mine, sir!

The man swooned like a woman in a tight corset and passed out. He remained unconscious through the night.

The demon was smug. It had made yet another conquest, and a good one at that—one with great potential.

The man who would be the first serial killer the world took notice of.

*   *   *

JACK'S DEMON

The next day, the man emerged from his lodgings to go about his business. He was a stock trader and made a good income, most of which he was applying to his own investments which is why he temporarily occupied such modest dwellings.

As he made his way through the crowds on the streets of London, walking when he usually would have taken a cab, he came upon a shop where cutlery was sold. An inner impulse directed him to enter the shop. He told the clerk he had need of a very large knife with a keen edge. He pointed to one on display with his left hand. His right hand was bandaged and useless.

He purchased the knife, had it wrapped in brown paper, then left the shop, mingling with the morning crowd until he reached the stock exchange.

The rest of the day passed without significant incident. The man was bothered by a few of his coworkers inquiring about his injured hand, but he shooed them away irritably, saying he had scalded himself while making tea.

After his work day was over, he returned to his rooms, had a small supper, and went to bed early.

That night the man awoke shortly after eleven. He arose from the bed like a sleepwalker, though a part of him was quite aware of what he was doing; he merely had no control. He was an observer of his own actions, trapped inside his own body. He dressed and placed the knife he had purchased inside his cloak.

He went directly to Whitechapel. He did not hesitate this time; he did not resist. He could not.

He prowled the streets for some time, passing whores, thieves and pickpockets, barely noticing men take their pleasure in the shadows, standing up against the women; barely noticing all that was going on around him.

He wasn't sure why he was here. Not yet. The demon had been silent, directing its energies into animating the man, not revealing a purpose. He did not recall the task the demon had put to him the night before.

Then he encountered a woman who might have been twenty or forty. Whichever age she truly was, life had taken its toll on her face. Her expression was that of a hardened, beseiged woman with little hope, though she flashed a fine, rehearsed smile at him. The man was thankful for the relative dimness of the street. The woman's countenance would be too unpleasant to contemplate in the light.

She's the one, the demon said.

The man reacted with shock; he'd almost forgotten the demon was inside him, forgotten that it was controlling him. He tried to ignore the impulses the demon was channelling through him, but he could not; he had been reduced to a minor role in acting out his own life.

"Want some fun, lovey?" the whore asked. Her voice seemed muffled as if in a dream.

"Yes," the man mumbled.

"Where to, then?"

"In here. This alley will do."

"Stand and deliver, eh?"

He nodded and followed her into the alley between two stone buildings. She leaned against a wall at the proper angle and hiked up her skirt. "Will you do me here, love?"

"Yes, I will. *I'll do you!*"

The next few minutes were a blur of actions, none of them his own—

He clamped his hand over the whore's mouth, sliced her throat once, twice, with his left hand, then let her fall to the pavement. Her skirt was still up over her bare abdomen. He thought he saw things crawling over her flesh—the worms of corruption and disease, perhaps.

Kill the worms, the demon spoke.

He carved her easily. It was as if he'd been trained to do this sort of thing.

He didn't throw up till he returned to his room and saw the blood on his face and hands.

* * *

As the weeks passed, the man became accustomed to the blood, the screams, the startled eyes, and the surging panic of his victims. He learned to feed off their fears just as the demon fed off their souls as they departed. He and the demon could hardly be sated.

He eluded the police without effort, the demon providing the instinct to know where they were and where they were not. The same instincts let him pass in and out of his lodgings without attracting notice.

The London papers were filled with outrage. The number of victims reported was up to five.

JACK'S DEMON

The man and the demon, who had become one thing now, one symbiotic entity, had actually dispatched twice that many victims. Some they had simply thrown into the Thames. Others were taken out of the city and hidden in the woods, left out in the open for the wild animals to feed upon.

The man, directed by the demon, wrote taunting letters to Scotland Yard and to the papers. He sent pieces of his victims in wrapped parcels to the authorities.

The demon was creating a legendary evil. He and the man were bonded perfectly. It seemed they would go on forever, man and demon, demon and man, ridding the world of whores, fostering panic and terror in the streets of Whitechapel beyond anything the great city of London had ever witnessed. The murders were so savage, so cunningly executed, that the man achieved a notoriety unheard-of in the annals of crime.

Nothing, however, was forever when dealing with man. The demon knew that in its innermost being but refused to confront it. There had always been an end.

*   *   *

This night marked the turning point—this night when the demon had compelled the man not merely to murder but to mutilate his victim in a frenzy that weakened the bond between them.

The demon had pushed his friend Jack too far. The killing and brutal eviscerating of the woman had sickened the man beyond the demon's power to contain him; he could not numb the man's sensibilities completely.

As a result, the man had acquired a different awareness of the demon, at last recognizing it for what it was: an infestation of evil, a disease within him that must be purged by whatever means.

He didn't want to be possessed any more. He no longer desired to be involved in the demon's scheme. The veil the demon had cast over his perceptions had been rent; the man realized the blood was real, the woman he had just butchered was real, that this was not a long, demon-induced nightmarish theater of the mind as he had fooled himself into believing.

The man turned away from this last victim violently, his cape swirling behind him as he strode out of the alley, planning to turn

93

himself in to Scotland Yard and proclaim to the world he was Jack the Ripper—and take his punishment. The gallows, at least, would free him of the demon, and if peace came only with death, then so be it. It was preferrable to the living hell of being a bloody murderer.

The demon rode with him uneasily, muttering inside his mind: *You can't do this, my friend. You and I are one. Just as I've been one with many great evils of the world before, now I am one with you, and you should be thankful I have made you a place in history. We have accomplished so much, you and I, ridding the world of whores. But there are many whores left. Shall we permit them to continue ruining the lives of weaker men than yourself?*

"Bugger you," the man muttered, picking up his pace.

Damn you! Have you forgotten I have complete control over you? I will make you suffer torments that our victims would gladly exchange for what we've inflicted . . .

"What *you* have inflicted, not I, though it is I who will suffer the consequences."

. . . It's what WE have done together, sir. You held the knife. You ripped them, not I. I am only the evil you needed to propel yourself forward, to commit yourself to the great task assigned you.

"Quit badgering me!"

But the evil was already there, a seed in you, a seed that can be found in many upright, seemingly moral gentlemen, just waiting to germinate —the common seed of evil in all mankind, of which you are a part, a glorious part now. Your deeds will be remembered forever. You will be famous!

"Infamous," the man spat.

Now, don't be curt with me. I am growing impatient with this whimsy of yours.

"You need me too. Otherwise, you could not perform your murderous deeds alone. Without me, you are nothing."

The demon remained silent briefly. That was true, but it would not admit it to the man. The demon would not let him go so easily, but words were having no effect. Pain would be more eloquent. He caused the skin on the man's left cheek to peel off and hiss with bloody steam as if a seering hot iron had been applied to his face.

The man bellowed. "Do what you will. I'll not . . ."

Skin ripped down his right cheek; his forehead exploded in blood blisters. His fingernails were plucked off by an invisible agency, one by one, making him screech with each new pain. The knife cluttered to the street, sliding away into the darkness.

Later, the blade would be licked clean by a stray dog, then picked up by a passing woman who would use it in her kitchen for the next thirty years.

"I won't surrender!"

Damn you! Damn all the weak lot of men. You are going to Hell! You will pay.

The man started running, pumping his legs hard to stave off the agony as blood ran copiously from every opening of his body. His coat and shirt were ripped asunder, his chest burst open and his heart was torn loose. He collapsed on a dark street, his head thudding on the pavement. As his last breath escaped, the demon removed itself and sat atop its former host.

Have a jolly time in Hell, dear fellow!

The demon smirked and bared his yellow teeth, then ate most of the man, belching mightily, then burning the rest of the man and his clothing in a fire summoned from Hell itself. The few ashes that remained were quickly dispersed by the chill autumn wind whipping down the street.

The demon allowed itself to feel a little sadness.

The wind picked up the demon and carried it into the ether high above the earth, where it made faces at the moon.

The demon was disappointed in Jack. Now it would have to find another host.

✻   ✻   ✻

Every demon since the beginning of time had possessed several hosts, and the possession was not always symbiotic. Sometimes the host was too eager, spoiling much of the demon's fun.

Jack's demon remembered Caligula. He was a violent, cruel man, even before the demon had taken up residence in him, and, after that, he becam so obsessively violent and obviously insane, the demon was itself repulsed. It preferred that violence be tempered with imagination; Caligula was merely a dull, mindless monster.

A good host had finesse. A good host was genteel. The perfect host also had good in him—which made the evil the demon compelled him to do more satisfying, more important, somehow. Good and evil were merely two sides of one essential element of man, and the demon fed on the manipulation of those apparently disparate forces. A totally evil man, such as Caligula or Atilla, and others the demon had known, was not much sport.

So before settling in another host, the demon waited.

After a while, the demon settled to earth, flitting from being to being, inhabiting men or women for only short times as it became quickly bored. It settled briefly in Chicago, during the World's Fair, and made a mad butcher of a man named Herman Mudgett. After he allowed the man to be caught and condemned to the gallows, the demon inhabited a succession of souls, sometimes varying its pattern of death and mayhem. For a time it was Typhoid Mary. Then it was a German killer who used a hammer to dispatch its victims. Once, it settled inside a young boy, just to see what it could do with a child's mind, but the child proved too unruly and had enough evil ideas without the demon's help, and the demon departed hastily.

No one was exactly like Jack, its most shining individual example of evil, its most notorious victim and accomplice in the modern age. Sure, people remembered his other triumphs, like Caligula and Atilla and Vlad the Impaler, but Jack—Jack had brought in the new age of murder with panache.

It *missed* Jack.

The demon still carried part of Jack's soul within its substance, and it regretted having been so precipitate in its anger, disposing of Jack all too quickly. Perhaps it should have used a different approach with Jack, appealing to his reason or his male vanity. Together, he and Jack could have dispatched many more victims, terrorizing London for years.

Because Jack had imagination; it was not only the demon that had guided his hand, despite what Jack had thought. His own innate evil had pursued the dread reckoning of whores as well.

The demon was disconsolate. Again, it rode the ether—for years—occasionally probing the earth for suitable habitations.

It witnessed the doings of its siblings: the infestation of monsters like Hitler and his minions, and in later decades, other types of killers, individuals who left their mark in the history of crime, but not quite with the flare Jack had possessed.

The demon was frustrated.

It grew angry at the whole lot of ordinary mortals.

*   *   *

JACK'S DEMON

The petulant demon ranged through space and time for a few decades, pouting and becoming ever more despondent and weary. It ignored the world and its continued wars and the unimaginative, insipid evils—guided by less sensitive demons—the makers of war perpetrated.

Evil—true evil—was high art.

The demon pounded itself over and over for having turned on Jack, one of the most potent, lasting evils it had ever fostered among mankind. Many decades after Jack's passing, people were still talking about him, still uncertain of his identity, still terrified by his dark deeds.

Finally, one day, as it was passing over the earth in its half-billionth orbit, it caught the scent of a fresh dawning of evil below.

The demon wisped down toward the world.

There were people roaming the face of the earth with Jack's genes in them, with the seed of his particular brand of magnificent evil. That first whore he had congress with—before the demon found him—had born his child—who went on to bring more children into the nastiness of the world, and successive generations of Jack's off-spring desseminated the evil over the face of the earth. It had spread throughout the populace like a virus, passed down through the human species until millions now carried that seed.

The demon swooped along a street in a small Midwestern town, keeping itself invisible, as it probed the town's citizens.

Everywhere!

Everywhere, it rejoiced, in everyone, there was a part of Jack still alive.

It informed its siblings, summoning them from the bowels of Hell in the center of the universe, and they raced through time and space to join the demon. Together, they would make good use of the seeds of evil. They would inhabit mothers, good husbands, handsome men and beautiful women, even men of God, finding countless hosts for themselves. The future of mankind, at the dawning of the twenty-first century, was theirs.

Eventually, they would touch every living being on the face of the earth.

At least once.

The Last Time I Saw Grandma

It was the last summer I spent with Grandma.

The energy that used to animate her every movement was waning. Her smiles were forced. Her attempts at idle conversation were labored and difficult. Her affection for me was mitigated by the ceaseless, numbing pain of the disease that was eating her from inside.

I was only twelve that summer, but I had learned enough of the nuances of adult behavior by then—mostly from observation of my constantly warring parents—to see Grandma wasn't entirely herself.

She was a dying person.

*   *   *

My first knowledge of her condition came when my mother was taking me to Grandma's house in Culver, Indiana, where I had been spending two or three weeks a summer since I was four. She told me to be especially kind to her mother and not to ask her to do anything that would make her have to "move around too much."

We were driving down from South Bend in the sluggish 1958 Plymouth station wagon which my mother preferred to the sleeker, meaner Buick my father drove. I glanced over at her and saw the sheen of tears on her eyes, and though I knew better than to pry for more information, I did anyhow.

99

"Is something wrong with Grandma?"

The muscles in Mother's jaw tightened, then relaxed. She sighed and squeezed the steering wheel till her knuckles went white. "No, Jeremy," she said, gulping back a flagrant lie, as I had often seen her do with my father when they were in the midst of a great battle. "She's just getting older. She *can't* get around like she used to."

I mulled that revelation over. Grandma was approaching seventy then. I had never thought she cringed from the onset of "old age." She certainly wasn't senile. She seemed—to me, at the time—to be sharper than my own mother in many matters, especially when it came to fixing suppers that I ate without protest, or when it came to letting me see my favorite television shows, even if they were on at a time that conflicted with her own viewing preferences. Of course, I was her only grandchild, and she liked to spoil me.

I liked to be spoiled too.

I didn't press the issue with my mother. I figured she must be wrong about Grandma. Though I hadn't seen her since Christmas, I knew nothing could really change her—nothing could possibly slow her down. She was indestructible. She would outlive all of us. She could conquer anything.

In my mind, I believed she could even conquer death.

*　　*　　*

The first evening of that visit, after a strained farewell to my mother, Grandma prepared a fantastic welcoming meal for me: chicken and home-made egg dumplings, biscuits with real butter and her own grape jam, green beans seasoned with her special Grandma secret spices, and my choice of chocolate cake or peach cobbler.

When it came to cooking, Grandma was one of the last of the old-fashioned grandmothers, the type we like to believe are still around, but exist nowadays only in the fantasies of advertising.

I hesitated politely when offered the two desserts.

"I know," she said, "why not have both?"

I smiled my acceptance. We were co-conspirators in a plan to keep me happy and stuffed with wonderful food—none of which my mother had ever bothered to learn how to prepare. She preferred to use the can-opener and instant or frozen foods.

Grandma rose from the worn oak table at which we sat in the

100

kitchen of her small, modest house, and went to the old gas range on top of which sat the pie and cake, made especially for me and waiting to be consumed.

At that moment, she was the same Grandma I always knew. A short, rather rotund—but not fat—woman with a round, cheerful face, shiny white hair, and glistening, deep blue eyes. She was clad, as always, in one of her many flowered print dresses.

But when she was halfway across the black-and-white linoleum floor she cried out in pain and clutched at her chest, snatching a wad of flowered fabric in her hand. She waited a few seconds, and the pain must have passed, and with its passing came my realization that she was changed.

She was changed in many ways too, and I just hadn't noticed them, because I didn't want to. I didn't want to believe my mother was right about Grandma.

For one thing, she was smaller—not physically so much. It was her presence as a person that had shrunken. The Grandma I had seen only a few seconds before suddenly didn't exist, and in her place was a frail impersonator.

"What's wrong, Grandma?" I asked, standing up quickly.

"Nothing, Jeremy."

She took a deep breath as I studied her face. It was then I recognized for the first time how death looked when it was infesting a human being. I saw it lurking in her eyes, ready to drag her down, and it was the scariest thing I had ever seen in my short life, scarier than all the monsters I had ever conjured up in my nightmares.

I thought I was going to cry but overcame the impulse. I was too big to cry openly then, especially in front of the only adult I truly loved.

"I'm okay." Her smile was tentative. She stood up straight, erecting herself in a robot-like movement, then continued to the stove to pick up the cake and cobbler, bringing them over to the table as I returned to my seat.

"I'll get you a clean dish." She went to the white-enameled cupboards and reached up for a plate. Out of the corner of my eye I saw her also getting a prescription medicine bottle, which she tucked into the pocket of her apron.

It was true, then. Grandma *was* ill.

I pretended not to notice when she slipped a pill between her lips and washed it down with iced tea.

The cake and cobbler didn't taste as good as they usually did, and

I refused her offer of seconds.

I slept uneasily that night. I couldn't dismiss from my mind what I had seen in Grandma's eyes.

*   *   *

The next day, Grandma served a big breakfast of pancakes with plenty of real maple syrup and eggs and sausage.

I was observing her closely now, watching everything she did, and I noticed how she moved differently, like a clockwork replica of my grandmother, stiffly doing the things she had always accomplished with such ease in the past.

She was also in her nightgown.

The Grandma I knew was always dressed the first thing in the morning. The nightgown clung to her, and I saw she had lost a great deal of weight, almost as if overnight, seeming even smaller than she had the evening before.

Nor was her table conversation the same. Usually she spent my first morning with her asking me about Mom and Dad, and how school had been this year and what I was doing to amuse myself.

Instead, she said, "You know, Jeremy, growing old is hard to get used to. You're only a young boy, and you can't know what it's like. It's nothing like anything you'll ever imagine."

"You're not old, Grandma."

"I am. Very old. My body has already given up the ghost."

I said nothing, wondering what she meant. I had a queasy feeling in my stomach.

"Your body and mind play tricks on you," she continued, "when you get old. You may think you're the same as always, but then one day, you forget something silly, and the next day, you forget something else, and then your body starts to die—without you even realizing it till . . ."

She didn't finish her sentence. She just stared at me, her eyes trying to convey a message my young mind couldn't fully comprehend.

I was a child, and I *knew* I was going to live forever, as all children know. My body could never do to me what she was describing; it would never turn against me. But I was forced to confront the fact this awful thing was happening in Grandma, and it made me angry.

"You're not going to die," I said, my eyes tearing. "You just can't.

THE LAST TIME I SAW GRANDMA

I won't let you."

"Everyone dies," she said. "Harry—your Grandpa—died before you were even born. My mother died when she was young—not much over forty. My father is dead, and so are lots of other people I loved. It's something you can't get away from."

"But I don't want you to . . ." I couldn't say the word.

"I don't want to," she said softly, shifting her gaze away from me. "Nobody does, but . . ." She sipped coffee and I could see her features struggling to assume the happy face she usually wore. "We shouldn't be talking about this. Go upstairs and get ready to go swimming."

I didn't feel like going swimming, but I couldn't think of anything else to do. I certainly didn't want to sit around talking about dying with Grandma.

I wanted to think.

I went down to the lake around which lay the town of Culver. It was only two blocks from Grandma's little two-story house. I splashed around by myself about half an hour, trying to shock the new knowledge of death out of my system, but the water therapy proved futile, so I waded out and lay on the beach, letting the July sun warm me as I contemplated Grandma's plight.

I knew she was telling me the truth about death, because she would never lie to me about anything. I just couldn't accept this particular truth. I also knew, with the certainty only a too self-assured child could have, that it just wasn't right for her to die. It was unfair.

I hadn't yet learned the world was not a fair place. In school, on TV, in our books, we children were constantly told what fairness was and how everything was supposed to be fair.

Then why was God being unfair? Why didn't he take all the bad people away instead of Grandma? What business had He depriving our family of the only loving, caring person in it?

It just wasn't right, I kept repeating to myself. And I guess that was a kind of prayer.

But really it was a criticism of God, and realizing that, I forced myself to quit thinking about it, knowing that criticizing God might get me in trouble, and that my prayers couldn't possibly be answered then.

* * *

Three days went by, and with each day's passing, I witnessed further signs of Grandma's deterioration. Her appetite was diminished. Her blue eyes were losing their sparkle. She fell asleep at odd times. Once or twice, I heard her throwing up in the bathroom late at night, while I lay awake trying to think how I might help her.

Then the doctor came.

It was Friday. Dr. Simpson was the only doctor in Culver, and he had delivered my mother. He was not much younger than Grandma. I had seen him in previous summers, driving down the street in his 1950 turquoise Packard, and I always thought he seemed too old to be much of a doctor. Now he seemed spry and strong compared to the withering shell that Grandma had become.

The doctor was examining her in the living room, and I stood outside the door, peeking around the edge. I flinched when he drew blood from her arm and again when he gave her a shot. He mumbled something to her, and I caught only a few words.

". . . weeks or so . . ." he said, scribbled on a piece of paper and handed it to Grandma. He turned and I darted away before he could see me.

After he left, Grandma gave me the piece of paper and a five dollar bill and had me go to the drug store. I came back with a bottle full of nasty-looking pills with a name I couldn't pronounce.

Grandma took two of them and sat down wearily at the table in the kitchen.

"I can't fix your supper tonight." There was a bit of shame in her voice. "I'm too tired. I'll give you some money, and you can go down to the diner and get yourself whatever you want."

"Aren't you coming with me?"

"I'm too tired even to eat, Jeremy. I have to rest. These pills are to help me sleep."

"But I don't want to leave you."

"I'll be fine. You're a growing boy. You need to eat. They cook good food down there."

"Okay," I said reluctantly. "I'll come back real quick."

"Don't rush yourself, honey," she said, and I smelled something antiseptic on her breath. "It's not good for you to eat too fast."

"I don't want you to be alone."

"I'll be okay. The doctor fixed me up just fine."

I gave her a curious look. I knew the doctor had fixed nothing.

104

THE LAST TIME I SAW GRANDMA

I thought he had made it worse.
But I kept that opinion to myself and did as I was told.

* * *

The streets of Culver at night were quiet and safe. It was a very small town, and during the summer, when there weren't so many boys at the local military academy, there were mostly locals on the street, people out for fresh air or just walking for the exercise. You could walk anywhere in Culver and not be far from anywhere else.

I saw no one on my way to the diner, and the place was almost empty when I arrived. Only an elderly couple and a dark, solitary man were there besides me.

I ordered a cheeseburger and a milkshake and French fries. I ate slowly, as I wondered what I should do. I considered calling my mother and having her come pick me up, because I didn't know how much more of Grandma's suffering I could endure.

But if I left, I knew I would never see Grandma again. This was the last summer I could be with her, because there wouldn't be another summer for her. I also would be deserting Grandma when she needed me the most, and that was cowardly.

Yet I wasn't doing anything to help her. I was probably in the way, and I could not change the fact she was dying.

What if she died while I was there?

That would be awful. Again, I prayed clumsily, not knowing what words could possibly persuade God to let Grandma live. I had never tried to reason with a Supreme Being before — at least not for anything so important.

I finished my meal and left the diner without ordering dessert, anxious to be close to Grandma if she needed me.

* * *

Footsteps sounded behind me as I walked back toward Grandma's house. Normally that wouldn't have bothered me, but I was so concerned over her condition I found myself less certain about other things I always took for granted — such as the safety of Culver's streets at night.

105

JAMES KISNER

I stopped and turned around. Half a block behind me, I saw a man's silhouette. He halted too.

The night seemed to grow darker suddenly. The maples, oaks and sycamores that lined the street and seemed so friendly during the day now formed a scary corridor through which I was afraid to pass.

I gulped as a chilling breeze wafted in from the lake. I was wearing shorts and a short-sleeved shirt, and I broke out in goosebumps.

I directed myself toward Grandma's house again and picked up my pace.

I heard the footsteps again.

Then I was walking even faster, and the man was too.

The next thing I knew I was running.

I sprinted up the steps of Grandma's house onto the front porch, and yanked the screen door open violently, then fumbled with the doorknob.

It didn't want to open.

I glanced back down the street and saw the lengthening, approaching shadow of the man.

Sweat poured down my face. My bladder was about to let go. Then I realized who the man was. I had seen him in Grandma's eyes.

He was Death.

*   *   *

My fumbling with the doorknob finally roused Grandma, and she came to the door to let me in.

"Jeremy! You're so white—and you're shaking. Whatever is the matter?"

My vocal chords didn't want to respond. I just pointed out the door toward the street.

Grandma propped the screen door open with her foot and looked up and down the street. "There's nobody out there," she said, stepping back in and letting the door close on its creaking hinges.

"Somebody was following me."

"Probably just one of the neighbors on his way home."

"No," I said. "He was after me. I mean, after you. It was . . ."

Someone rapped on the door. If I hadn't had the security of Grandma—even a frail, dying Grandma—next to me just then, I would have wet my pants for sure. As it was, I think I let out a childish yelp.

106

THE LAST TIME I SAW GRANDMA

Grandma opened the door without hesitation. Despite her present condition, she still remained essentially fearless in her own domain. The dark man I had seen in the diner was standing there—on the porch outside the door. He was thin and tall—over six feet I'm sure—and he wore a black suit and hat. His gaunt face had a look of fixed hunger and anguish, though he hid this with a twisted smile. I thought he was about sixty, maybe older.

"Hello," he said in a deep, resonating voice. "I've just moved to Culver, and I'm afraid—well, I hate to admit it—but I've lost my way."

Grandma's eyes met his, and I imagined I saw something pass between the two of them—a communication of sorts. Or was it the spark of recognition?

But I was sure the man was a stranger.

"I didn't hear of anyone moving to town," she said.

"I only moved in the first of the week."

"Oh? Where might that be?"

He gave the address of a house a couple blocks west of Grandma's place. It had been vacant every summer I has spent in Culver, and I had always assumed it was abandoned.

"So you moved into the Miller place," Grandma said.

"Yes," he replied—a bit too quickly I thought. "I'm fixing it up. I'm retired and want to settle some place that's peaceful and quiet."

There was a silence of several seconds during which I thought I could detect whatever strange quality dwelled in the man's eyes burning into Grandma's eyes.

I still couldn't find my voice, as if my larynx was actually paralyzed, and I desperately wanted to warn Grandma—to tell her who the dark man really was.

Grandma didn't seem to notice his odd manner. Usually, she had a sixth sense about strangers, being able to read their characters almost instantly, as she did when a salesman knocked on the door offering encyclopedias or insurance. But that sense wasn't working now— maybe because she was ill—because the man asked, "May I come in?" and she let him.

I huddled behind Grandma, trembling. I was about to scream.

All the dark man did was ask directions. Then he thanked her, smiled and left.

*   *   *

JAMES KISNER

That night as I tried to sleep, I heard a rustling noise upstairs in the old house. It wasn't the familiar night sounds of creaking or settling or the brushing of tree branches against the outside walls. It was inside the house. I climbed out of bed and went out into the hallway, and I realized the sound originated in Grandma's bedroom.

I approached slowly, my heart racing to get there ahead of me. The door to her room was open a crack, and I peeped into the somber place where I knew Grandma died a little more each night.

The dark man was in there, bent over my Grandma's body!

I could not see what he was doing, but I could hear the sound of sucking or lapping. I let out a startled cry and rushed toward the man, determined to save my Grandma.

I hit air. The man had vanished—evaporated—so quickly I had not even seen it happen.

I switched on the bedside lamp. Grandma's eyes fluttered open and stared at me without seeing. There was a trickle of blood running down her neck.

"Are you okay?"

She didn't answer.

I gently shook her to awareness. She rolled on her side.

"You're bleeding," I said, my voice cracking. "That man was here, and he bit you on the neck. I saw him do it."

"That's nonsense." She touched her neck, then pulled her fingers away and stared at the blood on them a long time. "It's only a mosquito bite," she said at last. "Now go back to bed."

I stared around the room. There was no sign of anyone lurking in the shadows. One window was up and the curtains were sucked against the screen by the wind. I didn't know what to make of it. How had the man disappeared so easily?

Because he wasn't a man, I realized. I started to explain this to Grandma, but she wouldn't let me talk.

"Go on," she said. "You were just dreaming." There was an impatience in her tone I had rarely heard.

I kissed her good-night again and returned to my room, wondering if I really was dreaming or imagining things.

I didn't fall asleep until almost dawn.

* * *

108

THE LAST TIME I SAW GRANDMA

The next morning, I didn't get up before eleven. Grandma had let me sleep, and when I finally came downstairs, she greeted me with more energy than I had seen her exhibit in some time. She was preparing a bountiful brunch for me.

Her skin, though still pale, seemed a bit pinker. I sat down to eat wordlessly, barely acknowledging her greeting and watched her moving back and forth around the kitchen.

I shuddered when I saw a Band-aid on her neck, but, again, I said nothing. I was too confused. If the man had hurt Grandma, why was she so cheerful?

It made no sense.

That afternoon, I watched quiz shows on TV with Grandma. Grandma was caught up in the excitement of *The Price is Right*, then became tearful at a sad episode of a favorite soap opera.

At two, she said I should go down to the lake and promised to have chocolate chip cookies ready for me when I came back.

I spent the rest of the afternoon bubbling around in the lake with some of the local kids, almost succeeding in not thinking about Grandma and the man in her room I thought I had seen.

When I returned at supper time, Grandma wasn't waiting for me in the kitchen as I expected.

She had left a note on the table, next to a plate of cookies that still steamed from the oven:

Had to go out. Supper's on the stove. Be back later.
Love,
Grandma.

She had never done that before. But the smell of the cookies — studded with chunks of black walnuts — permeated my senses and made me almost giddy with hunger. And on the stove there were stuffed pork chops and creamed peas.

I fed myself and washed the dishes, then went in and watched TV until I fell asleep on the living room floor.

*   *   *

It was after midnight when she came home. I awoke immediately when I heard the stairs creak, and saw her there. She stopped and stared at me a long time, as if she didn't recognize me.

I climbed up from the floor and went over to the staircase where

109

Grandma was frozen in mid-step. Her face was flushed as if she had been exerting herself. There was a new bandage on her neck, and there was fresh blood seeping from beneath it.

"Grandma . . .?"

"Hush, child," she said at last. "Don't ask all those questions I see in your eyes."

"But . . ."

"Listen, Jeremy, you have to promise me something."

"Cross my heart and hope to . . ."

"Just promise."

"I promise."

"Under no condition are you to leave your room at night. No matter what you hear—or *think* you hear."

"Why?"

"I can't explain right now. Maybe some day, when you're older. But just do as I say and don't stir from your room."

"What if I hear a burglar, or something?"

"There hasn't been a burglar in Culver since 1936 that I know of. Only a peeping Tom every now and then, and there's nothing for one of them to see here. If you hear any noise—*any* noise at all—it doesn't mean anything. You stay in your room. Promise?" I had never heard her speak to me in such a stern voice. "It's very important," she added, more softly.

"I promise."

"Good boy. Now go on up to bed."

She stood on the staircase and didn't move when I passed by her, didn't reach out to hug me or kiss me good-night as she usually did. She just watched until I reached the top of the stairs and was out of sight.

I was trembling by the time I got into bed.

* * *

For several nights afterwards, I heard scuffling noises coming from Grandma's room. I was tempted to disobey her several times, but then the noises would cease abruptly and silence would descend on the house.

One night, I saw a dark shadow flitting past my window, and I pulled myself under the covers to hide. Then I heard Grandma's familiar steps coming down the hall to check on me.

She knew I wasn't asleep. She just wanted to make sure I was okay. She stood in the door briefly, her breathing audible in the stillness, looking at me. Then she left quietly, explaining nothing. From then on, she visited me every night after the silence came.

She was changing again. Not becoming sicker—and not going back to her old self. She was being transformed in a way I could not even guess at.

It seemed now that her eyes were visible in the darkness, having acquired a cat-like glow. Her movements were more agile, her senses keener than ever before.

I knew better than to ask any questions, even though many came to mind:

Why are you letting Death visit you every night? Why is there a new bandage on your neck every day? Why are you getting better, Grandma? Why are you growing younger each day?

That's what I had decided was happening. Somehow Grandma was being rejuvenated. The differences were subtle at first: fewer age spots, and a gradual diminishing of the wrinkles in her face, but then the changes became even more dramatic.

One morning, I found the cup that held Grandma's dentures in the bathroom, where she had absent-mindedly left them. I brought them down to her, knowing she could not eat without them. I set the cup with the teeth down on the counter next to the sink, so she would find them and could slip them in without having to embarrass herself in front of me.

But she didn't put them in, not even when she sat down to eat with me.

Grandma had new teeth in her mouth.

They were pointed and sharp-looking.

* * *

A week later, Grandma died in her sleep. When I found her, I cried a long time. God had not answered my prayers. The dark man has hastened her death, just as I had feared.

I stopped crying eventually, then called my mother and Dr. Simpson.

"The big C got her," I overheard him tell his nurse. "Strange

111

how she looks better now than she ever did before—like she was recovering. Sometimes it seems like a relapse comes right before the end."

I looked past the doctor at the still form of Grandma. So that was it, I told myself. People got better before they die.

Death played games with us.

* * *

It was a hot, miserable day in early August. We all sweated in the small church in Culver, while the preacher told us what we all knew —that Grandma was a wonderful person and would be missed. He said God was taking care of her now, and I asked myself where God was when she was alive.

I didn't voice my feelings. Nor did I mention the dark man to anyone and the strange changes she had gone through. Everyone believed Grandma was taken by cancer, and I knew no one would give much credence to what I wanted to tell them. I also believed Grandma would have preferred that no one knew how it was before the end. It was better to let my parents, the other relatives and Grandma's friends believe the lies about her death—the lies about all death.

At the burial, in an old country cemetery on Highway 31, I stood by my parents, who were abnormally quiet. That spooked me as much as the occasion for our being there. I watched numbly as Grandma's coffin was lowered into the ground.

Then I saw *him* out of the corner of my vision: the dark man. He was huddling beneath the ancient oak trees, a shadow among the shadows.

I stepped back slowly from my parents, circled around the others gathered by the grave and walked toward the dark man, briefly forgetting that I was only twelve and about to confront a man who was much taller than I and surely much stronger.

"You killed her," I growled at him. "You killed my Grandma, just when she was getting better."

Most of the man's face was shaded by a wide-brimmed hat. His coat collar was drawn close to his nose, so only a small area of pale skin was exposed. His hands were narrow, with long fragile fingers that clutched his lapels together tightly. Even though I was half-crazy with outrage, I wondered why he wore so much clothing on such a hot day—and why he wasn't sweating.

His eyes were bloodshot, as if he hadn't slept in a week. They shifted away from me, scanned the crowd for reaction, saw no one was paying attention, then looked back at me.

I thought I saw something flickering in his eyes, as if insects were trapped inside and trying to get out.

He leaned down and opened his coat just enough to expose his purplish lips and whispered, "I'm the answer to your prayers," the dark man said. "You prayed, and He heard."

"I don't believe you!" I said.

"I'm the answer to your prayers," the dark man repeated hoarsely. "Someone always listens to prayers."

At that moment, my mother called to me, and I looked over my shoulder reflexively. When I turned back the dark man was gone.

*　　*　　*

In November Grandma came to visit me. She tapped at the window of my room in the middle of the night, and I got up and went to her without thinking. I didn't even question that Grandma had returned from the dead.

She didn't appear to be a ghost. She looked solid, fleshy and vital, and she was dressed in one of those familiar flowered dresses. She also looked much younger, with only a trace of gray in her hair, which had become light brown. Most of the wrinkles had vanished from her face, and . . .

But she was dead. I had seen her buried myself. I had seen her immobile form lying unnaturally in a casket, her face painted by a mortician to resemble a mannequin.

Then she smiled, and I knew it was my Grandma. She was the only person in the world who smiled at me that way.

She spoke, her voice possessed of the strong, vibrant assurance I remembered from every summer I had spent with her before.

"I love you, Jeremy," she said, "more than even my own children. Some day, when you need me, I'll pass on to you the greatest gift I know of—that of immortality. If you want it."

"But how . . .?" I started. I kept glancing at her hair, her sparkling

113

eyes, the glow of her skin. Was this semblance of youth another of death's tricks?

"You don't need to know how—yet. The stranger helped me. He showed me the way, because you prayed and someone answered." Her eyelids twitched, and I could read shame on her face just as I had seen that summer when she was too ill to fix dinner. "Maybe—maybe, it's not the best way. I don't know."

"What's wrong, Grandma?"

"Well, you have to drink blood . . ."

"Drink blood?" I echoed, shivering at the thought.

Her eyes turned up to me, moist now. "Don't think about it. It's not . . ." She glanced behind her, as a cat raced through the yard, running from nothing either of us could see. ". . . it's not as bad as you think. Like I said, it's a way, and there are only so many ways, I suppose. If you get used to it, if you accept it, and don't judge —promise me you won't judge me, Jeremy."

"I don't understand."

Her features assumed a kind of sadness. "I guess you don't. Some day, maybe you will, and I hope you won't judge me then, either. This way, if you want to, you can go on and on and on, just forever. Jeremy, and if you're given that chance, then there must be a reason. Because only a few people are given the choice."

"Are you . . . not dead?"

"Does it matter?"

"I guess not."

She sighed as the wind whipped her dress around her. She seemed to be listening to something. "I wish I had time to explain things better, but I have to go now. I just wanted you to know I'm okay, and I always will be, thanks to you and your prayers."

"Don't leave!"

"I have to. There are things I have to tend to. I'll always be close by, watching. I'll be back some day—when you really need me. When you're ready. It may be days from now, or weeks, or years, but when your time comes, I'll be there. You'll understand then."

"I want to understand now!"

"No, you don't. You don't need to know or understand anything except that life is sometimes a dream, and so is death, and you can wake up from either dream and go on."

"I . . ."

"Jeremy, always remember that I loved you. And promise me you

114

won't tell your mom and dad anything about tonight. They'll never understand."

"I won't say anything."

"I know. You're the best boy." Her eyes fluttered with the effort of crying but no tears came. Finally, she said, in a melodious, otherworldly voice that pulled at me, beckoning me to join her, "Just let me look at you one more time."

After that lingering, loving gaze, she seemed to float away. I opened the window and watched as she retreated into the darkness behind the house, suddenly becoming absorbed in it, as she returned to her new life.

A different kind of life, but life nonetheless.

No, it wasn't a childhood dream. I've considered that possibility many times these last thirty-odd years. Nor was it a fantasy or wish fulfillment. I knew the difference between reality and unreality then, as I do now.

It *was* Grandma I saw that night.

Later, I saw the year of her death etched off the tombstone the first time I visited it as a grown man. I saw her vacant grave a few years after that when they moved the cemetery to widen the highway. Both my parents were gone by then, so only I ever knew about that, and I offered no explanation to the authorities. They're probably still wondering what happened to the woman who had been buried there. I told them it didn't matter and that I would not sue them, which was really their major concern.

I accept all these things about Grandma, because I know they happened. I know that prayers can be answered in the strangest ways. I know there is a kind of justice and sense of right in the way the universe is run, even if we don't always comprehend it. Sometimes the world is fair, after all.

Grandma lives. There have been tough times during my life when I felt her presence, urging me on. And despite what some narrow-minded people might think, she's not a monster.

She never could be. Her life before and her life now are driven by love, and I know that whatever she has to do she does with the same sense of dignity and right that she always had. Someday, when I need her the way she needed me that summer, she'll be there for me. So I don't—I can't—judge her.

I was right from the very beginning.

Grandma really *could* conquer death.

115

It was a damn cold October morning in the woods, and all Kurt Kelly could think about was moose balls.

Kurt and three others, Bob Mickle, Ron Jergens, and Jimbo Long were out to hunt moose in the Superior National Forest in northeastern Minnesota.

Every two years Minnesota held a lottery and the various winners earned the rare privilege of participating in a moose hunt. This was the first time Kurt had won, and only the second time he had tried and he was not yet thirty. He was the envy of many older men who had been trying to win for years.

Winning had its conditions; you had to pay $250 for a permit and take three other hunters with you, and only one kill was allowed per hunting party. You also had to go to a class and learn all about moose and the dangers and perils of hunting the big animals—along with more rules and conditions.

Kurt was six-foot-one, well-fed but not fat, with sandy blond hair and dark blue eyes. He'd chosen his partners in the hunt well:

Bob was a good friend and an excellent hunter who had bagged quite a few deer in his day, though he had never shot a moose; Ron was a political choice, because he was Kurt's immediate superior at the office where he worked and asking him along would accrue innumerable ass-kissing points toward a promotion and year-end bonus; Jimbo was chosen for two reasons, one that he was an old friend of Kurt's father, the other that he had *actually* hunted moose before and could help the younger men.

Hunting moose was a lot different from hunting deer. Moose were big and sometimes mean, aggressive mothers. A bull might charge you just for the hell of it, and a charging animal that weighed almost a ton was something not to be fucked with; moose had balls. Jumbo-sized balls.

Though Jimbo Long was a friend of Kurt's family, he was also a liability. He was a big, gross man, about fifty-five, who liked to fart, belch and cuss. He smelled of perpetual gastrointestinal distress, stale bread, onions, cigarette smoke, and often, female genitalia. It was also obvious he hadn't much regard for bathing. His main virtue was his skill at tracking.

Kurt yawned and staggered into the shafts of dawning light penetrating the woods through the trees. He was a bit fatigued by the five hour drive up from Minneapolis, but he was up for the hunt. He reached into his hunting jacket and clipped mirrored shades to his glasses.

"Well, troops, are we ready to go after the fucker?"

Jimbo sat on the chromium running board of Kurt's Bronco, enjoying a last cigarette before the hunt began; he never smoked when he was tracking. He stood up and emitted a profoundly labyrinthine fart, which, if set to music, would sound something like "Yankee Doodle." "I'm ready," he said. "My butt's sore from riding up here, and I want to get my feet moving before the damn cold freezes up my blood."

"Let's do it to it," Bob joined in.

"Fucking Ay," Ron said. His cussing was clumsy. He was basically an executive with the mindset of a tightassed accountant, and he didn't really know how to be one of the guys.

Still, it was decided the moose's head would go to Ron. It was not only a smart career move for Kurt who had encouraged the others to agree; it was also the most practical choice. Kurt had no place to put the head; Bob didn't want it, and Jimbo already had three heads in his den and didn't want a fourth.

Kurt didn't actually give a damn about the head—as long as he got the balls.

Kurt had become obsessed with moose testicles ever since he won the lottery, craving a set of moose oysters to munch on for magical reasons. He hadn't been too great in the sack lately, and on some

118

subliminal level he believed he needed an infusion of male hormone to put the starch back in ol' Herkimer the Happy Muff Hound, as he usually called his pecker.

It was strange how Herkimer had quit functioning so soon after he won his chance at getting a moose.

* * *

Jimbo blew smoke rings. His breath condensing around the rings made them look like gossamer sculptures floating in the morning air. He farted again as he crushed the butt out. "Well, boys," he said, "first, we got to find the spoor of the fucking moose. We're close to marshy areas around here, where the moose like to feed, so this part of the woods should be full of the mothers." He squinted hard at each of the younger men, obviously regarding them as snot-nosed kids. "Y'all remember what you learned in class?"

The others nodded.

Jimbo decided to give them a lesson anyway. "Look for moose shit or a rut pit. Look for signs of grazing on the brush. Look for hoof prints."

"We know," Kurt said impatiently.

"But you ain't never actually done it. Can you tell moose shit from deer shit?"

"I don't know," Kurt replied.

"You find a rut pit, you know what moose come smells like?"

"I don't expect to put my nose in it, for Christ's sake."

"I was just asking," Jimbo said, pretending a hurt look. He was only having fun, joshing the youngsters. "Let's spread out then," he continued, taking command of the group. "First man who finds signs of a moose give a hollar. Then we'll all get together and track the son of a bitch down."

"All right," the men assented.

"Kurt and me will head north," Jimbo said. "You, Bob, go off east a little. Ron? You go off west a little. Be careful where you step, and don't fire your weapon. We have to be together when we shoot the thing."

"Aren't you going to use a moose call?" Kurt asked.

"Not till I see sign of the moose. I ain't wasting my breath in this fucking cold."

119

Kurt fell silent as they shouldered their rifles and split up. He reluctantly trudged along with Jimbo.

* * *

Kurt was carrying a 30.06 Browning with bolt action; Jimbo had a 300 Winchester Magnum. Both weapons were equipped with 3 x 9 scopes, giving the men advantage over the moose at up to 200 yards.

"I ain't been up here in a few years," Jimbo was telling Kurt, whispering hoarsely as he searched the ground for moose evidence. "It's like a whole goddamn different world in these woods. You could lose a buncha dinosaurs or space-ship aliens up here for years before anyone found them."

"We're not hunting dinosaurs."

"No, but we could bring one down if we saw him soon enough. My point is, son, there could be things in these woods that we don't know about."

Kurt shivered a little. It was mostly from the cold, even though he wore a down-filled, camouflage hunting jacket that was supposed to be protection against Arctic chills, but it was also partially from the thrill athrob in his body at the idea of killing something big and mean and powerful.

"Like what?"

"Fuck, I don't know. But every time I been up here, I always got a funny feeling in my gut. Like I should watch out for things. Of course, it's a goddamn park, and the state keeps watch, but still a motherfucking dinosaur might charge out of them trees as well as a moose."

"Bullshit." He could tell Jimbo was trying to spook him, probably for the sheer hell of it. *An old man's game,* he thought.

"Maybe. But you get to be my age, you learn to follow your gut instincts. Hell, if you don't, before you know it, you get fucked in the ass by fate."

"Very eloquent," Kurt said sarcastically. "You sound like an old woman talking."

"Old women outlive old men. Maybe because they obey their instincts. You don't see no fucking old ladies out here in this fucking

120

cold, freezing their nuts off—if they had any—just to shoot a god-damn animal that never did them no wrong. In fact," he paused, looking around significantly, "you don't even see no other hunters out. Kinda strange, ain't it?"

Kurt refused to participate in the game. Men of Jimbo's generation were always so goddamn wise, and he hated making small talk, anyhow. He kept thinking of that big shaggy scrotum hanging down between the legs of a bull moose. He shivered again, this time to the marrow of his bones. Would he be man enough actually to eat moose oysters? What kind of man did it take?

He decided to ask Jimbo about it, because he was a man who looked like he'd eat any goddamn thing.

*   *   *

Bob Mickle was a tall, thin man who had gone to high school with Kurt in Minneapolis. He had liked hunting since he was fourteen and his father had taken him out after deer.

It made him feel like Hemingway: the macho man against the elements, tracking the wary forest creature and blowing him away, then feasting on the meat. It was great fun.

He climbed up over a small ridge and saw an expanse of brush near a marshy area, but he saw no moose. He started to backtrack and go another direction when he heard a strange grunting noise.

A moose?

He crept toward the sound, his 30.06 rifle at the ready, just in case. His unclad ears stung with the cold, making it difficult to hear. Then he tripped over a rock and fell flat on his face.

"Fuck a duck!"

When he got back up to his feet, he had lost his orientation. He turned around slowly, trying to set his sights on where the sound had come from. He could not remember if he'd been heading north or south.

Then he saw the source of the grunting sound.

It was a medium-sized moose—a cow—and there was a big ape-like creature behind her holding her rear flanks in a tight grip with its massive hands. The creature was seven or eight feet tall and was covered with dark orange-red hair. The thing was making the grunting noise.

121

And the moose was bellowing. The ape-thing was fucking the moose, humping it for dear life.

Bob stared at the scene a few seconds, wishing he had a camera.

Then the thing must have come, for it stopped pumping the moose and backed off, disengaging its huge rope-like penis, grunting a noise that sounded like a word, like a name.

Bob could've sworn the thing said, "Charlotte."

He turned and ran. He could hardly wait to tell the others what he'd seen.

*   *   *

Ron Jergens sat on a fallen tree, sucking in great gulps of chilled air, which made his lungs ache even more. He was an indolent man with flabby muscles and not at one with the great outdoors.

I shouldn't've come on this trip, he admitted to himself. *I'm not a hunter. I don't want to kill anything. If Kurt wanted to make brownie points with me, why didn't he get me laid? Hell, he's got a sister . . .*

Ron got to his feet and started to head in the general direction he had seen Kurt and his gross son of a bitch uncle or godfather or whatever-the-hell he was go.

From now on, he was just tagging along.

*   *   *

"Hell yes, I've ate moose oysters," Jimbo Long told Kurt, without taking his eyes off the ground. "Deer nuts too, and wild boar nuts, bear oysters, beaver *cojones.* Down in Louisiana I even ate alligator nuts."

Kurt didn't think alligators had nuts, but he didn't challenge the older man's wisdom. "But what do they taste like—moose oysters I mean?" All this talk of balls was having a strange affect on Herkimer, who was stirring in Kurt's shorts. He was getting a hard-on up in these goddamn woods—where he didn't need it at all. Damn, Herkimer was a capricious beast!

"Good eating, son. Food of the gods, if you know what I mean. In the old days, back before we got so goddamn civilized, hunters used to just bite the nuts off the fresh kill and chew 'em up raw . . ."

122

Kurt's stomach lurched a little.

". . . getting *all* the juices out of 'em. Sometimes, the women would do it! How'd you like to get a knob job from one of them ball-biting bitches?" He nudged at Kurt with the barrel of the Magnum. Kurt drew away instinctively. "'Course nowadays we cook what we eat. I got a secret recipe for oyster batter. Cut up the nuts, dip the slices in the batter, and deep fry them fuckers. Taste better than pussy in April."

Kurt swallowed a bubble of stomach acid.

Jimbo stopped abruptly and looked Kurt square in the eyes. "What you so interested in moose nuts for, boy? Can't you get it up anymore?"

Kurt's face flushed. Fortunately, Jimbo looked away. "No, it isn't that. I don't know . . ."

"No need to explain to me, son. I had limpitis of the pecker before myself. Once went for two days without a boner."

"I just wondered . . ."

"Shush!" Jimbo stopped and knelt to the ground next to a small depression in the dirt in which was pooled a bit of opalescent liquid. He dipped his finger in the goop and brought it to his nose. "Moose come, boy. This here's a rut pit. Moose shoots his wad in there, rolls in it, and gets up a good smell to attract the ladies."

"I know," Kurt said, flinching.

"Still warm too." Jimbo wiped his finger on his worn pants and glanced around. About three yards away, he spied something. He got up, ran over and pointed triumphantly to a steaming pile of moose shit.

"We're hot on the trail of a bull," he told Kurt. "I'll wait here. Go round up the others."

*   *   *

Bob was heading back to the truck.

He wished he had a beer to steady his nerves, but they were saving the brews for celebration after they killed the moose. They had stopped in Isabella, a little town close to the park, and bought a case of Coor's for the occasion.

He was really glad to see Kurt running toward him, but in the excitement of hearing they were on the trail of a bull he forgot to tell him about the carnal knowledge he'd witnessed.

Well, it would be a good story for later.

*   *   *

After Ron caught up with Kurt and Bob, they all went to the place where Jimbo waited. The sun had risen to its nine o'clock position by then.

"About time," Jimbo snorted, flicking the bill of his flannel cap and pointing due north. "I got a feeling there's a big son-of-a-bitching bull waiting up there for us."

"Let's get him," Kurt said.

"Go for it," Bob said.

Ron yawned. He'd rather shoot beaver.

They walked slowly through the woods toward the marshy area Bob had seen from the other side. After they travelled a few yards, Jimbo took out his moose call, which he had fashioned himself from birch bark, and made a throaty bellowing noise through it.

No response.

Jimbo called again.

Without warning, out of a thicket to the right of them, a huge bull—at least seven feet tall at the shoulder—charged out, head down in challenge, its massive antlers ready to lock with another moose. Apparently Jimbo had issued a challenge. It was mating season, after all, and all the moose were horny and quick to fight.

Jimbo raised his Magnum and aimed it at the bull's broad chest.

Kurt aimed at the head.

Bob aimed at the snout.

Ron pretended to aim.

But the moose was on them too quickly. All they could do was scramble for their lives to avoid being trampled. Even Jimbo's trained reflexes failed him; his Magnum fired in the air as he dove for cover.

Ron wet his pants.

Bob blew a bush apart.

Kurt fell on his ass. As the bull galloped away, seemingly oblivious to the gunfire, Kurt caught sight of its bouncing scrotum. He jumped up and scoped the moose's ass with the Browning and fired.

His footing was unsteady and he tumbled over again.

Missed the fucking moose.

Looked like a fool.

Cussed a blue streak that almost thawed the air.

124

MOOSE OYSTERS

*   *   *

"Shit, piss and vinegar, mother*fuck!*" Jimbo raged. "How in the holy hell could *all* of us miss that big cocksucker?"

His young companions looked abashed — except for Kurt. He was angry too, mostly at himself. Then it occurred to him that if he had shot the moose in the rump, he would have destroyed its balls, and he was glad he missed. "Maybe he'll come back," he said.

"Goddamn it to hell." Jimbo spat on the ground, farted, and leaned up against a tree. "I hate missing one like that. Easy fucking kill."

"But he was too damn fast."

"Or else I'm too damn slow. I should've bagged him."

"We'll get another chance," Kurt said. "We know where he went."

"I guess," Jimbo said. "Let's go after him, then."

*   *   *

The moose's hoof prints were easy to follow. And Jimbo claimed he could smell him just a few yards ahead.

"We're getting close," he cautioned the others. "Have your rifles ready this time — *really* ready."

The others murmured assent. The only sound for the next few minutes was the cold wind blowing past their ears, the labored breathing of Ron Jergens, and the occasional farts Jimbo let.

Then they spotted something.

It charged at them, or seemed to.

Somehow, Ron squeezed off a shot and brought the moose down at twenty yards.

The men ran to the kill. The others looked at Ron and shook their heads in disappointment.

"What's the matter?" he said, his triumph at shooting the moose suddenly dissipating.

It was a cow, not the bull they had seen earlier.

Bob Mickle stifled a laugh; he was pretty sure he had seen this particular cow before. He wondered if she'd had time to douche.

"Fuck," Kurt said. "Let's go after that bull."

"We can't," Jimbo said. "Only one moose per party. That's the law,

125

and I ain't risking a fine to break it. We got our moose. Maybe it ain't
no big bull, but it's a moose."

"But . . ." Kurt couldn't explain to the others what he really felt—
how much he *missed* not getting those moose oysters.

"Forget it, son. There's plenty of good eating here too. She'll dress
down to 200 pounds or more. Let's get her skinned and start cutting.
We got to get the meat cold as soon as possible."

Kurt sighed heavily. Old Herkimer shrank up inside his body,
pulling most of his scrotum after him.

*　　*　　*

Ron turned away as the others peeled the hide from the moose,
beheaded and gutted it, and cut up the carcass. The smells coming
from the body were making him gag. At home, he couldn't even cut
up a chicken.

"Steak, hamburgers, stew," Jimbo said. "Good meat too. Not full
of chemicals like beef. Just full of juice." He hacked a sliver of flesh
from the exposed muscle and chewed on it tentatively and spit it out.
"Keep working, boys. She ain't cooling off very fast."

Ron peeked over his shoulder and saw Jimbo chewing the raw
flesh. He turned and stumbled into the woods to find a place to vomit
discreetly.

Before he could accomplish that, he ran into someone: A four-
foot-nine Indian and an eight-foot ape-like creature. The ape thing
grabbed him by the back of his jacket and jerked him off the ground.

Then the three of them returned to the butchering site.

*　　*　　*

"What the fuck?" Jimbo muttered, catching sight of the trio as
they emerged from the woods.

Bob and Kurt turned, seeing the Indian. They also saw Ron being
held aloft like a helpless kitten by a giant.

"Bigfoot," Jimbo said, his mouth dropping open in awe. "Fucking
Bigfoot."

"There's no Bigfoot in Minnesota," Kurt said.

"There sure as shit is now."

MOOSE OYSTERS

The creature dropped Ron. He half-crawled toward the other men. All of them were mindful of their rifles resting against a tree too far away to reach quickly.

The short Indian wore a parka and a plaid cap, much like Jimbo's. His multi-wrinkled countenance made him appear at least a hundred years old. He looked at the half-butchered moose, glared at the men with seering eyes, and said, "Spirit of the Woods think White man go too far."

The hunting party was silent a moment.

"What the hell do you mean?" Kurt said.

"Spirit not like what you do."

Jimbo Long finally broke out laughing. "Why, you little bastard. You ain't the spirit of shit. Come on over here so I can whip your ass."

"I not Spirit of Woods," the little man continued. "Him be." He gestured over his shoulder toward the creature standing behind him. "You call him 'Bigfoot.'"

The orange-red hair-covered creature stirred uneasily. Its face was gorilla-like but with a squarer jaw. Its hands were twice the size of any human's. Its penis, even in repose, was at least two feet long, and dangled half way to its knees, resembling a snake that had eaten a gerbil—and had just begun swallowing it. Its broad chest heaved with obvious anger.

"Jesus H. Tap-dancing Christ!" Bob said.

"Let's see him dance when I put a 30.06 slug between his eyes," Kurt said, running toward the tree where the rifles leaned.

"No shoot."

Kurt made it to the rifles, grabbed his Browning . . .

"No shoot!"

. . . raised it and aimed at the Bigfoot's ugly face.

"Shut the fuck up, Tonto!"

Before Kurt could squeeze the trigger, the Bigfoot opened its mouth and emitted a roar the shock waves of which jammed cable reception in Canada. He took two giant fluid strides covering half the distance between him and Kurt.

Kurt kept the giant in his sights. He had the trigger half way back. Two more strides.

Kurt steadied his shaking arms to fire, but the giant was upon him. It snatched the rifle from Kurt's hand and broke it in half as easily as one might snap a twig, then dropped the pieces and ground them into the earth.

127

The beast towered over him, snarling angrily. Kurt was unable to move. The last thing he saw was a large hairy hand reaching for his windpipe.

* * *

When Kurt awoke it was night, and his head was full of blood. His skin was icy, and he realized he was naked and hanging upside down, his feet bound by a piece of rope to a tree limb. There was a small fire burning somewhere and the acrid smoke assailed his nostrils. His eyes darted to the right and he could just barely make out the hulking forms of the Bigfoot and his Indian companion by the fire. They were ignoring him.

Maybe that meant he could escape.

He went through various contortions, trying to reach up to the rope that bound him. Men, he realized after several futile moments of struggling, weren't like foxes or even rats—they couldn't chew their legs off to get out of a trap.

Blood seemed to clog his brain now, and he was on the edge of panic. Then he twisted enough to see what was behind him:

Hanging upside down from other limbs were the naked bodies of his hunting comrades. Two of them were too far away to identify, but Jimbo's fat corpse was illuminated enough by the fire for Kurt to see he was undeniably dead. His torso was covered with blood, and chunks of flesh were missing.

Kurt lost the contents of his stomach, almost choking as he vomited upside down. When he finished, he called out to his friends weakly. "Ron? Bob?"

No answer.

Abruptly, he felt a hairy body brush against him, pulling the rope from around his feet. He was hefted in the air by the Bigfoot and taken closer to the fire, where the creature deposited him, then sat on its haunches to watch as the Indian spoke.

"Hello," the little man said simply.

Kurt hugged himself against the cold, conscious of his scrotum touching the ground. "What did we do to piss him off?"

"You kill Charlotte."

"What?"

"Charlotte. The moose you kill. She be his favorite. Spirit of the

128

Woods very sad. Charlotte was love of his life."

"Are you shitting me, Cochise?"

"No shit, White Eyes. No female Spirit around. Spirit take what he can get."

"There's a lot of other moose," Kurt protested, feeling foolish that he was even participating in such a discussion. But the Indian seemed to be serious enough.

"Not like Charlotte," the Indian said. "She not common whore like other moose. Save herself for Spirit."

Kurt stared at the Indian's puckered little face in disbelief. Then he laughed. "Hey, Hiawatha, I'll fix him up with my sister. She likes big guys with hairy chests. Really."

The Indian considered Kurt's proposition and frowned. "White woman too moody. Spirit no like."

Kurt's mind went blank; he cleared his throat. "Now what?"

"Spirit say it your turn."

"My turn for what?" Kurt's eyes shifted uneasily from the Indian to the Bigfoot.

"Spirit be plenty horny. Never get enough. Charlotte gone. You take place."

"Say what?"

"Bend over, White boy."

"No fucking way!"

Kurt started to run, but the Bigfoot grabbed him by the ankles, jerked him around and made him assume the position of a bitch about to be mounted. The giant fingers spread Kurt's cheeks. Slowly, it forced its enormous tool into Kurt.

Kurt yelped at first, then started whimpering.

The Bigfoot muttered something that sounded almost like words. Kurt moaned.

"No moan," the Indian said. "Do what Spirit say."

"Wh-a-a-at?" Kurt managed to utter.

"Him say you bellow like a moose."

"Oh, sh-eee-it!"

"Bellow like a moose. Him like."

Kurt caught his breath as the thing penetrated deeper and deeper. Then he really tried to bellow like a moose, hoping that somehow he might placate the thing and it would be over.

But the only sound he could make was a scream.

129

*　　*　　*

Outside their lean-to, the little man and the Spirit of the Woods held a wake for Charlotte. The beast grunted; the little man prayed, making the right signs for Charlotte's soul to pass over into the spirit world.

After the ceremony, they had the traditional funeral meal, consisting of bran muffins, braised toadstools and, of course, the main delicacy—which paid special tribute to Charlotte.

The Spirit of the Woods could speak a little, though only the Indian could understand it.

"What you call?" it asked the little man, holding up an oblong morsel that had been deep-fried in Jimbo-Long fat.

"Oysters," the Indian said in his regular voice, not the one he used to speak to white men. "Man oysters. Eat up, my friend; we have plenty."

The Spirit smiled as it took another helping of man oysters.

"Good," it said.

The Indian passed his friend a Coor's.

Scripture says: Except a man be born again, he cannot see the kingdom of God. Or words to that effect.

The Reverend Rockwell Healy tilted up the half pint of whiskey and drank, chugging it down in big gulps, shocking his body to its most alert state, so he could do the work of God.

Let it rip down the throat, he thought, burn out the demons, cleanse the gut of sin, make room for redemption, and put off damnation until tomorrow.

That was why God had invented whiskey. To give man a way out when the world intruded too much and Temptation curled its finger in his direction.

Not that the Reverend worried too much about temptation. He could control himself all right.

He stuck the bottle in his hip pocket and strutted out the door, past Lonnie, the chubby, fortyish organist who never wore a bra, past the altar, and past the huge cross on which hung a fearfully scornful giant wooden Jesus, His face tilted, His eyes cast heavenward, His wounds painted a livid red. It was a Christ who looked more like a boogie man than a Savior, and that was just right for the people who came to this church.

The Reverend arrived at his pulpit in under five seconds, like a ball player sliding into home plate. Sweat poured down his brow. It was nearly ninety outside, and probably hotter in the small, rough-hewn church. It was a good day to contemplate Hell.

And the Reverend was full of hell-fire today.

Jump-started by the whiskey, his mind was racing. He glared out at his flock—a sorrier bunch of sinners he had never seen nor judged in all his days as a preacher and observer of mankind's weaknesses and transgressions.

*　　*　　*

Scripture says: For what shall it profit a man, if he shall gain the whole world, and lose his own soul? Or words to that effect.

Reverend Healy's flock consisted of renegade, fallen former Baptists and Nazarenes who had forsaken their previous churches because they were too soft on them. They came from the small communities spotting the surrounding North Carolina countryside, one of the most beautiful places on earth, very much like Eden must have been, according to the Reverend. They were God-loving, God-believing, God-fearing folk, and they were damned sinners as well. They knew that it was the fate of man to sin: to commit adultery, to lust after another man's wife or another woman's husband, to covet your neighbor's house and land and pickup truck, to have sex with your children or your neighbor's children, to contemplate having sex with animals and objects, to piss in the mud and shit in the woods, to swear and blaspheme, to shoot people with the wrong color skin or cut off their balls and hang them, to foster corrupt politics and nepotism, to encourage gut toting and knife carrying—and to beat the hell out of anyone who denied them their right to sin—unless he was a preacher.

Sin was rampant among them. Sin was eating them alive. Sin was sweating out of their pores, creating the stench old Satan sniffed when he went looking for sinners. The Reverend had seen to it that they all realized the depth of their sins and how much sin had infested them, and he made sure they knew the dire consequences of their actions.

It was in Scripture, he said, all of it. All their sins had been sinned before, by the Old Testament people who invented sodomy and adultery and masturbation, despite God scourging their cities and turning them into pillars of salt. The New Testament people sinned too, even while the Son of God walked among them, teaching them the errors of their ways and showing them how they might be redeemed yet few heeded His teachings.

It was all told in Scripture—as the Reverend cited it again and again. Passage after passage, chapter after chapter, verse after verse spelled out the consequences of a continued state of sin.

"It says so right here," the Reverend would say, smacking his Bible, "or words to that effect."

Unless they sought redemption, he told them they were all going to burn forever in a literal Hell—a Hell he had conjured up that was hotter than the interior of a blast furnace or the inside of the sun. In this Hell dwelled Demons eight feet tall, wielding pitchforks six feet long with barbs on the end that pierced flesh by just grazing it. The demons would torment them as they were chained helplessly against the walls of Hell, while the Hounds of Hell gnawed their flesh; and the Hounds of Hell would chew them alive, for all eternity, spitting out their flesh, shitting it out, making them eat their own shitten flesh, while more flesh grew back in its place for the Demons and the Hounds to rend again and again—while fat, slimy worms crawled in and out of their bodies, over their tongues, burrowing through one ear and out the other, slithering up their noses, up their assholes, up their pee-holes and out again, carrying with them chunks of flesh, and more flesh, and more, and they would be scourged and damned and eaten alive forever more—feeling every agony as they would in life, only magnified a thousandfold.

All as they burned in an eternal fire.

That was Reverend Healy's message; it was the kernel of every sermon, even if he was waxing poetically about the beautiful country God had laid aside for them. Behind every statement he made was the implied damnation that awaited them for their sins, even the most trivial.

God was angry with them.

God cut them no slack whatsoever.

God would singe their asses forever.

The Reverend quoted Scripture to prove it, and there could be no argument with Scripture.

As the Reverend ranted, the fear of damnation rippled through the people in his flock: the skinny and old, the young and fit, the fat and the sloppy, the trim and muscular, the women, the men, the children. In all the pupils of their eyes, the irises constricted in terror, was reflected the enraged face of the Reverend, like a tiny demon

133

trapped in an even tinier crystal ball; his fierce visage, thus micro-
scoped, was still terrible to behold.

Righteousness animated his features: the shaggy eyebrows, the
dark gray hair combed straight back, the much-creased face, the
penetrating, burning eyes of fire hot enough to stoke the flames of
the Hell he described in delicious detail; the yellowed teeth, the
outrageous folds of skin that hung flapping beneath his chin.

His head was bigger than it should be. His body was a gnarled
oak somehow moving across the front of the church. His limbs were
sinewy and thick. He was as strong as a bull, as healthy as a lion, as
virile as a goat, and some said the Reverend was a hundred years old.

Every time the Reverend's voice raised, someone almost fainted.
His vision of Hell was beyond endurance for the weak of heart.

Yet they *had* to listen to him.

His way was the only way to escape eternal torment.

His was the only way to be born again.

Reverend Healy's Way.

*   *   *

Scripture says: Whosoever looketh on a woman to lust after her
hath committed adultery with her already in his heart. Or words to
that effect.

Reverend Healy's sermon gradually assumed a direction as he
started preaching on the varieties of adultery. He pounded the pulpit
as words of condemnation roared from his throat. He slammed the
Bible on the floor and danced on it. He threw himself to his knees
and bayed like a hound dog, like one of the Hounds of Hell.

Then he got mad.

He chewed the Devil's ass for getting into the souls of his people.
He challenged Satan to meet him right then and there in his church.

"Come on, Satan! Damn you! Come right down here and I'll fight
you to the death. You will not take over the minds and the hearts
of my people!"

A woman screamed and fainted, imagining she saw Satan coming down the aisle. No one paid any attention. Women were always
fainting in the thick atmosphere of Hell and brimstone pouring forth
from the pulpit. Sometimes grown men toppled over. Children wet

134

their pants. Often half the flock would start speaking in the Tongues; sometimes people were possessed by the spirits of animals. And on a hot day like this, some merely passed out from the infernal heat.

The Reverend kept challenging Satan, but Satan did not arrive.

"I knew he was a yellow-bellied coward," the Reverend said, facing away momentarily. Then he spun around and pointed at a woman in the front row, his eyes flashing open like spotlights. "But he's not afraid of you, Sister Bobbie! He'll come in the night and crawl into your bosom and eat out your heart and make you a condemned sinner."

Sister Bobbie, a flashy young redhead with hips that pivoted in the night, trembled.

"You have to be wary of the devil!"

"I will be, Reverend," she mumbled.

"Be watchful!"

"I will."

"Say it louder."

"I WILL!"

"God damn you, Satan!" The Reverend leaped down, grabbed Sister Bobbie by the shoulders and started shaking her. "Satan! Are you in this woman's body? Are you tempting her with adulterous thoughts?"

"NO!" Sister Bobbie screamed.

The whole congregation rose, alarmed and more than a little curious. The Reverend was likely to do anything. Once, he had torn a woman's clothes off to show how sinful the sight of a naked woman was, then preached over two hours about it, shaming every man who had looked upon her.

The Reverend slapped Sister Bobbie's face. He shook her so hard her red-checked dress started slipping off her shoulders. Men craned their necks, expecting one of her balloon-like tits to wiggle out on its own accord.

"Get out of there, Satan!"

Bobbie slumped against the Reverend, unconscious. He shook her back to awareness, kissed her on the forehead, and declared: "Praise the Lord! Satan has gone from this woman's body."

The congregation raised a chorus of "Amen's" that could be heard in the next county. Sister Bobbie had a smile on her face that would stop an army of Demons; tears flooded her eyes.

"You're saved, Sister Bobbie! Saved from the eternal torments of Hell everlasting. Saved from the temptations of flesh. Satan will never infest your poor soul again. He's a coward! God damn him! A coward who looks for the weak and the timid, who would take advantage of even a child's innocence to gain another soul for his legions in Hell! Sister Bobbie, you are born again."

The Reverend shook his fist and glared at the congregation. "I'm a one-man juggernaut, driven by the engine of the Lord. I'll kick the devil's ass from here to eternity and back. Who's next? Who else among you needs saving? Come forward! This is a day of salvation! This may be your last chance!"

People started down the aisle, many of them wet-eyed, trembling children, coming forward to be cleansed and saved.

"Come on, brothers and sisters. If you have the slightest doubt, if you feel Satan may be waiting outside for you—now is the time to get saved. You might get killed on the way home—so don't put if off, brother, don't put it off, sister! Get up and be saved, be saved, be saved . . . so you too can be *born again* in the flesh of the Lord!"

*   *   *

Scripture says: For many are called, but few are chosen. Or words to that effect.

Late that afternoon, the Reverend Healy was driven home by his wife, Edith. She was a short, pear-shaped woman, with her hair dyed black. Her brown eyes peered through thick bifocals. She was fifty-nine, six years younger than her husband.

"That was quite a sermon today, Rocky," she said in her soft Southern accent.

The Reverend smiled. "I really had the Spirit in me today. By God, I think Satan *was* in the church, and I kicked his ass good too."

Edith hesitated, then said, "You think you're too hard on them sometimes? I mean, what with people fainting and speaking in Tongues, and all that, some folks think you work your congregation up too much."

"Who thinks that?"

"Just folks." She turned the old Ford station wagon from the main highway onto a dirt road that led back to their house.

"That's what they want, Edith. If they want a preacher who will say it's all right for them to fornicate and commit incest and indulge

136

in bestiality, they should go find themselves one of those mealy-mouthed Baptists or piss-ant Methodists. I preach a hard sermon, I know. And I save a lot of people, so they can be born again."

Edith shook her head by way of criticism. "You can go too far, Rocky. You know, you shouldn't've picked on Bobbie Mason. Everybody knows she's been—been sleeping with another woman's husband."

The Reverend grinned. "I know that, Edith. Why do you think I picked her? She needed saving. She'll not commit adultery again, I'll bet."

"You're so sure, Rocky. So sure. I don't see how . . ."

"I preach the gospel, woman. You know what Scripture says . . ."

"I know, Rocky, Scripture says this, and Scripture says that—or words to that effect.' But these are just people—simple people who look up to you. People who are also scared to death of you."

He sighed. This was an old argument and always tired him. "Honey, I do it for their own good. You know those folks would just go on sinning and burn in Hell, if it wasn't for me. Especially in these times when Armageddon is just around the corner."

"They go on sinning, anyhow."

"But I save them. I give them the chance to be born again!"

"Is that all there is? To be born again? What comes after that?"

The Reverend frowned. "What have you been reading?"

"Nothing. I have a right to ask questions. If *you* can't answer them, who can?"

"Well, that's the damnedest question I ever heard. Sounds like something out of a Jehovah's Witness tract, or one of those slickery women's magazines." His face wrinkled in disgust. "What do you mean what comes after being born again? Everlasting joy—living with God and Jesus and all the good folks up in heaven. That's what comes afterwards."

"Oh."

"That's what Scripture says."

"Where does it say it?"

"Lots of places. We'll all be born again after the Rapture—or words to that effect. Now, don't rile me, Edith. I'm kind of tired from preaching, and I want to get some rest in before supper."

Edith remained silent. They were home now, a four-room house overlooking hilly countryside rendered in hundreds of shades of sparkling green by the summer sun. Edith parked, and she and the

Reverend went inside, he to take a nap, she to prepare his favorite Sunday dinner: fried chicken, mashed potatoes and gravy, grits, and cherry pie.

*　*　*

Scripture says: . . . and the sun became black as sackcloth of hair, and the moon became as blood . . . Or words to that effect.

The Reverend spent much of the week fretting about Edith. He was afraid for her soul. The way she had been talking recently— questioning his purpose and God's purpose, and asking questions about what came after death—he feared she might not be counted among those who were saved.

Why couldn't she just have faith, as he did? Why couldn't she see how fundamentally simple it was to get saved? It didn't require questions or thinking. It just required knowing what was right and doing it.

The Reverend didn't want to ascend into heaven and leave Edith behind—which would be a torment in itself. That idea troubled him deeply. Scripture said not all would be taken. How would those who were separated from loved ones cope in the afterlife?

But, damn it, you weren't supposed to question things like that. God had it all figured out, one way or another. He shouldn't let Edith's questioning make him waver in his own immutable beliefs.

She would change her ways eventually and come around to the solid truth he offered. She just had a weak mind, or perhaps she couldn't grasp the scope of his vision of life after death. Surely God would see that and make allowances for her and any others who questioned. As long as they remained fundamentally good and free of sin and actually believed in God and His son, and accepted the overall gist of it, God would deliver them. That was only fair, wasn't it?

The Reverend had to admit to himself he wasn't entirely certain what "fair" was in the eyes of the Lord, but he had the faith to know it would all be set right in the end.

Despite the Reverend's fretting and despair over Edith and others with shaky beliefs, Saturday night came fast. And with it, rather unexpectedly, came one of the signs of the dreaded End Times— of Armageddon.

BORN AGAIN

Everyone in the county watched, rapt with fear and awe, as the moon turned blood red.

The Reverend stood out on his porch in the night, swallowing God's whiskey in great gulps. "Come look at this, Edith."

Edith came out in her nightshirt, a flowered flannel garment that covered everything.

"Oh, my Lord!"

"The moon is covered with blood, Edith! Do you know what that means?"

"It's a sign. Not a good one, if I recall."

"It's not just any sign. It's in *Revelations*. The end of the world is nigh. By God, what a sermon I'll preach tomorrow!"

Edith stared at the full moon, looming large over the hills, its man-face an angry demon's now, as blood seemed to glisten on its features.

The entire countryside was bathed in red light. Edith ran back into the house, unable to endure the dire illumination.

The Reverend gazed at the moon with unsuppressed glee. This would remove all doubts anyone had. He kneeled on the porch, set his whiskey bottle at his side, and prayed.

"Thank you, God. Thank you for this sign. I shall deliver unto you all my people. Many of those who seek the Rapture shall come from my flock. They will be born again to dwell with you in the house of Heaven."

He bowed his head. His soul swelled within him; he thought he might burst with joy. How fortunate he was to live in this day and age—to be there at the final accounting—to be present at the end of the world!

He could barely sleep that night. He would not have slept at all if he hadn't drunk a full pint of whiskey.

*   *   *

Scripture says: . . . there shall be wailing and gnashing of teeth. Or words to that effect.

Early next morning, the Reverend awoke alone. Groggily, he arose and shuffled to the bathroom to take his morning leak and shave. It was unseasonably cold, and his feet stung on the bathroom floor

139

tiles. He left his pajamas on as he lathered his face. He picked up his old Gillette and started to scrape his right cheek, then jumped back from the mirror.

As he almost fell backwards, he felt pain in his right ear—piercing pain that told him what the mirror reflected was true. He leaned forward and touched his ear—or what remained of it.

Half of it had been torn off. Or bitten off.

"Edith!" he yelled in shock. "Come here!"

Edith didn't answer.

"Where is that woman?" he muttered.

His fingers trembling, the Reverend doctored and bandaged his ear and finished shaving. Maybe his wife was outside, doing some early morning chore.

What the hell had bitten him? He was sure he'd locked the door last night.

Maybe a possum had gotten in, but he never heard tell of a possum biting half a man's ear off.

He remembered the bloodied moon of the night before—the sign of the End Times. The Bible hadn't said how it would affect animals. Maybe they were going crazy out there. How else could soul-less beasts be expected to behave? They would be destroyed in the pandemonium at the end of the world, and they must be sensing this.

The Reverend shook his thoughts of animals away, dressed quickly and went out into the kitchen, expecting to smell bacon frying. But the dishes from last night were still in the sink, untouched, and the stove was cold.

"Edith?"

He wandered outside. The car was parked out front, so his wife hadn't gone into town for groceries or anything like that, as she sometimes did without waking him. The Reverend went around to the back of the house calling her name, but his instincts told him she was nowhere around. Had she left him? She had been awfully critical of his sermonizing lately. Maybe she wasn't strong enough to share his righteousness, and the moon's transformation had scared her into leaving him, so she would not have to face the end.

How foolish could she be? Didn't she know there was nowhere to hide? Leaving him on the eave of the Rapture was the worst thing she could do.

Maybe Satan had gotten to her!

The Reverend's stomach asserted its needs, so he returned to the

140

house and made himself breakfast: two eggs, grits, three slices of bacon, and toast, washed down with plenty of coffee. He wanted to be alert for his sermon. During the night he had dreamt up a humdinger.

He'd have the women peeing their pants. Grown men would be begging for salvation. That blood-covered moon would have them all half-scared for their lives.

As well they should be.

He chewed his food slowly, thinking and wondering if the other signs of Armageddon had manifested themselves. Was the sea boiling? Were rivers running red with blood? Would the sun "become as black as sackcloth"?

A chill constricted the muscles in his jaws, and he stopped eating. Good God! This was The End. Everything would perish. Everyone would die.

And he was wasting his time eating breakfast.

He had souls to save—the last of the damned who could maybe be born again before the final wrath of God descended on the world. His physical needs were trivial.

Yet, he was hungry.

He arose, popped a strip of bacon in his mouth to appease his hunger, and rushed into the bedroom to dress for church. As he was about to depart, he noticed Edith's nightshirt lying on the floor.

There were bloodstains on the front of the garment.

"Oh, Lord God Almighty!"

* * *

Scripture says: Why should it be thought a thing incredible with you, that God should raise the dead? Or words to that effect.

The Reverend was late for church that morning. He stayed at home briefly to put in a call to the sheriff and got an answering machine on which he left an angry message.

He waited a few minutes, then remembered the true urgency of this day—that of saving souls. If something had happened to Edith, he would find her later—perhaps in heaven. He could wait no longer. His flock needed him.

"Damn that sheriff to Hell," he muttered and climbed into the

Ford. He started it after two tries, then lurched along the dirt road to the main highway, trying to get used to the feel of driving again. He hadn't been behind the wheel in five years—since he had lost his license in Tennessee for drunk driving—on the same night he had received the call from the Lord to become a preacher.

As he drove along, he became uneasily aware of how little traffic there was. There were no other vehicles to be seen at all, not even an out-of-state truck or tourists passing through. He turned on the radio and there was only static on all channels.

An awful thought occurred to him. What if the Rapture had already taken place? What if the Lord had already called the faithful unto His loving arms?

Had he slept throught it?

Could a man sleep through such a momentous event? No. The Lord would have jerked him up out of the bed if the Rapture had happened.

Maybe the lack of people on the road was due to their all seeking salvation at their various churches. Anyone with any sense at all would be in a church on this portentous day.

Mildly relieved, the Reverend turned on to the steep, rocky road that led to the church. His teeth rattled as he crossed over the rickety wooden bridge and parked out in the clearing near the church. There were no other cars. Shaking his head, he strode toward the front entrance of his church, a feeling of forboding building within him.

He sensed something was very wrong. When he entered the church, he knew it for sure. There was not a single soul inside.

He strode down the aisle, conscious of his footsteps echoing in the empty House of God, and stood behind his pulpit, waiting.

He waited for an hour. Two hours.

As noon approached, it started getting dark outside.

The Reverend went to one of the side windows and, shading his eyes against the glare of the sun's corona, witnessed the first total eclipse he had seen in his life.

"Black as sackcloth," he muttered. Another sign. Another confirmation he was right. So where were his people?

He could hear animals running about in fright in the underbrush and the woods behind the church. Birds chirped nervously. Some of them seemed actually to scream.

The earth trembled slightly. Turning, the Reverend saw the cross tilt; the rough-hewn face of Christ seeming to glower at him.

142

Frightened, he raced to the pulpit for sanctuary. Now closer to the large rood, he thought he saw real blood streaming from the Savior's wounds.

He reached for his whiskey bottle, but before he could get it to his lips, it turned completely black outside, as if God had snapped off the light of the sun with a switch.

A pain tore through his chest.

The Reverend slumped, fell forward and died.

*　　*　　*

Scripture says: And the fifth angel poured out his vial upon the seat of the beast; and his kingdom was full of darkness; and they gnawed their tongues for pain. Or words to that effect.

Things chittered and whispered and moaned as true night claimed the countryside. The smell of fresh death was thick in the air, thicker than the North Carolina humidity.

Armageddon, such as it was, could be said to have passed, taking with it the last opportunities for salvation. If there had been a Rapture, it had passed too, without a great impact.

Behind remained the dead.

The Reverend Rockwell Healy swam toward a kind of perilous consciousness. He finally broke through the caul of numbed sensibility wrapped around his head, and sat up, a taste of bile on his tongue, while his temples pulsated, not with pain, but with spasms of displaced energy, in a dimly-perceived cloud of awareness.

Was he, the Reverend mused, truly dead? Had he come back to life? If so, where was the gateway into Heaven?

He realized he was still in the church, and it was almost as dark inside as it was outside. He pulled himself up unsteadily. He noticed red moonlight streaming in the window next to the pulpit. Looking at it filled him with anguish and a peculiar dread, so he turned away.

He heard movement in the church. People movement. He smelled people scents, unfamiliar ones, yet undeniably human.

"Who's there? Is that you, Edith?"

"We're all here," a hoarse woman's voice replied.

Someone turned on the overhead lights.

The Reverend staggered to the pulpit and gazed out over his congregation.

They returned his gaze.

With dead eyes.

Edith was in the front row, naked. His own lifeless eyes wide with shock and dismay, the Reverend scanned the rest of the congregation. Others were naked as well. Most had blood on them. Some were missing limbs. Parts of faces were torn away. People were clumsily copulating in the pews, oblivious to those around them. Women were fondling other women. Men were kissing other men. Children were peeing on the floor.

Every sort of fornication and abomination was going on in *his* church!

After a few seconds, he also noticed there were twice as many people as there should be. The extra people he recognized as folks who were supposed to have been long dead. Some of them still had clay on their putrescent faces from digging out of their graves.

He had preached at many of their funerals.

The Reverend stepped back, his mind overwhelmed, as he saw that the outside of the church was surrounded by more apparently dead people. He recognized the sheriff out there among them. And his deputies. And many other people he knew. They all stood by, evidently waiting for something to happen—a confrontation of some kind, the Reverend guessed. Perhaps a final reckoning.

Were these the leftovers, the Reverend wondered—the people who had *not* been snatched up by the Rapture?

If so, why was his whole congregation here? Had he failed to save *any* of them?

Why was he *here?*

The Reverend's face twisted in anger. His flock had not heeded his many warnings. They had gone on sinning, not realizing that the consequences were real. Any minute now, he expected the floor would split open and swallow them all in Hell-fire.

Maybe there was hope. There might yet be time for him to save some of them. He lurched forward and grasped the edge of his pulpit. He grabbed the Bible and lifted it above him, his pale hands trembling.

"You're all damned!" he screamed with great effort. "Each and every one of you! You must listen to me—now! Stop that fornicating in my church! Stop those evil acts! Stop sinning in my sight and in the eyes of the Lord. Stop it now, before I call down the wrath of the Almighty God to damn you to Hell for all eternity!"

For a moment, the congregation seemed stunned. People halted in mid-sin. Dead eyes rolled heavenward briefly, then dropped back in place to stare at the madman in the pulpit, the man who was dead but had yet to realize it fully.

Edith stood and stepped forward. One of her fingers was missing, its jagged stump seeming to point at her husband.

"Can't you understand?" she said. "You're dead too, Rocky. We're all dead—every last one of us. *This* is the blessed afterlife you promised us."

"Edith . . ." The Reverend started to relent, then the old fire returned to his eyes. "No, by God, I'll not believe it. You're all possessed by Satan."

"The moon, Rocky. It was the moon."

"The moon changed us." Sister Bobbie was naked too. "A sign of the Revelation and Armageddon, just like you told us. When all God's chosen would be called to his bosom." One of her mighty breasts dropped off, shorn from its moorings by a jagged bite; it was already infested with worms. "Except all that happened was we died, and we were *born again*—just like you said—like this. This is what we waited for."

She paused and grinned with defiance and a different variety of righteousness from any the Reverend had ever pursued. "Now we're doing whatever we like. We've been fornicating, and running naked in the street and killing people who weren't already dead, and we've been eating them—and each other. And it doesn't matter because there's no pain. Nothing hurts. We're not in Hell. And not in heaven. This is what happens. This is the Rapture. This is our reward. This is what we *didn't* sin for." She laughed and a few of her teeth dropped out.

The Reverend touched his ear and cast a glance at Edith. The dried blood stains around her mouth told the whole story. He had provided a morning snack.

"No," he said, his voice cracking with determination. "No! This is all an abomination in the sight of the Lord. You have been tricked by Satan. He is setting you up to bring you down to Hell! Do as I say. Get to your knees now, and pray before it's too late!"

"Rocky . . ." Edith ascended to the pulpit. "It's already too late. We're dead now. Don't you understand? This is what the *real* eternal life is—not the fairy tale that stupid book tells you."

"Are you telling me *no one* was saved. No one was born again?"

"Yes—and no. We're born again all right, and this is it. I don't in

145

particular believe it's being saved."

The Reverend stared at his own hand, discovering for the first time that it did not have real life in it, at least not what he had expected. It was animated and he could control its movement, but it didn't seem to matter to him the way it should. He glared at his wife, his mind still fixed on the idea that had driven him so many years.

"Edith, stand back! It's Satan behind all this! I'll preach him out of here!"

She snatched his Bible from the pulpit and started chewing on it, spitting out shreds of paper and leather binding. After a few quick bites, she removed it from her mouth.

"This is not the truth. This is lies, lies, lies!" She tossed the ravaged book out into the congregation, where its destruction was completed by teeth and clawing hands. "There never was any heavenly plan."

"Are you saying I was wrong?" the Reverend asked, his voice dropping a few decibels.

"Of course you were."

"Why didn't I die sooner then, like the rest of you"

"Only one reason I can think of," his wife replied. "I think God —if there is one—saved you . . ." Her blood-stained teeth flashed. ". . . for us."

"No!"

"Yes . . . dear."

She threw herself on the Reverend and pressed him to the floor, biting deeply into his shoulder.

The rest of the congregation went on sinning. Only it was no longer sin.

It was recreation for the dead. After a while, they went up and took their taste of the Reverend too.

* * *

Scripture says: Marvel not that I said unto thee, Ye must be born again.

The Reverend was home, having no idea how he had arrived there. He stood on the porch, as he had the night before, and marked the progress of the blood-red moon across the sky. It was, he guessed, three or four o'clock in the morning, not that time made any real difference any more. A chilly wind whipped through the trees, embracing the Reverend, but he didn't pay it any mind, since he didn't feel it.

Something snapped inside the house, and he went inside to investigate.

He heard the frantic scratching of tiny claws on the linoleum in the kitchen. He crouched down and peered across the floor to the space underneath the sink.

A mouse struggled in a trap the Reverend had set a few days go when he had found droppings on the floor. The tip of the small creature's head and its front paws had been caught in the bow which had missed getting it in the neck. Instead of enjoying instant death, it was suffering.

The Reverend crawled over to the mouse. Since much of the flesh on his legs was missing, it was difficult, but at least it wasn't painful. Nothing was.

He watched the mouse writhing, fascinated by the desire of even the most odious vermin to want to live, to continue its existence even if there was no particular reason to do so.

Why, he wondered. Did the mouse have a God of its own, and did it believe it would be taken in a special Rapture?

He held the mouse's tail and gently sprung the bow off its paws and head. The animal squeaked and urine ran down the Reverend's arm as it wriggled in his grasp.

Why struggle?, the Reverend thought. He would have spoken aloud, but he no longer had vocal chords. Nor had he a nose to smell the mouse's odor. His congregation had left very little flesh on his bones, after Edith had taken a few choice morsels from his body.

Despite the lack of physical pain, the Reverend was deeply hurt by the way he had been treated. He felt there was some genuine vengefulness among his flock. But he forgave them.

Even though he was dead, he still saw no reason to allow Satan into his heart, whose work this travesty of the afterlife must surely be.

Somewhere, he thought, *things are different, maybe not on this earth, but on another planet, or in another life, and being born again meant just that. Maybe only this little corner of North Carolina was singled out for a hideous afterlife, because Satan had chosen it. Maybe in other places, other times, people were ascending to heaven. Only we here are too short-sighted to see it, or even know of it.*

He held the mouse aloft, watching it with his good eye. Then he popped the creature in his mouth, chewed it ravenously, and swallowed. The warm flesh tasted very good.

Maybe not, he reflected dismally.

The mouse was only an appetizer. The Reverend's hunger still asserted itself, as it never had in life—maybe because he needed to eat to replace his flesh. *So that it might be gnawed away again?* he mused ruefully. He tried to laugh; his vision of Hell was tame compared to the reality.

He remembered that Edith lay in the bedroom, in a kind of stupor. She offered real sustenance, and he didn't mind that her flesh would be cold.

Outside, souls roamed the countryside. The Reverend could hear them, wandering aimlessly, looking for food, dead or alive. He hoped they didn't hate him too much.

How was he to know things would come to pass this way?

Somewhere . . . maybe on the dark side of the moon . . . or in the heart of the jungle . . . or in a place no one had discovered on this earth, there had to be righteous people who deserved to be saved. God's promise couldn't be a lie.

It just couldn't!

He heard sundry gnawing sounds outside. Things eating other things; things allowing themselves to be eaten. He would join them eventually, he supposed. He had no choice but to become one of ∟ them. Right now, he had plenty—just waiting for him in the next room.

Yet where was the kingdom of God—if not here after death?

He went into his wife, his eye burning with some of the old righteousness that was now hunger, and crawled toward her. He hoped she would understand his needs, and she would not resist. She might not even stir. Or she might even offer herself as a feast for him. Willingly.

In a way, he speculated, it might be a pleasurable experience to be eaten. Maybe that's why the mouse allowed itself to be caught, and the fly dove into the spider's web. The animals knew what was right. Being eaten could be defined as the ultimate form of communion. The true communion.

This is my body; this is my blood.

Before the Reverend Rockwell Healy began to feed, his thoughts were again disrupted with the annoying query his mind had persisted

148

BORN AGAIN

in posing ever since he had come to awareness in this new life.

For the thousandth time, his decaying brain fixed on the question that could not be answered.

Why had he been born again?

Fugyu

Every night he disposed of another one, sometimes two. It was his chosen task, and though he didn't relish it, Elmer knew his work had to be done.

Elmer had determined that not everything that resembled a human being was human. He had come to realize many so-called people were, in fact, mere soul-less shells, who contributed nothing to the world. It was his duty to extract them from society, as if they were rotten teeth.

Now that it was summer in New York, and the weather was more agreeable, he had better opportunities to do his duty.

With a clear conscience and a bag of Oreos, Elmer set forth every night in search of the non-human elements of society.

They were easy to identify, because they used a shibboleth, a single word, that let Elmer know who they were; that word was "fugyu."

*   *   *

Annie Halstead trudged along lower Fifth Avenue, her gaze averted from the sun. She carried two cloth shopping bags, both of ancient origin, perfectly balanced on either side of her. The bags contained the necessities of her life: food, trash, gum, toilet paper, spare underwear, wads of tinfoil and waxed paper, matches and candles, sandwich bags, and bottles and cans of sundry things, some open, some not.

JAMES KISNER

She had many toothbrushes in her bags, all picked up from the streets, which she used for such tasks as scrubbing the rim of a can before opening it or applying shoe polish. However, she never brushed her teeth.

Annie was two inches above five feet, having shrunken four inches the last five years, the shrinkage having occurred since she had become a denizen of the streets. Part of her diminution in size was due to age and osteoporosis; part was due to the attrition of living in the streets, which might eventually erode her into nothingness, though she never pondered that possibility. As she had grown shorter, she had also acquired a pronounced dowager's hump, making her resemble a distaff version of Quasimodo.

Though Annie ate at infrequent intervals, she was still quite obese, because her diet consisted of mostly carbohydrates or sweets. She weighed close to two-hundred pounds, not counting clothing, bags, or dirt. Her head was large and fat, her neck bloated with a goiter, her rust-colored eyes buried in a crazed matrix of infinite wrinkles. Her ragged teeth were piss-stain yellow, surrounded by purple leathery lips. On her upper lip a hair-studded mole rode precariously, at an oblique angle to her left nostril. Her skin was the color of bleached meat and had the texture of a shrivelled orange. Her fingers were like sausage links, with thick battered nails bitten down to the quick. Though her hands were broad and gnarled, they were surprisingly nimble when she needed them. Her feet were chunky pyramids of flesh and callus, clad in black leather men's work shoes from Sears with broken, knotted laces.

She wore a brown dress with frayed short sleeves and a scooped out neck that revealed about twelve inches of cleavage between her massive spider-veined breasts. The dress, over a decade old and patched in many places, tended to shift over her protuberant, rolling stomach as she waddled her way along the sidewalk; it stopped two inches below each swollen knee. Beyond her knees, she wore a mismatched pair of nylon hose on her calves, one taupe, the other nude, both rolled up to below the knee.

On her head was a black felt hat that she had found in a trash bin on 42nd Street. It bore the logo of the Guns N Roses rock group — which meant absolutely nothing to her.

Annie possessed a distinctive presence that removed her from the ordinary legions of bag ladies in New York. There was her lumbering girth, but by far the most overwhelming aspect of her personna was her smell. She bathed, on average, about twice a year, if she remembered to bathe at all. As a result, there were sores on her body from dirt abrasion, as well as a miscellany of slow-healing, festering infections. Dirt and crud had collected in the crevices and valleys of her skin. Between her legs a gritty substance reminiscent of a vile French cheese had formed.

Annie's smell was her built-in defense system. Nobody, not even the most whacked-out, screwed-up crack user would get within ten feet of her. Dogs turned and ran as soon as they got her scent. Cats tried to cover over things that dropped from her. Squirrels went mad at her approach.

Birds wouldn't even crap on her.

* * *

It was a typical night for Elmer. He had discovered a soul-less being half a block off Broadway, uptown, only a few yards from the glitter of nightlife, a wretch living in a cardboard carton, adrift in his own filth, a man whose wrinkled countenance was etched in shifting, spidery shadows from the moon overhead.

Elmer approached the man's cardboard box and bent down to address its inhabitant. The man's smell assaulted his nose and eyes, but Elmer had learned to tolerate such inconveniences in his job. "What is your name?" he asked.

The man drew himself closer into the box, like an insect hiding from the light. Only his eyes were visible, picking up a stray reflection from somewhere, perhaps from the point of Elmer's knife peeking out from behind his back. He made an animal sound that could have been choking or his stomach rumbling or the subtle whispering of his body decaying.

"What is your name?" Elmer repeated. Soul-less things rarely had names.

The man's face leaned forward into the dimness. Across the street a group of youths passed by, laughing and swearing as they passed a quart of beer among themselves. Neither Elmer nor the man paid any attention to them.

The man looked up into Elmer's face and squinted. Elmer was thin, six-two, thirtyish, balding, his eyes dark and ashine with purpose. He wore a gray windbreaker, a T-shirt under that, jeans, and Nike athletic shoes. He didn't look the least bit threatening; he had made a study of how to appear ordinary, so that he would blend into just about any crowd.

The man in the box snorted by way of saying he did not wish to be bothered.

Elmer reached into his jacket pocket with his left hand and pulled out a dark round object.

"Want an Oreo?" he asked.

The man's eyes focused on the cookie briefly. "Fugyu," he replied.

Having uttered the magic word, the man had identified himself for certain.

"Fuck you too," Elmer said. He reached out and sliced the man's leathery throat with a fillet knife, then jerked back to avoid the gush of blood. When he was sure the man was dead, Elmer said a little prayer to God for making it so easy, then he ate the Oreo.

It tasted of blood.

He put his knife in his pocket, then took a large plastic trash bag from underneath his windbreaker and wrestled the man's body inside.

He wasn't worried about being seen or being caught. Since he was doing such necessary work, he knew that an entity watched over him — a guardian angel perhaps. He lifted the bag over his shoulder and headed east, away from Broadway, until he found an alley with a light shining in it. At its end was a large metal trash dumpster.

He deposited the nameless thing in the dumpster among the litter and garbage of a restaurant.

His task accomplished for the evening without mishap or flaws, Elmer went home to his small two-room apartment. After stripping down and taking a quick shower, he had another Oreo and a glass of milk before crawling into bed.

He slept very soundly.

*   *   *

Annie Halstead sat on a bench near Washington Square. She was chewing on a peanut butter sandwich and watching the birds. The birds were feeding on the carcass of a small mongrel dog.

The sun was warm on Annie's skin, intensifying the smell rising from her flesh, until some people complained and a cop ran her off.

She told the cop, "Fugyu," in her gravelly voice and waddled away, bags in tow. She wandered around Greenwich Village, causing pedestrians to cross to the other side of the street and scaring small children and animals.

She stopped briefly on Sixth Avenue and picked up a half-eaten submarine sandwich and placed it in one of her bags. She also found a broken beer bottle. She stuffed it in a bag as well and continued on her way. Eventually, she ended up by Union Square, where she was disoriented for several moments and unable to decide which way to turn. The streets seemed to go off in every direction.

Finally, she simply sat down on a bench and waited. She was still there when darkness came. She slept in a sitting position, her ragged breathing echoing in the night.

Summer was a good time for those who lived in the streets.

*　　*　　*

By day, Elmer's work was abysmally commonplace. He filleted fish at a market on the lower east side. None of his co-workers suspected he was a man with a mission. Nor did he want them to know. He kept his distance, even from the women on whom he sometimes cast lustful gazes. There would be time for women later in his life, after he had accomplished his secret work.

His work was a matter of conscience, based on a sacred trust between him and the Supreme Being. That's how his mother would have advised him to handle it.

She had told him that God had a purpose for every living soul and that one day his purpose would be revealed to him. That concept had sustained him through many lonely years, through many nights of anguish as he struggled with the flittering things in his mind, the things without voices that caused him to awake in the middle of the night, sit up and stare at the wall in the darkness.

Once, when he awoke, he saw something dancing on the wall, a gathering of tiny, shifting shapeless bits of matter on its blank surface. At first he had thought the tiny things were a manifestation of an evil presence sent to torment or test him. Then he realized they were only molecules—molecules dancing on the wall.

When we are asleep, Elmer told himself, molecules move about. Like elves.

155

* * *

Elmer's purpose had been revealed to him as he was riding the subway home to Brooklyn one evening. Before he reached his destination, he was witness to an angry sermon delivered by an old black woman in a purple coat who sat south of him in the car. She talked loudly about Jesus and how without Jesus a person was condemned to hell.

She was still preaching as the train came to her stop. She paused in the doorway and barely finished her tirade before stepping onto the platform. Her last words were, "You'll find out! You'll find out about the wrath of God! You *better* be believing in Jesus."

A person in rags sitting next to the door muttered, "Fugyu," as she exited.

The juxtaposition of events was not lost on Elmer's intelligence.

The woman was a messenger from God; the man in rags was a thing without a soul; hence, it had dismissed the woman with the magic word used by its kind.

Something clicked in Elmer's mind, and it was obvious to him what the two events meant. This incident was a message, perhaps divine in origin, that the homeless had to be eliminated — it pointed to Elmer's purpose in life.

After all, only a soul-less being would reply "Fugyu" in answer to a sermon — only a being without respect for God, because it had no god, and, by extension, had no purpose itself and was only cluttering the earth with its presence.

Elmer set out to confirm his understanding of the message in case he had misinterpreted it. The next day, a Saturday, he went up to a homeless man who was begging in front of the Kentucky Fried Chicken on 34th Street. He was shaking a Styrofoam cup full of quarters, muttering something about needing help because he was homeless.

"Do you believe in Jesus?" Elmer asked him, remembering the old woman's sermon.

The man kept shaking his cup without acknowledging Elmer. He repeated his question.

"Hey, man, you going to give me a quarter or not?"

"No."

"Then I don't believe in Jesus, and you can fuck off."

"What is your name?"

"Fugyu, man. Now get outta my face!"

That was the second time Elmer had heard the awful imprecation "Fugyu" invoked. He didn't respond. Instead, he walked away from the man, weaving through the crowds on the street without looking at anyone.

From this encounter he was able to sort things out mentally. It was all fairly obvious. The streets were full of soul-less things. Perhaps these damned things were creations of Satan, simulacra of people, whom he had sent to confound the rest of humankind.

It made a great deal of sense. If he were Satan, he would send legions of non-beings into the world to cause confusion and unrest. What better way to confound real people than with pseudo-people?

In his heart, Elmer knew he was right. The whole concept felt right. He had found his purpose.

Within the week he had decided the means by which he would embark on fulfilling that purpose.

His first slaying of a soul-less thing was difficult, as he expected it to be. The similarity of the soul-less thing to something human grated against Elmer's sensibilities. He had to keep telling himself a soul-less thing deserved to be removed from the face of the earth.

The thing he found that night was a wino, a derelict who had passed out on the stoop of a run-down apartment building near the market where Elmer worked. It was late March and there was a lingering winter chill in the air.

Elmer had nudged him to consciousness with his foot and asked him the vital questions—the test questions.

To the first question the wino replied, "Jesus lives in a whiskey bottle."

To the second question, the wino replied, "Fugyu."

Elmer produced his knife, the one he used at work to fillet fish flesh, and stabbed the man in the chest.

The man screamed and clutched his wound. Blood spurted on Elmer. Panicking, he fled.

That night, in his apartment, Elmer consoled himself with milk and Oreos. He felt he had botched the job. The soul-less thing's wailings could have attracted attention to him. And he had allowed himself to be soiled with the thing's pseudo-blood.

From then on, he decided, he would cut their throats.

After he adopted that means of dispatch and learned to step back when the blood flowed, he found the work grew easier and easier. It also helped to bring along a bag of Oreos.

*   *   *

Before dawn, Annie's face was tickled by dew which formed on her as if she were a tree planted in the Square. The moisture made her cheeks twitch, but she did not awaken.

She was adrift in a perilously happy dream, one that brought her such wonderful feelings she might choose never to wake up. She was a Queen—no, a Goddess—a beautiful immortal with magic powers. She wore a crown festooned with rare jewels, and an ermine robe with a white mink collar and fringe. Her body was covered with a gossamer white dress that barely concealed the slim, nubile form beneath. Her breasts were pert, small and manageable, not the twin sacks of blubber she had to heave around in reality. Her pubic mound was a prim puff of golden blonde, scented with the exquisite musk of youth.

She marched regally along an endless red carpet with pile two inches thick, her petite feet clad in silken white slippers. On either side of her were fawning worshippers, men and women alike, who tossed tributes of gold, silver, platinum, and jewels in her wake. Beyond the people was a vast rolling plain of rich green, dotted with fruit-laden trees, filling the air with the aromas of cherry, apple, and lemon.

A gold scepter appeared in her right hand, and she waved it in blessing of her admirers. The scepter was topped with a shimmering, multi-faceted sapphire, surrounded with different shades of cat's-eye jewels.

The scepter was also magical. When she touched it on the head of a bowing worshipper, that person was transformed, changed into a glowing being of light that flew away on the crimson-orange ether of which the sky here was colored—and became a star.

All the stars in the heavens were her creation. It was the greatest honor she could bestow upon anyone.

Abruptly, the dream changed locales, and Annie feared she was no longer a goddess. She needn't have worried. She cast her eyes down and again beheld the beautiful nymph-like body in which the dream had molded her.

158

FUGYU

She was sitting at the head of a long table, set with fine china, gold-tipped eating utensiles, and fine crystal goblets. An array of elegant fare lit up her eyes: stuffed pheasants, roast suckling pigs, rack of lamb, and exotic vegetables and fruits. There were also many desserts, including tortes, petits fours and flambés, and every form of chocolate delicacy in the universe. There was champagne and all types of fine vintage wines.

And caviar. Tons of it.

Sitting along the edge of the table were her dinner guests, all of them famous people, some of them movie stars, other stars of the arts — ballerinas and classical musicians — and painters and sculptors. They all waited patiently for her to begin eating before they dined themselves.

She picked up a tiny bell and tinkled it, signalling the beginning of the feast.

She daintily took a knife in one hand and a fork in the other and carved herself a chunk of roast pig, her senses overwhelmed by the juicy aroma of the steam issuing from the cut in the pig's side. She dropped this on her plate and picked up a sterling silver shaker, holding it above the meat and tapping it.

Instead of salt, fairy dust sprinkled over the pork, enhancing its aroma.

Annie sawed off a piece of the meat and brought it to her mouth, stopping just short of her lips.

Maggots were squirming in the meat. She dropped her fork and saw that the piece on her plate was also infested with worms. She looked up and all the food on the table had become putrid and vermin-infested.

Her guests had become skeletons.

She grabbed her scepter from her side and reached out to transform things to the way they were, but the scepter was now an ordinary stick. Even worse was the realization her arm had become a mass of bloated fat.

The dream was slipping away.

"Get a move on, lady," a voice said. It seemed to be coming from the roast pig.

Annie blinked.

"Move it," a cop said. "Jeez, what a smell."

Annie looked around. The sun was up now. Traffic had filled the streets. People were hustling about.

She glared at the cop, muttering, "Fugyu," before hefting her bags and shambling away, heading north.

The dream was still lingering in her mind, making her wonder if it was a rememberence of a past life or a portent of life to come. She played with the notion briefly, then the protective cloud that kept her from thinking too much descended, and she continued wandering without apparent purpose, until the moment when fatigue or some other biological urgency would bring her to a stop.

Her breasts, however, were swollen, as if with milk. They had been that way ever since she'd been wakened by that rude cop who deserved no better than a "Fugyu" for a morning greeting.

*   *   *

Elmer's summer was very busy. He rarely missed a night. In his own way, he was terrorizing the city, making people dread to open dumpsters, fearing they would find a slashed derelict inside.

Eventually, the media caught on, and the newspaper, radio and television reports were filled with dire warnings to street people, warning them against being out alone.

Elmer was glad he was getting notice for his work; he even imagined himself being interviewed on TV, lauded as a hero for ridding the city of unwanted, unnecessary non-people.

But the TV people never would do that. They spoiled the whole thing by making the homeless look like *victims*.

Elmer snorted at that notion.

How could soul-less things be victims? Society was the victim of them. He, Elmer, who had to get close to them, who had to handle them and kill them, was their worst victim.

The news people always got things screwed up.

Then came the copycats—the anonymous killers who did what Elmer did thereby diminishing his accomplishments. Soon just about every dumpster in the city had a corpse in it by morning.

Elmer was disgusted. As with many people of insipid intelligence, he thought he was the only one capable of conceiving of this grand scheme. Now there were others getting in on it.

He almost came forward to identify himself, but so many others had already done that, he didn't expect he would be taken seriously.

160

FUGYU

He trudged through every night, still pursuing his task, but not nearly so satisfied as he had been.

* * *

Those of the homeless who were aware of the world around them were at first afraid of the shadowy killing thing which had come into their world. The fear gradually changed into anger, then the anger became a kind of strength. There was talk of unifying to catch the thing, which they had dubbed the "Angel of Death," since the police were clearly unable—or pehaps even unwilling—to track the person down. After all, the killer only struck those who were derelicts or otherwise burned-out wretches; he didn't bother families. No one really missed a few less winos or crazy street people, not even the other homeless.

Unification also required money and effort. Money could be begged, but true effort was difficult to orchestrate. Among their numbers, the homeless counted many feckless souls who were inclined not to do anything about anything.

So most of the homeless just huddled in the darkness at night, hoping the Angel of Death would not visit them.

But he did. Quite often. He came in many guises, offering death. And sometimes cookies.

By the end of July, the story of the homeless killer was receding behind the imperative of other, more exploitative news, such as which wealthy Manhattan resident was sleeping with which foreign beauty, what foolishness the President was up to, or which rock singer was the most perverse.

Many of the copycat killers had sluffed off, leaving Elmer to continue virtually alone, keeping at his task doggedly with almost no interruption—depositing bodies in dumpsters night after night.

He no longer bothered to wrap them in trash bags. He had decided it was unnecessary, and, besides, it was becoming expensive.

Since a divine entity watched over his work, Elmer easily eluded policemen or detection by anyone else. He was as invisible as any Ninja could hope to be.

He was invincible as well.

* * *

161

Annie was not aware any Angel of Death was invading her universe. She was only aware that it was getting very hot in the city—so hot she had considered taking a bath, although the crust of dirt covering her had become so comfortable in its own way, she hesitated to disturb it.

She ultimately decided against the bath. She might take one in the fall, if it was really necessary.

Besides, her breasts were now so swollen they hurt. She did not want to touch them unnecessarily, and bathing would require that she did, if only to remove the top layer of scum.

She ambled along the streets, her smell gathering greater strength, her breasts about to burst through her dress, finding comfort only at night when she could slip into the world of dreams.

She was always a goddess in her dreams, the slender young woman with a perfect body. In some of the wonderful excursions into the dream world, she offered her breasts to be fondled by her worshippers. Once, when her breasts were stroked, they produced cream, which was lapped up greedily by her minions. When she awoke, her breasts always ached. She feared they might explode eventually, taking her away into dreamland forever.

*　　*　　*

By September, Elmer was growing weary. There were so many soul-less wretches in the city and he was only one man. So a depressing number of homeless remained. It was as if they multiplied when he wasn't looking. Perhaps Satan, the dark Lord of Fugyu, was making them with a hellish cookie-cutter, stamping out two for every one Elmer destroyed.

Eventually, Elmer took a week off and sat around in his apartment watching TV, eating Oreos and drinking beer. At night, he watched the molecules dance on his walls until he drifted into a fretful slumber, marked by dreams of spinning, blood-flecked Oreos.

During the day, his thoughts were preoccupied with how he would continue his divine assignment. It was very important, but the strain was eroding his purpose, and he definitely needed more sleep than he was getting lately. One day he had almost sliced off his own thumb with his fillet knife at the market, he was so bleary-eyed and fuzzy-headed.

FUGYU

He wanted to keep his thumbs and fingers. He wanted to keep his job.

He took another week off. His task had become thankless, and though he had a purpose, it was less rewarding when only he knew about it.

That had to be sufficient, he realized. Only he appreciated the good work he was doing. He would have to await the judgment of future historians before he gained the recognition he deserved.

So, somewhat refreshed and revitalized by his two-week hiatus, he took to the streets again.

*　　*　　*

In early October, Annie found a purple tweed coat in a dumpster — just the sort of garment she needed for the coming winter. The coat was the shroud of an old black woman whose throat had been cut. Annie unpeeled the coat from the corpse and donned it without pausing to consider why the black woman was in the dumpster, or how she had become dead. She did appreciate that the woman's coat held residual body heat, which made it even more desirable in the early morning's chill. Fortunately, there was very little blood on the coat itself.

After she took the coat, she foraged in the bin for other treasures. But the dead woman's blank stare began to get on her nerves, and she stopped her rumaging, settling for half a box of stale Cheese Nips someone had discarded and a cracked 45 record.

She took one last look at the dead woman and closed the lid. As she trod along the alley, something jiggled in the dark recesses of her skull—in the space where her mind had once dwelt: There were fewer homeless on the streets than usual. That black woman had been one of them; Annie thought she recognized her from somewhere.

Something wasn't quite right in the world.

She vaguely recalled hearing a rumor about someone killing street people. It was something that had been going on around her which had bounced off her defocused awareness, but now it became more real.

She didn't like the idea at all. Being homeless was bad enough, but to be a target was very upsetting. Annie vowed to do something about it, if she got the chance. What she would do was an amorphous proposition in her mind, however, so it didn't have much tenacity.

Then Annie forgot every thought she'd just had as she found a perfectly good screwdriver lying in the alley. She bent over and picked it up, straining mightily to upright herself as her engorged breasts were tugged by the force of gravity.

She fought the force and just barely defeated it, gaining her balance more by effort than by grace.

She wondered if her breasts would ever go down. Maybe if she pricked them, they would deflate like balloons.

That was painful even to contemplate. Annie dropped the screwdriver in one of the bags and moved on.

*   *   *

Elmer had trouble getting up that morning. Killing the black woman had been difficult, because she didn't want to be killed and had fought back, trying to gouge him with her fingernails. She had kicked him in the shins too and was about to jam her knee into his groin, when Elmer simply decked her. He had to cut her throat while she was unconscious, so he hadn't had the chance to offer her an Oreo. She was also heavier than he expected, making him expend more energy than usual dragging her to the nearest dumpster.

His task had become very tiresome. By the time Elmer reached his apartment, he collapsed on the bed without undressing. He slept only a couple of hours, then awoke abruptly, as if nudged by something sharp.

He had rolled over on his back and the fillet knife had nicked him. He went into the bathroom and hiked up his shirt to inspect the wound. He saw a tiny dot of blood on his back. He wiped it away with a piece of toilet paper and dabbed alcohol on it. It stung then hurt no more.

Elmer splashed cold water on his face, then hot. He lathered and shaved, exhorting himself to wake up—that he had to go to his job in a semi-alert state.

The black woman's outraged face hovered in his memory. What if others started fighting back?

That was absurd. They had no right to fight back. They should let themselves be removed without protest.

164

FUGYU

Elmer hurriedly dressed and took the early morning subway into Manhattan.

* * *

Annie found herself headed toward the sanctuary. She was driven more by instinct than by design. She did not want to end up in a dumpster like the black woman.

She dimly recalled a colony of homeless people like herself living on the lower east side, near the river. It was a place where her smell would hardly be noticed, and she would be surrounded by others like herself, who had no direction or particular purpose in their lives. She could hide out there until such time as she felt safe to wander the streets again.

She could crawl into a box and be alone with her dreams.

* * *

Three o'clock was quitting time. Elmer washed his hands vigorously to remove the fish smell, then combed his thinning hair carefully. He had decided to take in an early movie this afternoon, go home afterwards and get to bed early. He simply had no reserves of energy left to pursue his task this evening. If the soul-less ones proliferated one night, then so be it.

As he said good-bye to his boss and the Puerto Rican girl at the register, he turned into the street.

He halted.

On the other side a bloated ugly thing had appeared. It was wearing a purple coat and a small black hat. It was something akin to a woman.

It was a soul-less thing.

Something stirred in Elmer's chest—a yearning—a compulsion to do the necessary. He checked his back pocket for the fillet knife; he had put it there automatically, without thinking, despite his resolve not to do any work tonight.

He darted into the street, was cursed by a truck driver, and followed the ambling whale-like woman.

As he watched the massive jowls of her ass scrunch and roll

165

together when she walked, Elmer realized she was a sign from God. Here, God was saying, was the ultimate abomination—remove *this* from the earth!

It was a challenge and a test of Elmer's faith in himself. He knew he must not fail.

The woman wandered around in circles, going up two blocks, down one block, west three blocks, back east a block, south another block, until she arrived at a ramshackle community near the river.

Elmer knew this place. It was a colony where many homeless people lived. It was a small city with a miniature skyline made of cardboard cartons and wooden crates. There was a fire going in an old oil drum at its entrance. The place was surrounded by a make-shift fence constructed of boards, bits of wire strung across railroad ties, and, in a few places, cinder blocks or bricks piled up.

The woman stopped there, mumbled at a tall black man, and lumbered on in.

Elmer drew back.

Why hadn't he come here before? Here was the source—the place where the homeless multiplied as if in an ant hill! He could have saved himself a lot of footwork.

Elmer watched the woman enter a crate. He noted its location and retreated. He would wait until it was dark before taking action. In the meantime, he would go to the movies as he had planned, and that would give him a chance to gather his remaining strength.

Once he removed the ultimate abomination, the woman, he would set the colony on fire, destroying the source of the soul-less, nameless things.

His task would be completed.

*   *   *

Annie settled comfortably into the crate she had been assigned by the man at the entrance. He said she could stay only one night unless she came up with some money. She wasn't worried about that, since she was sure there was money somewhere in one of her bags.

She slumped against the side of the crate and closed her eyes, feeling a bit safer.

She fell asleep and became a goddess.

166

FUGYU

* * *

After the movie, through most of which he had slept, Elmer stopped at a convenience store and purchased a small box of Oreos. Then he headed east toward the homeless encampment near the river.

It was dark by the time he got there. He approached the place slowly, orienting himself carefully with regard to the position of the crate where the ultimate abomination had taken up residence. There were several rows of boxes and crates, arranged symmetrically, thus proving even the lowliest of people—that is, non-people—had a sense of order.

But it was too early for Elmer to act. There were too many of the colony's inhabitants up and about, eating, talking and cursing. There were many intelligible "Fugyu's" among their chatter.

He backtracked a few yards and found an old, abandoned truck, a rusted hulk with no doors. He crawled up into the truck's cab and lay down, sliding quickly into a peaceful sleep.

He awoke in the deepest black of night. His limbs were cramped from his precarious position on the old truck's ragged seat, and he sat up and stretched. He climbed down and looked toward the river.

There was almost no light in the encampment, except for the dying flames in the oil drum at the entrance.

Elmer moved along the rubble-strewn ground in a near-crouch, his eyes straining to adjust to the darkness. The boxes and crates were ebony forms, barely distinguishable from the night. He went to the entrance and stood briefly by the oil drum, warming his hands by holding them above the small fire.

He listened and heard ragged snores, wheezing slumber, vague sleep mutterings, and tubucular gasping all about him. Then the smells of the homeless assailed him. He almost choked on the mixture of odors—of rot and mildew and unwashed skin—but managed to keep from coughing and revealing his presence. He felt like dirt was crawling on his skin.

His hands warmed, Elmer peered out into the camp. He wasn't sure he could pick out the crate in which the abomination slept now. Everything looked the same.

He took his knife from his pocket, filled his other hand with Oreos, then ventured into the darkness. A few feet inside the camp, his eyes adjusted to the shadows and he could make out the forms of the

167

homeless in their shabby dwelling places. He would work his way to the old woman somehow.

He approached a wino slumbering in a refrigerator carton to his right.

"Where is the old woman," he asked, "the one who came in today?"

"Fugyu," the wino said.

"Fuck you too," Elmer mumbled without bothering to offer the man an Oreo. He drew back to plunge his knife into the wino's throat, but he suddenly found his arm immobilized, being pulled hard, nearly wrenched from its socket by a tall man, who he knew must be the sentry of the place.

He twisted around and could barely make out the form of something grotesquely obese with an unhumanly stench standing before him.

"Fugyu" the ultimate abomination said.

"Let go!"

The man exerted more pressure on Elmer's arm, pulling it up behind him.

Suddenly there were lights in the camp. The winos, the street people, the old women, the lost people of the world, all had lit candles, so they could see the Angel of Death.

Abruptly, the wino Elmer was going to kill arose, produced a razor blade and slashed Elmer's free hand.

Elmer stuttered with pain; he couldn't quite make a scream rise from his throat.

The tall black man pinned both Elmer's arms behind him. The ultimate abomination stared in his eyes. Her purple coat hung open, and his eyes were drawn to the expanse of breast exposed below her swollen neck. He imagined he could see moss growing on her skin, especially in her cleavage. The black man pushed him closer, until Elmer was almost nose-to-tit with her gargantuan breasts.

"I have cookies," Elmer said desperately. "Oreos. I'll give them to you."

"We know who you are," a man in rags said.

"The Angel of Death," another man croaked.

"No, not me," Elmer protested. "I just wanted to help, to give you some food."

"Fugyu!" the woman said.

"Bullshit!"

168

FUGYU

"Nobody fucking else don't care about us, so we got to take care of you ourself."

"Take off his clothes!"

"Cut his nuts off!"

"Throw him n the river!"

"Stick a spike up his ass!"

No one made a move. They were shouting wishes, not deeds, not reality—words meant to threaten and make the Angel of Death withdraw from their midst.

Annie was disgusted. Had she known her sanctuary was populated with ineffectual cowards, she would not have come here.

A portion of her dreams slid down between the cracks in her brain, animating her, propelling her forward with an unspoken imperative. She felt her skin tingle with purpose.

"Let's just kick his ass," the black man said.

The goddess had emerged from the cocoon of the ultimate abomination. The goddess had the jeweled scepter in her hand. She would transform this intruder into a dungbeetle.

Annie the goddess stepped forward. The others watched, wondering what she intended to do with the screwdriver in her hand.

She thrust the tool into Elmer's stomach. The man holding Elmer dropped him, as surprised at the blood spurting forth from the wound as Elmer was.

Elmer dropped to his knees, clutching the shank of the screwdriver.

Annie saw that he was transformed, but not enough. "Fugyu," she said and sliced Elmer's cheek with the edge of a 45 record, which in her mind was a silver platter.

Elmer let go of a tittering scream, like a woman frightened by a mouse.

The goddess took her regal staff, a broken beer bottle, and carved her sign on the intruder's forehead.

She stood back briefly.

It seemed something was churning inside her breasts.

Other beings, inspired by Annie's actions, scuttled forth from the darkness, leaving their candles behind them. They ripped Elmer's jacket and shirt off, yanked his trousers and shorts down. Someone yanked on his privates; someone else buggered him with a corkscrew. His lips worked at wailing with the pain of it all, but he was unable to complete the sound because one of the soul-less things had sliced his throat with his own fillet knife.

Annie stumbled into the midst of the others. They fell back from her presence, astounded by the sight of her now exposed breasts.

"Fugyu," she pronounced imperiously in her goddess voice, and stuck her blood-flecked sausage fingers between her cleavage. She tugged at one of her breasts and lifted it, struggling with its dead weight.

Despite the pain making it hard to focus, Elmer was fascinated by the size of Annie's jagged-edged purplish brown nipple with its encircling aureole—that seemed like a bruise or a stain that spread over the face of the breast like a blotchy mask.

He could see molecules dancing in the end of it.

She pointed the distorted nipple at him and squeezed. The goddess in her would drown him in her cream—providing him a death as grotesque as he deserved.

Fluid jetted out the end of the humongous bag of flesh. But it was not cream.

Elmer clutched at his steaming face.

Acid. Acid had come from her dug.

Annie squeezed the other breast directing the squirting fluid in a line down the center of Elmer's body. He thrashed with pain.

Her breasts finally emptied, Annie tucked them in awkwardly. She felt a great sense of relief. But she was no longer a goddess. The Angel of Death had used up all her cream.

She went to the crate and dragged out her bags, then trudged out of the camp, pausing only once—to retrieve an Oreo that had rolled from Elmer's pocket. She popped it in her mouth whole, grinding it with her few teeth, then tottered out into her world, the streets.

While Elmer's flesh melted, the others descended on him with their knives and icepicks and razor blades and can lids, and other weapons.

Later, the members of the colony left pieces of Elmer all over the city, but the pieces were so small no one noticed them. The integrity of their souls reaffirmed, the homeless retreated into their spaces and themselves became invisible, except when they came forth for a handout.

Annie had few thoughts or memories of what had happened—only the lingering sensation of something on the tip of her tongue—something exquisitely, addictively sweet—some kind of cookie. She wanted more.

FUGYU

Her life settled into its familiar routine; she reclaimed the streets as her own special world, her designated universe, and was caught up in a unique kind of bliss, having realized that she had been a goddess in one life or another. She need fear nothing from now on; she was invincible.

She would occasionally pause on a street corner, regarding all the rest of humanity through a squint and shake with a combination of self-assured knowledge and laughter.

Then she would say, "Fugyu," and wander on, searching the city for Oreos.

Rick Hautala

Stories and Tales of the *Little Brothers*

Dedication:

To Steve Bissette, with *mucho* thanks *amigo!*

also, special thanks to: Paul Mikol, Scot Stadalsky, Matt Costello, Chris Fahy, Roman Ranieri, Craig Goden (of *Time Tunnel*), Michael Zulli, Carmine Leo, Larry Fire, and Dominick Abel.

Introduction to *Untcigahunk*

Of all of my novels, it seems *Little Brothers* is the one for which most people ask me to write a sequel. I have no problem with that idea since I'm particularly fond of the main characters, Kip and Watson, and I certainly wouldn't be opposed to returning to Thornton, Maine, sometime—say five years after the close of the novel, to pick up what happens with the next appearance of the "untcigahunk." Certainly, if you've read the book, you know it's been left wide open for a follow-up.

Problem is, years ago, maybe even as far back as when my first novel was published, I made a personal vow—foolishly, and in jest, but possibly all too true—not even to consider doing a sequel to *any* novel of mine unless or until a movie was being made of the original. At least as of right now, my "little brothers" aren't slated for the silver screen; so to maintain my honor, I have to make it clear that the following collection of stories, under the general title *Untcigahunk*, are not—in any way—a sequel to my novel.

The origin of these stories is quite simple: I got a phone call one day from Steve Bissette, a friend of mine, asking if I would be willing to "expand" on the original concept of *Little Brothers*. He wanted me to write a handful of stories, a couple of different episodes about *other* appearances of the "little brothers" which he and Michael Zulli *(The Puma Blues)* would then adapt into comic format for Steve's magazine, *Taboo*. Not a sequel, mind you. None of the characters from the original book would have a major role in any of the stories (although "The Birch Whistle" happens at the same time as the novel, and a

175

younger Police Chief Parkman from the novel has a cameo in "Love on the Rocks").

I liked Steve's suggestion because it sounded like fun; it gave me the impetus to go back to the situation I had created in the book and re-explore it, to look at it from several different angles.

As it turned out, I was between books; one novel was in the galley stage, and my next book was a completed first draft that was marinating before I started revising it. So I sat down at the keyboard one morning, fished around a bit to get a handle on the suggestion Steve had given me—"Something to do with an archaeologist and Indian petroglyphs"—and BANG-O, I got one. "Love on the Rocks" took several days to write and revise; then I sent it off to Steve.

He liked the story, and his enthusiasm sparked another idea based on reminiscences of my grandfather's cow barn, so I wrote "Deal with the Devils." When that was all set and ready to send off to Steve, while I was jotting a quick note to accompany the story, another idea hit me, so I wrote "The Birch Whistle." And not long after that, Steve and I were having a laugh about the idea of "rabid squirrels"; thus "Chrysalis" was born. Then, in thinking about a prologue for the whole thing, I came up with "Little Brother" and the other two "myths" as framing devices. (I should apologize here for playing fast and loose with the Micmac Indians' mythology. Although "untcigahunk" is the Micmac word for "little" or "younger" brother, that's all I borrowed from their traditions.)

Once I had all these stories and tales, I figured I could take a break. Steve and Michael had plenty of material on hand to get started drawing, and I was busy revising that novel. Then Paul Mikol called, inviting me to join in Night Visions 9.

I liked that idea, and I figured, because these stories would only see publication in comic book format, Night Visions 9 would be a terrific opportunity for me to present them first as I had originally written them. So here they are—Untcigahunk, the un-sequel.

Enjoy!

— Fall, 1972 —

— 1 —

"You know, from this far away, if you squint your eyes, doesn't it sorta look like an ant hill?" Stan Walters said.

He and his older brother, Chet, were lying back on their elbows on a grassy slope, watching the Maine state highway construction crew at work. Both boys had heard plenty about the project to straighten out Route 25 south of their home town of Thornton; day after day, their father complained about how many extra miles he had to detour so he could make it to work on time in Portland. In the distance, bulldozers, dump trucks, and men moved through billowing clouds of yellow dust that rose like sulfurous smoke into the heat-hazed July sky. All sound was lost in the distance except for the blaring *beep-beep-beep* of the backing-up warning buzzers as the heavy equipment carved away the hillside.

Stan's eyes darted back and forth, trying desperately to keep track of all the activity. "Look at everything they've dug up. I'll bet I could find some really neat rocks for my collection down there."

"You know what I think?" Chet said lazily as he slid a spear of grass between his two front teeth and smiled. "I think you've got rocks in your head!" He swatted Stan on the shoulder. "Naw—just kidding. But you know what pisses me off is how they're ruining Watchick Hill. Damn! There ain't gonna be nothing left of it by the time they're through."

Stan smiled at his older brother's use of profanity. Chet had just

177

turned thirteen, and he took every opportunity to swear like a pirate whenever there weren't any adults around. Chet's swearing in front of him made Stan feel older, accepted—well, at least a little bit.

"I know, but look up there. See all those holes in the hillside?" Stan said excitedly. "There's gotta be more than twenty holes up there where they've been blasting. I think they might have opened up into a whole bunch of tunnels or something. I can just imagine the different kinds of rocks they're turning up—"

"Yeah, and I can just imagine the reaming we're *both* gonna get if we're not home in time for supper," Chet said. He hoisted himself to his feet, brushed off his butt, and started down the grassy slope to the road where Stan had left his bicycle. "And if you don't get your sorry ass moving, I'm gonna take your bike and ride it home."

"Oh, yeah? The hell you are!" Stan yelled as he leaped up and started running.

The race was on.

Chet had a good head start, and even though Stan knew it was hopeless, he ran full tilt boogie down the hillside, his arms pumping madly as he chugged through tall, summer grass that whipped at his legs, threatening to trip him up. He watched in frustration as Chet easily outdistanced him. Once he was beside the bicycle, Chet turned and crossed his arms triumphantly over his chest while he waited a moment. When Stan was no more than ten feet from him, he picked up the bike by the handlebars, spun on his heel, and started running. After a few quick steps, he vaulted onto the seat and started pedalling furiously. Derisive laughter curled like a scarf over his shoulder as he sped away.

"*Come on, Chet!*" Stan shouted. "*That's not fair!*"

His breath came into his lungs hot and hard as he cupped his hands on his knees and leaned forward, expecting at any second to puke his guts out. Sweat poured down the sides of his face and stung his eyes. His lower lip was trembling as he watched his brother easily put distance between them. For several pounding heartbeats, he watched helplessly, waiting for Chet to turn around and come back; but without even a backward glance, he rounded the curve and disappeared out of sight.

"*Fuck you, you bastard!*" Stan wailed, shaking his clenched fist at the empty road. It was safe to swear—Chet was too far away to hear him, anyway. But he wasn't about to start crying. No way! Crying was for *babies!*

− 2 −

After a quick supper of a hamburger, French fries, and green beans—and a brief tussle with Chet for taking his bike—Stan went up to his bedroom. He grabbed his flashlight and the burlap bag he used to collect rocks and ran back downstairs. As he raced out the front door, he shouted to his mother that he was going outside to play.

"Where are you off to?" she asked.

"Just out," he replied, letting the screen door slam shut behind him. He was halfway down the walkway to where Chet had left his bike when she leaned out the front door and called to him, "Just make sure you're home before dark!"

Pretending he hadn't heard her, Stan slipped the flashlight into his hip pocket, wrapped the burlap bag around his handlebars, and started pedalling furiously down Elm Street. He had only one goal in mind; he had to get out to the construction site and check it out now that the highway workers were gone. This was probably his best chance to find some neat rocks for his collection.

His feet were a blur as he sped around the curves and up and down the slopes of Route 25. The closer he got, the more his excitement rose. It felt like a bubbling gush of cool water inside his chest. In spite of the cool evening air washing over his face, the exertion made him break out into a sweat. When he saw the flashing yellow warning lights up ahead, he squeezed the hand brakes, coming to a stop where the road changed from asphalt to hard-packed dirt. He swung off his bike and walked it along the stretch of stripped highway.

The hillside was strangely quiet in the gathering gloom of evening. White barricades with flashing yellow warning lights lined the strip of gravel they had laid down for the road base. Along both edges of a long, deep trench were round, black metal balls. The wicks at the top flickered with fat orange flames that gave of thick, sooty smoke. The yellow dust had settled, skimming everything with a hazy coat that reminded Stan of the scum of pine pollen that floated on Sebago Lake when he went swimming in early summer.

But it was the scarred hillside towering up against the darkening sky that riveted Stan's attention. Deep gouges lined the steep side of the hill where the men had blasted away the red granite ledge. Huge blocks of rock jutted out from the dirt like the rotten, crooked

179

teeth of a long-buried giant. In the dimming light, Stan could see high up on the hillside more than a dozen dark tunnel mouths, looking like black, sightless eyes. Piles of rubble lay at the base of the hill, waiting for the men to return in the morning to be loaded up and trucked off.

Did they even bother to check over these rocks to see if there was anything valuable? Stan wondered. Did anyone even bother to look inside those tunnels? Watchick Hill could be honeycombed with caves that could be part of an old gold mine, or loaded with Indian arrowheads, for all anyone knew.

He stared up at the nearest cave opening, no more than forty feet up the hillside. It looked three, maybe four feet wide. Stan couldn't stop wondering what might be hidden in there.

"Only one way to find out," he answered himself aloud.

Unwrapping the burlap bag from the handlebars, he leaned his bike against one of the barricades, jumped the trench, and started up the hillside. The slope was steeper than it had looked. He had to lean way forward and paddle his hands on the ground in front of him for balance as he made his way up. Loose soil kept slipping out from underfoot, and just about every step started a mini-landslide. He found that by cutting across the face of the hill first one way, then the other, he could zigzag back and forth. Before long, he arrived at the narrow slanting ledge in front of the open cave mouth. Another, stronger shiver rippled through him as he got onto his hands and knees and stuck his head into the dark hole. The air inside blew cold and dank from the tunnel into his face.

"What the—?" he whispered. His voice echoed from the deep recesses of the cave with an odd reverberation. He knew if air was blowing *out* of the tunnel, that meant there had to be another opening somewhere at the other end.

Stan's footing wasn't all that secure. One foot kept skidding out from underneath him on the tilted, dirt-coated ledge. He knew if he didn't find the courage to crawl into the tunnel soon, he would have to climb back down . . . before he fell down. Glancing at the roadbed forty feet below, he tried not to imagine how much it would hurt if he slid all the way in the dirt and gravel. And what if he started a *big* landslide, enough to cover him beneath tons of dirt and debris?

He had to decide—soon! Night was coming on fast, and the workers would be back in the morning. Even if he left for home right now, he wouldn't be back before dark, so it was a safe bet that

180

he'd be grounded for a couple of days, at least. By the time he was un-grounded, the whole hillside would probably have been hauled off. If he didn't check out this cave now, he wasn't *ever* going to get to check it out!

But did he even dare go in there?

After glancing over his shoulder at the blaze of sunset on the horizon, he took a deep breath, tucked the burlap bag into his hip pocket, took out his flashlight, and clicked it on. Holding his breath, he got onto his hands and knees, and edged into the doorway. The oval of light illuminated a hard-packed dirt floor. Cool—actually *cold* air raised goose bumps on his arms as he skittered forward. Because of the low ceiling, he had to feel blindly for a handhold to pull himself all the way inside.

Even with the feeble glow of the flashlight, Stan felt deep rushes of nervousness as he started along the stone-lined tunnel. The walls seemed to narrow gradually, squeezing in on him from all directions. More than once, he considered backing out and was grateful, at least, that Chet wasn't here to ride him about being a sissy.

But maybe being a sissy wasn't such a bad idea, Stan thought as he inched his way deeper into the earth. After each lunge forward, he would look back over his shoulder almost longingly at the receding oval of burning, orange sky and think how pitifully small his flashlight beam was.

"Damn it!" he muttered, when his hand holding the flashlight hit the ground hard, and the light flickered. His voice reverberated oddly in the narrow confines of the tunnel, but even before the echo died, he thought he heard something else—a soft, hissing, scratching sound—like ripping wet cloth. He froze, directing his light ahead and craning his neck forward as he listened tensely for the sound to be repeated. He was positive of only one thing: *he* hadn't made that noise!

Ripples of fear raced up his back. In spite of the coolness inside the tunnel, sweat trickled down the sides of his face.

"All right, all right now," he whispered, trying to reassure himself as his eyes darted around, following the dodging flashlight beam. "Just take it easy . . . take it—"

His throat closed off, stifling a scream that would have resounded throughout the entire mountain when his left hand, reaching forward, touched . . . something. He jerked back too quickly and bumped his head against the tunnel roof. The impact stunned him, and the flashlight dropped from his hand. It winked out the instant it hit the ground. Dirt and grit showered down like rain on a tin roof as he reached forward, furiously groping for his light. His only fear was that he would touch that . . . that *thing* again. At last, his hand closed around the metal cylinder. His heart was pounding hard as he clicked the switch uselessly back and forth.

The light was dead.

For several seconds, Stan remained motionless, listening to his racing heartbeat until it started to slow down. A sheen of sweat had broken out like dew on his forehead. He couldn't stop thinking about whatever that was he had touched. It had felt cold—almost dead cold, clammy and sticky, like a dead animal or something. The tunnel was too narrow for him to turn around, so, still shaking, he started retreating backward, fighting the urge to scramble out of there as fast as he could.

But wait a second! he thought, suddenly halting his backward retreat. He hadn't found any rocks worth beans, but what if that thing was something . . . neat?

He crouched in the pressing darkness, feeling equally compelled to go forward to find out what that thing *was* and to get the hell out of here while he still could . . . at least until he got another flashlight. His pulse thumped heavily in his ears as he debated which way to go; in the end, his curiosity won out. His whole body was trembling as he started forward again, reaching blindly ahead until his fingers once again grazed the squishy, cold, *dead*-feeling thing. He jerked his hand back, fully expecting the thing to move even though he knew, just by the touch, that whatever it was, it wasn't alive. It may have been once, but it was stone cold now.

"Oh, *shit!*" Stan whispered when—again—a soft, rustling noise echoed from deep inside the cave. It sounded like someone dragging something heavy over the dirt floor. Although the sound had definitely come from up ahead, in the echoing darkness, Stan had the illusion that, like the rock walls, it was all around him, threatening to come crashing in on him any second. With steadily rising terror, he grabbed the burlap bag from his hip pocket, spread the mouth wide, and, without touching the thing any more than he had to, shoved it into the bag. The mere touch of it made him feel queasy, and he was relieved once he had it bagged.

The cave was too tight for him to turn around, so he started working his way backward, probing his path with one foot so he wouldn't lose his way or go screaming out off the ledge and down the slope.

CHRYSALIS

As he dragged the bag along behind him, his fear-heightened state made the return trip seem infinitely longer. He tried to sort out his impressions of what the thing he had found might be. It had felt rubbery and cold, just about the size of a football, maybe a little bit narrower; it felt like it was composed of thick, segmented rings like donuts that came to a blunt point at either end.

The sun had set by now, so even when he was near the cave entrance, he wouldn't have known it except for the strong draft of cool, fresh air that curled around him. He shivered, wondering what the hell this thing was. It made him feel woozy, almost sick to his stomach just remembering how squishy and cold it had felt. Try as he might, he couldn't get rid of the thought that he had discovered a dead man's severed arm.

Finally, over his shoulder, Stan could see the circle of star-lit sky drawing ever closer. He sighed deeply with relief when he felt his foot kick out free in the open air. Scrinching up his legs, he spun around and hung his feet out over the ledge. Just as he was about to push off down the slope, he heard again that hollow rasping sound—much louder now, and coming closer. Its rippling echo filled the cave.

Whatever it is, it's coming this way! Stan thought with a white bolt of panic.

Intense pressure squeezed his stomach as he leaned back, stuck his feet out in front of himself, and began a slow, controlled slide down the slope, clutching the burlap bag tightly against his chest. It may have been just his imagination—it *must* have been—but he was *positive* that the instant he pushed off the ledge, something rushed up to the cave mouth and either threw something at him or else made a quick grab at him. He had no idea *what* it was, but he felt *something* whisk by his head close to his ear like a bat, unseen in the dark. He didn't have any time to think, though, because just then one foot snagged on a rock and catapulted him forward. Before he could recover, he was tumbling head over heels down the gravely hillside. His long, trailing scream filled the night as he and a wave of dirt and gravel rushed headlong toward the roadbed.

Stan was knocked nearly senseless when he came to rest flat on his back at the bottom of the hill. Loose dirt hissed like an angry snake as it slid down in his wake. Shaking his head, he leaped to his feet and hurriedly brushed himself off with one hand. There wasn't a square inch of his body that didn't feel battered and bruised, but a quick inventory proved that he wasn't hurt except for a single stinging cut above his left eye. He sure as hell *felt* as though he had just been put through a high-speed meat grinder. Unbelievably, he had managed to hold onto the burlap bag throughout his fall. He wanted like hell to see what was in it, but there wasn't enough light to see by. The image of a dead man's severed arm rose again sharply in his mind, making him feel rubbery and sick.

He was dazed from his fall and kept rubbing his head to reassure himself that it was still attached. Lit only by the flames of the smudge pots and the blinking yellow warning lights, the night pressed in around him tightly. For a panicked instant, he imagined he was still inside the cave. His head throbbed with pain as he started toward the road. He had to stop every few steps, shake his head, and hope that the waves of dizziness would pass soon. Once, when he turned and looked back up the hillside at the cave mouth, he saw something moving up there. He tried to convince himself it was just a trick of the darkness, but it sure as hell *looked* like something dark shifted against the darker black of the cave opening.

Trembling, he was just turning to leave when a hand shot out of the darkness and grabbed him by the neck.

— 3 —

"I *knew* I'd find you out here!"

Chet's voice drilled into Stan's ears as he spun him around and gave him a solid push that sent him staggering backwards. Stan's mouth opened, and his lips moved, but the only noise he could make sounded like air hissing out of a punctured bicycle tire.

"Mom's been hollerin' and hollerin' for you for the past half hour," Chet said. "I figured you'd be out here collecting rocks, right? His face glowed eerily in the flickering strobe of the warning lights.

"God *damn*, you scared the *shit* out of me, you motherf—"

"Ut-ut," Chet said, wagging a warning finger underneath Stan's nose. "Better watch your language, or else I'll tell mom. You're in enough trouble as it is. Hey! What you got in the bag?"

Chet made a move to grab the bag from him, but Stan swung his body around protectively.

"None of your damned business," he shouted.

"Ohh . . . ohh, little mister foul-mouth," Chet said, taunting. "Com'on. Lemme see." He darted first one way, then the other in an attempt to get at whatever it was, but finally he gave up. "Well, it better not be any more rocks. God knows your junk takes up enough space in the bedroom as it is. We'll just see what you have to say once you get home, wise guy. Mom is *royally* pissed you weren't back when she said to be."

"Yeah, well, I just sorta lost track of the time," Stan replied weakly. He was still a little dizzy from his fall, and his pulse hadn't slowed down from the surprise Chet had given him. He was trying his best to control himself, but he felt like he had to go to the bathroom r-e-a-l bad.

"Come on, then," Chet said. He suddenly darted ahead of Stan, heading toward the open trench. At the very edge, he leaped up into the air. The flashing lights made his movements strobe like an old-time movie as he hung suspended against the night sky for an instant; then he landed with a grunt on the other side. One foot caught at the edge of the trench and knocked dirt down into the darkness below. He looked back at Stan, his face horribly underlit by the flickering orange flame of the smudge pots.

"Hey, man — if you don't get a move on, I'll take your bike again!" Chet shouted. His mouth hung open; he looked like he was about to say something else, but he cut himself short when a faint noise from down inside the open trench drew his attention. Craning his head forward, he looked down.

"Hey! What's the matter?" Stan yelled, remembering the odd noises he had heard inside the cave. His hand clutched the closed mouth of the burlap bag as the image of a dead, severed arm rose up in his mind. Maybe the rest of this dead guy is buried down there!

Chet didn't say anything as he stared into the dark trench, waiting tensely to hear the sound repeated. When it didn't come again, he muttered a swear and kicked some loose gravel down into the trench. When there still was no response, he straightened up, looked smugly back at Stan, and then started walking away. As soon as Chet's back was turned, Stan thought he saw a shadow shift within the darkness of the trench.

"Hey, Chet!" he called, his voice tight with fear. "Wait up!"

"No way! You wouldn't show me what you've got in the bag, so I'm not gonna wait for you!"

The skin at the back of Stan's neck prickled as he eyed the opened trench and recalled the hissing, dragging sound he had heard inside the cave.

"Come on! Wait for me!" Stan shouted. It took effort to control the wavering in his voice.

"Come on, yourself, then! Move your lard ass!" Chet shouted back, his voice receding into the darkness.

Stan was about to yell again, but when he opened his mouth, a clump of dirt at the edge of the trench slid noisily down into the darkness below. One of the smudge pots teetered at the edge for a moment and then fell. It sputtered as it rolled into the ditch, the flame blazing higher just before it winked out. At that same instant, Stan was positive he heard a short, barking yelp of pain. Slinging the burlap bag over his handlebars, he took off down the road like a shot, hoping like hell to catch up to his brother.

− 4 −

"I was up in my tree house, mom. Honest!" Stan said. Cringing inwardly, he glanced over at Chet, just waiting for him to tell her the truth. Even when his brother remained silent, Stan was convinced it was only so he could use this little white lie against him some other time.

"Is that how you got so dirty, and how you got that cut over your eye?"

Stan shook his head, trying to think of an excuse, but his mind was a blank.

"Well, you know what I think about that tree house of yours!" Lisa Walters said.

"I must've dozed off or something, 'cause I never even heard you calling for me. Honest, mom!"

CHRYSALIS

"I swear to God, I'm going to have your father tear that—that *monstrosity* down this weekend," Stan's mother said. The scowl on her face deepened as she placed her hands on her hips and glared at Stan. "I don't want you up there in the trees like that. Why, just this morning, Mrs. Emerson was telling me about the problem they're having out there in Cornish and Limington with rabid squirrels. She—"

Before she could say more, first Chet, and then Stan started snickering with repressed laughter. One boy set the other off, and before they could stop themselves, both of them were fighting hard not to roar in hysterical laughter.

"Oh, so you think it's *funny*, do you?" their mother said, glaring back and forth between the two boys.

"Come on, mom," Chet said, snorting back his laughter. "You got to admit that the idea of . . . the idea of a—" He couldn't force himself to say any more when he looked at Stan, and another gale of laughter took hold of him. In an instant, Stan lost control and was howling, too. He lost control, imagining himself cornered in this tree house, held at bay by a rabid squirrel looming in the doorway. No, not one—a whole *pack* of little gray squirrels, foaming at the mouth as they moved slowly toward him. The image sent him into a paroxysm of laughter.

"Well, you boys just go ahead and laugh," their mother said angrily. "You know, it isn't just dogs and foxes that get rabies. Squirrels— even field mice can get the disease." She let her voice trail away as her two sons continued to blubber hysterically. "But right now, I want the both of you to march yourselves up to your bedrooms. *Move* it! And you—Stanley Walters! You march yourself into the bathroom right now and take a shower!"

"Okay, mom," Stan said, still unable to stop chuckling as he started up the stairs. It was almost enough to make him forget how much he still hurt from his roll down the hillside; but as funny as his mother's irrational fear was, the idea of being attacked by a rabid squirrel wasn't what occupied his mind as he undressed and stepped into the shower. He felt at least a bit relieved that he hadn't lied to his mother; he *had* been in his tree house just before coming into the house. He had climbed the rickety ladder up into the darkness and deposited the football-shaped thing, burlap bag and all, in the safety of his tree house. After his shower, as he settled down to sleep that night, he couldn't stop wondering what the hell that thing was. He could hardly wait until morning when he would even risk the danger of encountering a rabid squirrel to go up to his tree house and find out what was in the bag!

– 5 –

"I'm not hungry!" Stan said. "I'll eat something later!"

The screen door slammed shut behind him, cutting off his mother's shouted advice that breakfast was the most important meal of the day as he raced out across the back lawn, heading straight into the woods that fringed the yard. About a hundred yards along a narrow path, he came to the towering oak tree that supported his tree house. Without a backward glance or any hesitation, he scampered like a monkey up the slats of wood he had nailed into the tree trunk as a makeshift ladder. He was panting heavily as he poked his head under the canvas sheet he used for a door. It took his eyes a while to adjust to the gloom inside the tree house, but after a moment, he saw it, over in the corner, right where he had left it.

After waiting in the entrance for a moment, he hooked the canvas onto the nail he used to hold the door open and entered. Shadow-dappled sunlight angled across the rough plank floor, but it didn't quite reach the burlap bag in the far corner. A winding tension gripped Stan's throat as he crawled over to it on his hands and knees.

"Now, let's just see what we've got here," he whispered, his voice hissing like sandpaper in the moist gloom. His hands were shaking as he picked up the end of the bag, sucked in a deep breath, and held it before dumping the thing out. It hit the floor with a dull *thud* and rolled to a stop in the darkest corner of the tree house. Stan sat back on his heels and stared at the object long and hard. Just like last night, he was strongly and equally drawn and repelled by the thing, whatever it was.

In rough outline, it was indeed about the size of a football, but there the similarity ended. It had a thick, doughy look to it and was pinched at both ends into a blunt point. In the dim light, the thick, segmented rings were the color of sour milk, white blending into dull yellow. In the middle, where it was thickest, it was about half a foot thick, maybe a bit more. Although the diffused sunlight didn't quite reach it, it glistened, almost as if it had its own internal light source.

"Goddamn, but don't that look like a maggot," Stan whispered. "A big, bloated *maggot!*"

He didn't quite dare get any nearer to it. Just the thought that he had picked up and carried a monster maggot all the way home sickened him. And God-All-Mighty! Even though it had *felt* dead, the thing sure as heck *looked* like it might even be . . .

"A*live!*" Stan whispered, sitting back and prodding it with the toe of his sneaker.

As soon as he touched it, the maggot-looking thing twitched. The middle segments puffed up, making both ends contract and point at each other like a fat, crescent moon. Squealing in surprise, Stan jerked back and banged his head on the low ceiling of the tree house. Curlicues of light wiggled across his vision as he rubbed the back of his head and stared in utter disbelief at the thing.

It had to be a maggot or worm or cocoon of some kind, he could tell that much—but what? What kind of worm or slug ever got as big as a football?

Tense seconds passed as Stan sat there, just staring at the thing, waiting for it to move again. When it didn't, he tried to convince himself that it hadn't moved the first time; it must have just been his imagination . . . or a shifting shadow that had made it *look* like it moved. How could a worm that big even exist, much less be alive?

After a minute or two, when the thing still hadn't moved, Stan scrambled out of the tree house. Climbing up onto the pitched roof, he reached up and snapped off an oak branch about two feet long. After stripping off the leaves and twigs, he swung back down onto the platform and re-entered the tree house. With the stick held out in front of him like a sword, he cautiously approached the giant maggot again.

"Just what in the hell *are* you," he whispered. His hand trembled as he reached forward and gently prodded the thing. He expected the sharp stick to pierce it easily, but the milky white skin had a rubbery resistance that deflected it. No matter how hard he pressed against the thing, even hard enough to make it shift across the rough floor, he couldn't puncture it.

"Well, then, maybe a knife," he said aloud. He reached for his front pocket, then sighed out loud when he remembered that his mother had taken his jackknife away from him last week. Frustrated, he whacked the middle of the maggoty-looking thing with his stick. In a flash, the worm twisted around and flipped over. Stan screamed so loud it hurt his throat when he saw the underside. It looked . . . weird, all puckered up and wrinkled like a dirty sock turned inside out. Inside the fat, folded wrinkles, it looked almost as though there was a face—a twisted face, distorted and squashed flat against the

189

thick, milky wrapping. Round, bulging eyes stared unblinkingly at him. Squashed up flat on each side and running halfway down the length of the thing, were what looked like the faint outlines of two arms ... arms that ended in small, flat, clawed hands.

Stan was barely aware of the whimpering sound he was making as he scurried toward the tree house door. He felt his way blindly with his hands and feet, unable to tear his eyes away from the distorted face that steadily gazed at him. He tried desperately to convince himself that there couldn't really be a face—an almost *human*-looking face—on the underside of this thing. No matter *what* it was—a slug, a maggot, or whatever—there was no *way* in heaven it could have a *human* face!

His whole body shook as though he were being jolted by a powerful electric current as he swung over to the ladder and started down. Halfway to the ground, he let go of the steps and sprang out into the air. Landing on his feet, he ran as fast as he could back to the house.

– 6 –

Throughout the morning, Stan was uncharacteristically silent—enough so even Chet commented on it. After lunch, he went right out and mowed the front lawn without his father having to tell him more than once. When he was done with that job, he even offered to rake up the clippings, a job Chet usually did whenever Stan did the mowing. A couple of times during the day, Chet tried to talk to him, to draw out of him whatever was bothering him. Several times Stan was tempted to spill his guts and tell Chet all about the *weird* human-faced maggot-thing he had stashed up in the tree house, but he kept his peace, all the while wondering if he truly had seen what he thought he had seen ... and if those bulging, round eyes had seen *him!*

Supper came, and although Stan was still withdrawn, he was also starting to feel nervous and anxious ... curious. He continually bounced his legs up and down as he ate. Although he was hungry, he had to leave his slice of lamb untouched because the light beige color of it reminded him of the thing in his tree house. Once supper was over and he was free to go do whatever he wanted—at least until dark—he felt drawn, nearly compelled to go out to the tree house just to verify that he had seen what he thought he had seen. Anticipation gnawed at his nerves like a worm working its way to the core of an apple. Before long, he knew he *had* to go out there, only this time he'd be prepared. Although he knew his father kept a pistol in his desk drawer, Stan didn't dare go quite that far. But he did manage to sneak his jackknife out of his mother's top bureau drawer. With that, Chet's flashlight, and a length of rope in case he had to tie the thing up or whatever, he left by the back door and disappeared down the trail leading to the tree house.

When he got to the tree, he stood for a moment, looking up at the underside of the tree house. Never, in all the years since he and some of his friends had built it, had it ever seemed so scary, so ominous. The dark, jagged timbers of the roof line and flooring were black, dimensionless blocks against the paling evening sky. The sheet of canvas hung down over the door like a sodden blanket, and Stan couldn't stop wondering what in the name of Sweet Jesus was behind that curtain.

"I'll take the human-faced giant maggot behind Door Number One," he whispered, chuckling to himself for courage as he started up the ladder to the platform. His breath caught, dry and scratchy in the back of his throat as he pulled back the canvas door covering. Before entering, he folded the blade out of his knife and held it out defensively in one hand as he snapped on the flashlight. Bending low, he went inside.

The sun was setting behind his back. It angled across the tree house floor with a wash of bright orange that illuminated every detail of the rough planks of the floor and walls. The quiet of the evening magnified every sound around him—the harsh rasp of canvas, the creak of rusty nails in weathered wood, the swish of leaves as the branches supporting the tree house bent beneath his shifting weight. The oval of light from his flashlight darted like a laser beam over to the corner, his eyes desperately seeking the maggoty thing. As soon as he saw it, his heart started pounding hard in his chest; tears started in his eyes.

"You bastard!" he hissed as he swept the beam of light back and

191

forth over the tangled, white mess that littered the tree house floor. "You lousy, scum-sucking, rotten, *bastard!*"

He couldn't believe what he was seeing. The only thing his brain could register was—whatever that thing had been, it was gone now, smashed and ripped and torn into hundreds of tiny, fleshy shreds. The floor was saturated with a thick, gooey liquid that had dried into a black crust on the old wood.

Stan had no doubt who had done this; it *had* to have been Chet, the *prick!* Sometime in the afternoon, probably while he was mowing the lawn, he must have come out here, found what Stan had stashed up here, and destroyed it. Why? Simply to piss him off, of course— just like he *always* did!

"I'm gonna get even with you," Stan said, his voice vibrating with a snarl as he probed the remains with the tip of his knife. Even with a sharp blade, the outside covering resisted cutting or puncturing, as if it were some kind of thick, white rubber. He still couldn't quite bring himself to touch what was left of it, so he sat down and used his foot to push the remains of his prize into a pile over in the corner.

Once he had everything all gathered up, though, he realized that something was dreadfully wrong.

"There isn't enough stuff here," he whispered. His eyes darted back and forth, following the beam of the flashlight to see if he had missed any.

As he was looking, a faint scratching sound from overhead drew his attention. Cringing backward onto the floor, he was just swinging the flashlight around and up when something dropped onto his back.

Stan realized instantly whatever this was must have been clinging to the underside on the ceiling where he couldn't see it. He let loose a wild scream that almost completely masked the high-pitched chittering sound close to his ears as tiny, sharp claws punctured his neck and ripped into the back of his head. His mind went white with terror as his skin was ripped away. Blood flowed hot and sticky down his back. He swung out wildly with both hands, batting behind his head in a desperate attempt to dislodge the thing, but all to no avail. Whatever it was, it had wrapped its tiny arms around him like a clawed leech. Stan's jackknife slipped from his sweaty grip as he thrashed around on the floor. The flashlight beam swung wildly back and forth, sweeping the inside of the tree house like a searchlight as he repeatedly hammered at the slick, skinny body that had attached itself to him.

A rabid squirrel, he thought through a numbing flood of panic.

192

It's a goddamned rabid squirrel!

As he rolled back and forth on the floor, he reached out blindly for his dropped knife. Several times he raised his head and slammed it back hard against the floor, hoping to kill the thing or at least knock it unconscious. With each impact, the creature let out a sharp, high squeal, but it dug its claws into him all the deeper. Finally, knowing it was his only hope to get free of the thing, Stan started toward the door. He needed room to move. If he could get outside, get down to the ground, he just might be able to get rid of the thing by banging it against the tree trunk or something. He knew that he didn't have much time. Tiny, razor-sharp teeth were burrowing deeply into his shoulder muscles, sending burning jolts of pain throughout his body.

But in his pain and panic, Stan over-reacted. Doubling his legs up underneath himself, he pushed back as hard as he could. Too hard. He shot out through the doorway and started falling . . . falling. Branches whipped past him as he plummeted downward. For a frozen instant, he knew he was going to die as soon as he hit the ground, but then—miraculously—the underside of his left arm hooked over one of the lower branches. For an instant, his fall was halted, and in that split second, his other hand reflexively shot out and grabbed the branch. The impact jerked his body hard, slamming his teeth together hard enough to bite off the tip of his tongue. The force also was sudden enough and strong enough to knock whatever the hell that thing was off his back. Muscles straining, Stan struggled to hold onto the branch. From down below, he heard an ear-piercing squeal when the thing hit the ground with a sick, heavy *plop*. Then came the rustle of leaves as whatever it was scurried off into the deep brush.

"Jesus Christ! Stan! What the hell are you *doing?*"

The shout boomed like thunder through the woods. Frantic and wild-eyed, Stan looked all around, trying to find the source of the voice. Tears, sweat, and blood streamed down his face and neck. His whole body throbbed with the effort of hanging onto the branch. Down below, he heard the heavy tread of footsteps coming closer. In the dense twilight brush, he finally made out his brother's face, glowing eerily like a pale moon as he stared up at him.

"How in the hell did you get yourself—"

Chet was cut off by a loud cracking sound as the branch suddenly snapped. Stan pictured himself as nothing more than a piece of dust, being sucked into a vacuum cleaner as his body plummeted toward the night-stained ground. He landed with his left leg cocked behind his back; but he was unconscious by the time he hit the ground, and he never felt the painful *snap* that broke his leg in two places ... at least not until several minutes later, once Chet had raced back to the house for help and returned with his mother and two guys from MedCu.

– 7 –

With its red warning lights flashing, the ambulance raced through the night, taking the curves of Route 25 perhaps a bit faster than it should have. Stan's leg was completely numb; he half-suspected it had been cut off. The physician's assistant had given him a shot for the pain, but his neck and shoulders still felt like they were burning. His eyes were narrowed to slits as he looked up at his mother from the ambulance stretcher. The physician's assistant, whose badge read *Cochran,* was also leaning over him.

"I *told* you I didn't want you going out there to that tree house," his mother said. Her voice was a perfect mix of anger and concern as she stared down at her boy. "I *never* liked you playing out there!"

Stan wanted to say something, but he knew, if he opened his mouth, the only sound he'd be able to make would be a faint whimper ... or else a scream. In spite of everything Cochran had done, cleaning and dressing the wounds, he still thought that giant maggot *thing* was clinging to his neck, digging and gouging into his flesh.

"I'll just bet it was one of those squirrels I warned you about. It was, wasn't it?" his mother asked, unable to keep the sharp accusation out of her voice. "Just like I was telling you yesterday ... it was one of those rabid squirrels."

Cochran cocked one eyebrow and looked at her with a half smile as if he thought she was kidding; then he looked at Stan, who shook his head in weak denial. Tears threatened to spill from his eyes, but he wasn't about to let himself cry; not in front of his mother and this guy he didn't even know. No way! Crying was for babies!

"Well, whatever it was, Mrs. Walters," Cochran said mildly, "it's too bad it got away." He looked down at Stan and gave him a light but bracing touch on the back of his hand. Turning to Stan's mother, he said softly, "We'll have to keep a watchful eye on those cuts for a few weeks to make sure they don't get infected."

Stan's mother bit down hard on her lower lip, sighed deeply, and shook her head. "If only you had listened to me, Stan," she whispered. "If only you had listened."

− 8 −

"Look out!" the man riding up front with the ambulance driver suddenly shouted.

They were approaching the construction site where the state highway workers had been blasting away at Watchick Hill. The asphalt abruptly ended, and the road changed to hard-packed dirt, but that wasn't what had drawn the man's attention. Off to his right, in the flickering light of the yellow warning light, he had seen a dark blur of motion. Before the driver could respond to his warning, something small and fast-moving darted out of the woods, heading straight toward the trench on the opposite side of the road. The driver hit the brakes, but it was too late. The tires skidded on the gravel just as a heavy *thump* sounded from underneath the ambulance.

"Aww, shit! You hit him!"

"Hey! Watch your language up there!" Cochran said.

"What the hell−? Was that some kind of dog or something?" the ambulance driver asked. His expression was tight as he played the steering wheel back and forth while stepping down hard on the brakes. The ambulance swerved to a stop as the siren died with a descending *hoot.*

"Come on, man," the passenger said. "You can't stop now. We have to get this kid down to Maine Med."

"Shouldn't we check it out. If that was a dog, we have to report it," the driver said.

"We have to get this kid to Maine Med. We can check whatever the hell that was on our way back."

They delivered Stan and his mother to the hospital and, once the paperwork was completed, headed back up Route 25 to the Thornton Fire Station. As they neared the construction site, the driver slowed down, scanning both sides of the road.

"I know it was around here someplace," he whispered. A second later, he saw a dark lump of . . . something on the road up ahead. He braked, jammed the shift into park, and opened his door. As he stepped out into the night, the other man got out and walked around to meet him at the front of the ambulance. Both men focused on the dark splotch in the middle of the road.

"What in the name of—?" the driver muttered.

Flattened onto the hard-packed dirt was a tangled piece of dark, scaly flesh. Blood and purple guts had spurted out of its opened mouth; huge, rounded eyes bulged up out of the eye sockets, glistening like exposed bone in the bright headlight beams. Not quite daring to touch the thing, the driver knelt down and stared at the array of tiny, pointed teeth that lined the squashed lower jaw. The body—at least what was left of it—looked like a long, flattened tube with distorted hind legs and long, thin arms that were tipped with flat, clawed hands.

"What the fuck *is* that thing?" the driver said.

"Looks to me like somebody else ran over it after we did," the passenger replied. "Either that, or else you really creamed it. You *were* going kind of fast."

The driver wiped his forehead with the flat of his hand as he leaned closer, tensed, half-expecting the thing to leap up at him. "You ever see anything like this?" he asked, barely able to restrain the nervous quaver in his voice as he stood up and looked back and forth between his partner and the splattered roadkill.

"Nope," his partner replied coolly. "Can't say as I have. But I'll tell you this much; whatever it is—or *was*—it sure as shit wasn't no *dog*. Come on. Let the crows have it. Let's get our butts back to the station."

The driver stood there for nearly a minute, his eyes glued to the strange mess of twisted flesh on the road. Then, heaving a deep sigh, he followed his partner back to the ambulance, got in, and drove away.

— A Micmac Indian tale told around the campfire —

– 1 –

How the earth and water came to be, no one but Old One knows. How trees and rocks and animals came to be, no one but Old One knows. The earth and sky were made by Old One. He sang a sacred song as he molded them; he carved the earth with swift, gleaming rivers and filled its depths with surging oceans. He sang another sacred song as he stamped his foot on the ground to make deep valleys and pushed up mountains that reached to the sky. Singing another sacred song, he placed the sun and stars and moon in the sky and set them on their courses. Taking soil and spit in his hand, he sang many sacred songs as he fashioned all the creatures that live on the earth, in the air, and under the waters.

But after all this work was done, Old One was lonely.

When the sun fled from the sky and the moon shined her cold light over the land, Old One would sit huddled by the campfire in front of his wigwam, filled with sadness.

"What's the matter, Old One?" Brother Wolf asked one night, seeing how sad Old One was.

Old One smoked on his pipe and didn't answer as he looked up at the stars, his creations, and thought long. He saw the stars' beauty, but he felt their loneliness, too. Looking across the land, he saw the valleys and mountains he had made, and the gleaming rivers and

197

oceans he had filled; but they, too, filled him with a deep longing. He knew in his heart that none of his creation mattered unless there was someone to look at it, someone to appreciate its beauty.

"I'm lonely, Brother Wolf," Old One said after a while. "I look around me and see what I have made and it saddens me."

"The world you have made is very beautiful," Brother Wolf said. "The woods and plains are filled with animals and birds. The waters are alive with fish. The hunting is good, and all that is strong grows and prospers."

"That is not enough," Old One said sadly. "I feel the loneliness of the world, and I need someone . . . someone I can talk to. Someone who can share with me and enjoy the beauty of all that I have made."

"Every day after the hunt I come to you and we talk long into the evening. Am I not company enough for you, Old One?" Brother Wolf asked. He lowered his head and pointed his sleek black tail to the ground as he waited for Old One's reply.

Again, Old One smoked and thought long before speaking.

"No, Brother Wolf," he said, "your company is not enough. The world needs Human Beings, creatures created in my image who can truly enjoy what I have made."

"But Old One," Brother Wolf said, scowling deeply, "would not creatures made in your own image also share your powers? I mean no disrespect, but would it be wise to give Human Beings such domination over your work? Perhaps they will make things and do things to your creation that are not part of your plan."

Old One laughed loud and long, and smoke as thick as storm clouds billowed from his nose.

"Brother Wolf," he said sagely, "I have no plan other than to do what I have said. In the morning, I will take more soil and spit, and I will sing a sacred song as I fashion some Human Beings for my world."

Brother Wolf bowed so low his snout nearly touched the ground as he shook his head from side to side.

"Meaning no disrespect, Old One, but I think that would not be wise."

Saying that, he bid Old One good evening and skulked away; but in his cold, animal heart, he held resentment for Old One for not telling him that his company was enough to give him pleasure. He resolved, that very night, to wait for the dawn and, before the sun could light the land in the morning, he would steal it and hide it in his den.

– 2 –

Old One slept, and the night was long, seemingly without end. He was not aware that while he slept Brother Wolf had stolen the sun. When Old One awoke refreshed, he sat and smoked, waiting for the sun to rise. After a long time when it didn't come, he grew impatient and called Brother Bear to him.

"Brother Bear," he said, "I feel in my heart that many hours, perhaps many years have passed in darkness, yet the sun has not brought his light and warmth to the land. Do you know anything about this?"

Brother Bear shook his head sadly. "I do not, Old One," he said. "Like you, I have slept long and have awakened to find the world still dark. You created the day and the night, the sun and the moon, so you must know if this night will last forever."

"We shall see," Old One said, stirring the coals of his campfire. There was little wood, and the fire was no more than a feeble orange glow in the darkness. "If the night lasts too long, I will either find the sun or else sing a sacred song and make a new one."

After that, Old One called to him Brother Deer, Brother Fox, Brother Rat, Brother Raccoon, and many others. They all said to him what Brother Bear had said to him, and Old One answered them as he had answered Brother Bear. Before he could call Brother Wolf to him, however, Old One found that he was growing tired. Remembering his resolve to create the Human Beings today, he set about his work in spite of the darkness. By this time, his campfire had burned out, and he could no longer see in the darkness to gather more wood. Digging blindly into the earth, his creation, he took a handful of soil, spit into it and, singing a sacred song, began to fashion a Human Being. But working in the dark, he was unable to see his handiwork. It was only by touch that he fashioned a Human Being like himself who walked on two legs like Brother Bear but was naked.

"To you, Little Brother, I give the gift of life," Old One said. With that, he blew gently onto the molded soil until he felt it stir with life. Carefully, he held his new creation close to his face and addressed it thus:

"Also to you, Little Brother, I give command of the earth. All of the animals I have created are for you to—"

He intended to say *"for you to enjoy,"* but before he could continue, Brother Wolf came sniffing to Old One's campsite. Old One heard him prowling in the darkness and called out to him, "Brother Wolf, why do you come to me, skulking in the darkness?"

"I have heard from my brother animals that you are displeased, Old One," Brother Wolf said softly. "You have been asking my brothers if they know where the sun is."

"And you know," Old One said, seeing clearly into Brother Wolf's heart.

"I do," Brother Wolf replied, "for I have taken the sun from the sky and hidden it inside my den."

Old One's heart flashed like lightning with anger, yet he said nothing.

"I was saddened by what you said to me last night," Brother Wolf went on, "that my company was not good enough for you. I stole the sun to prevent you from making Human Beings."

"Go! Now!" Old One said, his voice trembling like distant thunder in the darkness. "Return the sun to the sky or else you and all of your children will perish."

Without another word, Brother Wolf departed back to his cave where he retrieved the sun and placed it back in the sky. As soon as the warm yellow light touched the land, Old One looked into his hand and saw what he had created from soil and spit and by singing a sacred song in the darkness.

The Human Being was short and stunted. His body was covered with a thick, scaly skin like that of Brother Lizard. The back of his head was pointed, and his face projected forward like Brother Rat's. His eyes were round and bulged from his face like twin full moons. His shoulders were broad, like Brother Buffalo's, but his body was narrow and had long, dangling arms that ended in wide flat hands upon which were long, curved claws like Brother Mole's. He stood shakily on thin, gnarly legs that bowed outward at the knees like no creature Old One had ever created.

"You are a disappointment to me, Little Brother," Old One said, looking earnestly at his creation as he placed it carefully on the ground. "I thought, working in the dark, that my hands and my sacred song would guide me, but now that Brother Wolf has returned the sun to the sky, I see that I was wrong. You are not what I had in mind at all. You are not a Human Being."

Little Brother looked up at Old One but, because Old One had not given him the gift of speech, said nothing. The sudden blast of sunlight hurt his rounded, bulging eyes, and he shielded his face from the day's warmth as best he could with his wide, flat hands.

"No, Little Brother, I am sorry, but you are not a creature of the daylight," Old One said solemnly. "You are a creature of the dark, and to the darkness below the earth I will send you. But to show that I am kind, I will allow you and all of your children to come up to the upper world once every five years, there to see my creation and all the animals which I have created for you to—"

Again, Old One intended to say *"for you to enjoy,"* but at that moment, Brother Wolf returned, approaching Old One with his head bowed and his snout scraping against the ground.

"See what you have done!" Old One said, clenching his fists and shaking them over his head until the wind rose high in the sky. "Because I was not able to see, I have created *this,* not the Human Being I intended. And it is all your fault, Brother Wolf. Because I have to banish this pitiful creature to the dark caverns below the ground, I will also have to punish you. You, Brother Wolf, will become a child of the night as well; and every night, you and all of your children will howl at the full moon, the pale reflection of that which you tried to steal from me!"

— Spring, 1977 —

— 1 —

Eddie LeFevbre figured he was approaching the bridge at a rate of about twenty-five feet a day. By his calculations, he was going to be in just the right spot by Thursday—Friday at the latest. Being the flag man on this stretch of road construction along Route 25, ten miles north of Thornton, Maine, was one boring bitch of a job. But even if he *did* have to stand here, freezing his ass off in the cold drizzle or sweating it off when the sun came out, it was a damned sight better than staring at three concrete block walls and one wall of iron bars every day for the rest of his life.

Spring was here, and Eddie had spring fever—bad. So bad, in fact, he didn't really give a shit about what he planned to do, even if it all went to hell. He was serving a life sentence for killing a man in a fight outside a bar in Portland. He wasn't getting any closer to having his ass back on the street . . . not with a ninety-nine year sentence hanging over his head.

Every day after lunch, he walked up to the bridge, pretending to be interested in checking out what the construction crew was doing. In fact, he was scoping out the area. The bridge they were repairing spanned a good seventy-five foot stretch of the Saco River. Straight down, the water looked shallow, maybe four feet deep at best. It was white-capped with rapids that raced over the stony river bed, but that wasn't what interested Eddie. What had caught his eye was the sharp right hand turn the river took about a hundred yards downstream. A huge patch of briars covered the near side of the river bank, and from there it looked like nothing but dense pine forest stretching, as far as he knew, all the way to the distant, purple-hazed mountains in New Hampshire.

Fred Webster, the guard from the prison who watched Eddie and the other two prisoners on work release, usually took a nap in his car after lunch. Eddie knew Webster had a mean-looking shotgun in the front seat with him, but he was willing to bet — even his life — that he could get down to the fast-moving water and swim clear around the bend before Webster or anyone else knew he had bolted.

"But *plu-eze*, don't fling me inta that briar patch, Brer Fox!" Eddie whispered, chuckling to himself as he looked at the tangled mess of thorns. He took the cigarette from his mouth and snapped it out over the railing. It twisted end over end before landing in the raging water and was instantly whisked out of sight. Eddie smiled with anticipation, thinking that Thursday, or Friday at the latest, he was going to be just like that cigarette, bobbing and floating down the river . . . to freedom!

— 2 —

"Don't be such a retard about it, okay?" Mark Murray said. Flames from the campfire lit up the sneer on his face before he leaned his head back and guzzled Rose from the bottle. Smacking his lips with satisfaction, he gasped and wiped his mouth with the back of his hand.

"I'm not being a *retard*, all right?" Janie said. She was sitting in front of the fire, huddled in her thick sweater against the chilly spring night. At least the cold rain has stopped, she thought as she looked from Mark's glazed eyes to the dark sky overhead. A crescent moon looking like a scimitar ripped through the fast-moving cloud cover. A few pale stars winked in and out of existence.

"Then what *are* you being?" Mark asked sharply. He tilted the wine bottle to his lips again and took several more noisy swallows. "I mean—besides a raging bitch!"

"Yeah, well fuck you," Janie snapped, narrowing her eyes as she looked at him and wondered how the hell she ever could have convinced herself she loved this jerk. Okay, so he knew how to make her squeal in bed; that was lust, not love!

"All I'm saying is, you're a damned idiot if you think you can read *any* of that shit," Mark said, slurring his words. "*No* one can decipher that shit!" He hooked his thumb over his shoulder in the direction of the stream bed, but it was too dark down there for either one of them to see the carvings Sarah had found on the slanting rock ledge above the stream. "You're starting to sound like that guy from . . . wherever the hell he's from—that guy who says these petroglyphs are . . . are Egyptian hieroglyphics or whatever."

Janie held her hands out in front of her, then—in exasperation—clenched them into fists. "I'm not saying I can *read* them all. Well, not word for word, anyway. Actually, I don't think they *are* words per se. I'm just saying—"

"You're just *saying* they're some kind of—*what?* Some fucking warning, right?" Mark said. He leaned back for another chug-a-lug of wine, but the bottle was empty, so he tossed it off in the darkness where it made a hollow thump behind him.

Janie shrugged helplessly. "Well . . . yeah, sort of." She scratched her head and closed her eyes as she tried to measure her response. "I mean, I think it says something about some kind of cycle—something that looks, at least to me, like some kind of danger. I can show you if you'd just take a look at the rubbings I did. There's this wolf figure, you see, that—"

Mark cut her off with a loud snort of laughter as he stood up and kicked viciously at the fire. Sparks cork-screwed like trailing comets into the night sky.

"Are you trying to start a forest fire or something?" Janie asked with a bitter edge in her voice.

"Fuck you," Mark said with a hardened sneer. He wobbled on his feet and stared at her with an unfocused glaze in his eyes. "*Fuck* your rock carvings! And fuck *you!*"

Janie grimly shook her head as she looked up at him. "No thank you. Not tonight," she said between clenched teeth. She got up and went over to the tent they had pitched under the trees. After unzipping the fly screen, she grabbed Mark's sleeping bag and flung it out onto the ground, just missing the fire. "You can sleep it off outside, thank you very much!"

— 3 —

"I feel like such a damned idiot," Mark said the next morning. He was curled up in his sleeping bag, leaning against a tree trunk when Janie came out of the tent.

"You *were* a damned idiot," she said, scowling as she looked at him. Kneeling by the campfire, she stirred the coals, trying to bring them to life, but the fire was nothing but cold, gray ashes. Without a word, she got up and went off into the woods to collect an armload of firewood. When she returned, Mark hadn't moved; he was still huddled in his sleeping bag.

"Do you plan on staying there all day?" she asked snidely. "I could use some help getting breakfast going, you know."

Mark nodded and eased himself out of the bag. He looked rumpled and dirty, and his eyes were red-rimmed. Janie wished to Heaven that he had a monster headache, too.

"I *was* pretty obnoxious last night, wasn't I?" he said, more comment than question. He walked over to where Janie was trying to get the fire going again and placed both of his hands on her shoulders.

She cringed under his touch and looked up at him with a fixed smile. Shaking her head, she said, "I think it's getting to be the dominant characteristic in your personality."

"Can you forgive me?" he asked, massaging the knotted muscles in her neck.

Janie didn't look at him again because she knew damned well there would be that earnest, little boy pleading look in his eyes.

"You *do* have to understand that I—we're both under a lot of pressure here," Mark said earnestly. "I mean, we've got less than a week left, and we haven't done a tenth of the work we should have done."

LOVE ON THE ROCKS

Janie sniffed with laughter. "That was before we found those petroglyphs."

"I know, I know," Mark replied, hissing between his teeth. "You've spent a lot of time working on them, but I've been thinking, you know, that something's happened here that we haven't even noticed."

'Oh—and what, pray tell, might that be?"

Mark shrugged nervously, then walked around in front of her and knelt down. He picked up a stick and poked at the cold fireplace between them.

"I think, what with all the pressure I've been feeling—we've *both* been feeling to get this excavation done, we've kind of let what we feel for each other go by the boards." He reached for her hands, but Janie didn't connect with him. Her lower lip bagan to tremble, and her eyes teared up even as hot rage filled her.

"I think," Mark continued, "you know, what with the budget cuts the department just found out about and my having to get my thesis done this year—or else—we're forgetting how much we love each other."

Janie looked at him with a cold, steady gaze. "*You're* the one with all the pressure," she said in a low, measured, voice. "*I'm* just along for the ride, remember?" She almost said something about just being here to keep his sleeping bag warm but let it drop.

"You're more than—"

"And if *I* want to spend my time working on translating those stone carvings, even if I'm not even close, well then—that's my choice. *I* don't have to have any fieldwork done on time for you or Professor McCray or *anyone!*"

Running his hands through his disheveled hair, Mark nodded agreement. "So does this mean you forgive me?" he asked.

If he hadn't poured it on so thick with his hurt little boy voice, Janie might have said she forgave him. Instead, she bristled, jabbed her forefinger across the campfire at him, and said, "Look! You get to work, digging down into that damned trench of yours all you want, all right? Just leave me the fuck alone!"

"Hey, hey! All right!" Mark said, nodding agreement but still looking at her with a downcast expression.

"And don't make fun of me if I tell you what I think these carvings mean, all right? It's none of your damned business, anyway!"

207

– 4 –

Eddie could barely contain his excitement as he rode out to the construction site early Thursday morning. As Webster let the men out of the back of the van, he even commented that Eddie seemed awfully darned chipper, but Eddie just said it was the warm, sun-shiny day that was lifting his spirits after such a bleak fucking winter. Those spirits soon fell when Webster directed Eddie to the other end of the flag line, a good hundred yards over the bridge and away from the river. His good mood rapidly evaporated as he stood with his back to the bridge, stopping and starting the thin flow of traffic on Route 25.

The chattering of jackhammers and the rumbling of huge dump trucks rolling by worked on Eddie's nerves all morning. The vibrations transmitted through the asphalt, shaking the ground so much he started to worry that it would loosen the fillings in his teeth. With warming sunshine on his back, he maintained his position until Tom Eckert, one of the other prisoners, relieved him for lunch at twelve-thirty.

Today or never, Eddie decided, as he took the bag containing his tuna fish sandwich, a small bag of Doritos, and a can of Coke and sat down in the shade by the roadside. Webster kept an eye on him while he ate his own lunch in the comfort of the van.

"You miserable mother-humper," Eddie muttered, chewing his sandwich as he eyed the parked police van. Was it just his imagination, or was Webster watching him just a bit more suspiciously today? Eddie knew he couldn't make it to the river from here. Webster would be on the radio the second he started to run, and no doubt he'd unlimber that mother-fucking shotgun before he took twenty paces. Sure as shit, Eddie knew he'd be nailed—lose his work release for sure, if he wasn't outright killed.

No, Eddie thought, he *had* to get his ass up there on the bridge where he could jump off right into the Saco River. The swift current would carry him away faster that he—or Webster—could run. Problem was, how was he going to get up there without warning Webster.

"Awright, break's over," Webster shouted, leaning out his window. With a flick of his hand, he gave Eddie a "get-along" signal.

Eddie crumpled up the trash from his lunch and tossed it into

208

one of the orange and white barrels lining the construction site. Instead of heading straight back to his position, he started over to Webster's van.

"Hey, you got a smoke?" he asked, patting his empty shirt pocket. He had thought to toss away his full pack with his lunch trash so this would look good.

"Fuck you, no," Webster said with a snarl. "'N you don't need one, either. Get your fuckin' ass back to work."

Eddie almost said something, but then, shrugging, turned away and started walking toward Tom. Apparently satisfied, Webster eased himself down in his seat and leaned his head back. With one quick glance over his shoulder—*You're so fucking predictable, Webster*—Eddie walked right past Tom and headed to the bridge.

"Be right with yah, Tom," he said. "Gotta bum a smoke."

"I have one," Tom said, but Eddie pretended not to hear him as he strode right out to the middle of the bridge and, without hesitation, swung his leg up over the guard rail.

"Hey!" someone shouted. "Get the fuck away from there! What the fuck you doing?"

Eddie glanced behind him and saw Tom and Webster as well as several construction workers looking at him. After a quick glance straight down at the raging river, he turned back to Webster and waved his hand at him. "Bye-bye," he called.

Webster stumbled as he leaped from the van, his shotgun in hand. "Hold it right there, Eddie!" he shouted as he brought the gun up to his shoulder.

"Fuck *you!*" Eddie shouted as he raised his middle finger high in the air. He swung his other leg over the railing, stood for just a second on the edge, and then pushed off. At the peak of his jump, he heard the scattering of shotgun pellets whistle over his head, followed instantly by the *bang* of the gun.

His arms and legs flailed wildly, trying to stabilize him in his fall. All sound was lost in the whooshing of air in his ears. After a fall that seemed to take forever and be over in an instant, Eddie hit the water. Icy cold gripped him, and he was tugged away by the current as if by strong, unyielding hands. Spinning around madly as he careened off rocks, he caught a few fleeting glimpses of the activity on the bridge. Webster stood with one foot up on the railing and his arm braced at his side as he took aim. Expecting the swift current to sweep him away, Eddie laughed as he watched the shotgun kick

209

back. He didn't hear the report above the roar of the water, but the pellets made little *zip* sounds when they hit right in front of him.

"Missed me, you asshole!" Eddie shouted, laughing hysterically as he floated away. He figured they couldn't hear him, so he raised one hand and waved to the men lining the bridge. His glee instantly died when, spinning wildly down the rapids, he was suddenly pitched up on a spit of land. Fighting for balance as the water tried to tug him off balance again, he lurched up onto dry land just as another spray of bullets ricocheted with loud whining sounds off the rocks beside him.

I've got to get the fuck out of sight, Eddie thought as he staggered away from the river. The roaring of the water masked all other sounds except his labored breathing and the wet *slap-slap* of his feet on the rocks. Before he rounded the bend in the river, he looked back at the bridge once more. His heart dropped when he didn't see Webster up there any more. He was either back at his van, radioing in for help, or else he was coming after him. Eddie looked frantically back and forth for the best escape route. A desperate idea hit him when he saw the huge tangle of briars not more than a hundred feet up on the river bank. If he could hide deep enough in the briars, maybe Webster would assume he had jumped back into the river and continued on downstream. Once the police had gone past, searching for him far to the south, he could wait until night and then, under cover of darkness, head north, maybe to Montreal.

Every muscle in Eddie's body screamed in agony as he raced around the bend and then up the slope toward the briars. Any second, he expected Webster to round the corner and see him. His ears tingled, just waiting to hear the blast of the shotgun and feel the searing pain as the bullets entered his body. His lungs ached with every breath he took, but he pushed himself to make it.

"Go, you mother-fucker, *go!*" he grunted as he leaped from rock to rock and then scrambled up the weed-choked river bank. Without any hesitation, he ran straight into the tangled thicket, unmindful of the sharp thorns that ripped his clothes and flesh like hundreds of tiny insect bites. Dropping onto his hands and knees, he crawled along on the ground until he was well inside the twisted mess of brush. Once he was positive he was out of sight, he collapsed onto his back on the damp soil and, panting heavily, stared up at the blue sky, cross-hatched by the dense spread of thorny branches.

Eddie could hear the distant sounds made by his pursuers far down

210

by the river. From the scattering of shouted comments and replies, he realized Webster had convinced several of the construction workers to help run him down. Wincing from the pain of hundreds of lacerations, Eddie got onto his hands and knees again and burrowed deeper into the briars. Water and sweat mingled with the blood running down his face into his eyes. He didn't think any of the men would be crazy enough to venture into the thorny barricade — not unless Webster was offering one hell of a reward.

Eddie tensed and turned around when he heard a faint rustle of vegatation behind him. With the steady roar of the river filling his ears, any sound could be distorted and magnified; but it sure as hell sounded like *someone* was crawling in the brush nearby.

"All right, you son-of-a-bitch," Eddie muttered. He moved into a low crouch, clenched his fists, and got ready to fight. He hoped to hell it was Webster, even if he did have a rifle; he wanted to whip the shit out of that asshole just for refusing him a cigarette after lunch, if nothing else. The bastard had it coming!

Eddie looked left and right, trying to pierce the vegetation, but he didn't see anything moving until it was too late. The thorns and the ground around him suddenly erupted as dozens of small, brown animals burst up out of the soil. Eddie's first — and practically final — thought was that it was a pack of oversized groundhogs or something, but then he saw the nearly human wrinkled, brown faces and the curved, black talons reaching for him. Unblinking eyes burning with hatred and hunger stared at him from the dense shade of the thorns as the creatures, chittering shrilly, tore Eddie to ribbons. In less than a minute, he was nothing more than a twisted pile of shredded pink meat and broken bones.

– 5 –

After a hurried breakfast, Mark went to the excavation site to start his day's work. Last summer, he and two other graduate students from the University of Maine in Orono had discovered several post molds. After probing, they had discovered this ancient site a hundred feet up from the stream bed. Three feet below the ground level, beneath a thick layer of silt where the stream had overflown some time back in prehistory, they had struck an ancient shell heap—a prehistoric Indian garbage dump. For the past month and a half, Mark had been digging a trench, exposing a nearly eight foot face of sedimentary layers that were loaded with artifacts—broken pottery, plenty of arrow heads, and numerous other chipped stone fragments. He knew he was working against time as he spent all morning digging out another layer of the hard-packed substrata.

A hundred yards downstream from their camp, Janie was up on a narrow ledge about twenty feet above the water. She was so involved doing graphite rubbings of the carved inscriptions on the cliff face that she didn't notice when two uniformed policemen, one with a German shepherd on a leash, came out of the woods near the tent.

"'Morning," one of the policemen called out as they walked toward her.

The voice surprised Janie, and she almost lost her balance when she turned around quickly to see who it was.

"Oh—hi," she said nervously as she carefully climbed down the cliff to the ground.

"I didn't mean to startle you," the policeman said as he and his partner came closer. "I thought you heard us coming."

Shrugging, Janie walked toward them, not knowing what to say. The German shepherd stood stiffly at attention, so Janie kept a reasonable distance away. The only thought in her mind was, what the hell are two cops doing out here this time of day? She and Mark had permission from the Forestry Service and the University to be out here doing their work.

"I'm Officer Parkman, from Thornton, and this is Patrolman Fielding," the policeman said. He paused and looked around, scanning the tent site and the twisted lump of Mark's sleeping bag. "I thought there were two of you out here."

Pointing in the direction of the trench, Janie replied, "My partner's Mark Murray. He's over there. What's the problem?"

Parkman nodded. "Mind if we call him over here? I want you both to hear this." Without waiting for her reply, Fielding went over to the trench and signalled for Mark to come up.

A second later, Mark clambered up over the side, blinking like a mole in the bright sunlight. His face, hands, and clothes were layered with dirt, and in his hand was a small, pointed trowel.

"Look, I uhh—I don't mean to alarm you," Parkman said, "but we think there might be an escaped murderer in the area."

Mark scratched the back of his neck and shook his head. "Sorry, Officer. We haven't seen anyone."

Parkman took a deep breath and scanned the woods around them. The forest rippled with the bright green of newly sprouted leaves. Overhead, thin white clouds rode across the bright blue sky. The distant song of morning birds was lulling, peaceful. The policeman let his breath out slowly.

"Well, I don't know what to tell you," he said. "This fella, name of Eddie LeFevbre, jumped off the bridge into the river up on 25 this morning. Best as we can figure, he's heading down to Kittery. Least that's where he's from, so we figure he's going that way, but I dunno—"

He turned to look at Fielding, who shrugged and said nothing.

"God*damn!*" Parkman muttered, shaking his head. "I don't know if I should tell you folks to leave until we run this guy down, or if—"

"If you don't mind, officer," Mark piped in. "I've made some fairly significant discoveries in this area. Those rock carvings up there aren't the only things, either. I've got an *extremely* rich excavation site. I have three days, counting today, to finish up my work here, and I can't *afford* to stop now because, frankly, I don't think I'll get the funds to come back here later this summer."

Parkman sighed deeply. "Look, this convict is considered extremely dangerous. I don't have the authority to clear you out of here, but I'll tell you—for your own safety—you might want to consider leaving until he's been apprehended."

Mark looked at Janie, then back at the cop. Shrugging his shoulders as though helpless, he said, "I appreciate your concern, but I've got important work going on here. Besides, I don't see where we'd be in any danger. Like you said, he's probably miles from here by now."

"Probably, but I wouldn't bet my life on it," Parkman said before he and his partner turned to leave. Janie walked over toward Mark as they both watched the two policemen and the dog disappear into the dense brush. Without another word, Mark walked quickly back to the excavation and disappeared inside.

RICK HAUTALA

– 6 –

"Will you *please* look at this," Janie said.

She and Mark was sitting beside the campfire. Supper was over, and night was fast approaching. After an exhausting day digging in the trench, Mark looked through slitted eyes at the paper she was holding out to him. Within the wide swatches of black graphite marks, there were numerous lines, circles, and other markings. Some of them looked vaguely human although most were horribly distorted figures.

"Looks just great," Mark said, sounding sleepy and uninterested.

"No—this," she said, tapping one of the marks with her forefinger. "See this?"

"It's a bunch of lines and squiggles," Mark said after pretending to study the markings for a few moments.

"Well these *squiggles,* as you call them, are repeated here—here —and *here,*" she said, jabbing the paper every time for emphasis. "And do you want to know what I think these *squiggles* mean?"

"Why do I have the feeling you're going to tell me?"

"I think they mean there's some kind of . . . danger around here. It's clearly a warning of some kind because of the—"

"Jan*ie* . . ."

"Because of the prostrate figures underneath each one. This is a wolf or coyote, but all the others look human. And see here, these circles? They appear in regular order, but look carefully; every fifth one is hollowed out, so the rubbing is a completely black ball, not just a circle. You said yourself that there was evidence the Indians who lived here suddenly abandoned the place, right?"

"Yeah, but I don't pretend to know *why,*" Marked snapped.

"I think these carvings have something to do with it. I think they explain the whole thing if we only knew how to read them."

"So what?"

"So—?" Janie said, sighing deeply as she looked up at the darkening sky. Deep in the woods, a night bird began to sing, lending an eerie note to the descending night. Shivering, she picked up a stick and poked the fire, raising the flames higher. "So, I think there might be some connection between these rubbings and what you've been digging."

"Jesus *Christ,* Janie, of *course* there's a connection," Mark shouted.

"We don't have exact dates on either the shell heap or your carvings, but I'd say it's a fairly safe bet the same people are responsible for both. What's the big deal?"

Before Janie could reply, the silence of the night filled with a deep-throated rumbling sound. Janie started and inched closer to Mark's side of the campfire.

"What the devil was that?" she whispered.

Mark tensed and looked around them. With his finger on his lips, he hissed her to silence.

"What if it's that escaped murderer those cops were talking about?" Janie said, her voice no more than a harsh rasp in the gathering gloom.

"There's no escaped murderer around here," Mark whispered. "What that sounded like was—"

He cut himself off when the sound came again: a low, crunching sound of dirt and rocks tumbling down a hill.

"Oh, shit!" Mark yelled suddenly as he bolted to his feet. "That's coming from the trench! *Shit!* I *thought* it looked a little unstable. I shouldn't have dug under that last bit of ledge."

He ran over to the tent and scrambled around until he found the flashlight. He snapped it on and swung the beam over toward the trench. A thin haze of dust filtered up into the air, sparkling in the light. Without another word, Mark raced over to his work site, all the while dreading what he knew he would find there.

Janie remained close to the fire, watching Mark's frantic activity. As obvious as it was that the problem was in his excavation trench, she couldn't get rid of the idea that this had something to do with the murderer the policemen were looking for.

"Oh, *Jesus!* Oh *shit!*" Mark shouted when he saw the dirt walls of his trench crumbling inward. Looking up at the sky, he shook his clenched fists in anger. Almost two months worth of painstaking, intensive work was being lost in the few seconds it took the dirt walls to collapse and fill the trench.

But when Mark looked more closely, he saw that the trench wasn't filling up! The thick dust rolling upward was as thick as smoke, making it difficult for him to see exactly what was going on, but he was swept by the dizzying illusion that all the sand and rocks were funneling down through a hole in the bottom of the trench.

"Oh, boy! This is fucking *weird*," he muttered as he crouched on the edge of the trench and tried to figure out what was happening. It looked as though the ground he had been standing on all day had

215

suddenly opened up into some underground tunnel or subterranean stream. What it looked like was a huge ant lion trap—those little funnels of sand where the insect in the bottom pulls the sand inward so fast any crawling insects—their food—can't escape, no matter how hard they try.

The flashlight beam projected a thick, yellow cone that swung back and forth along the length of the trench. Choking on the dust, Mark leaned closer, trying to figure out exactly what was happening to his excavation. He didn't see the pair of thin, clawed hands reaching up out of the loose earth until it was too late. Before he could scream, the fingers encircled his throat. Needle-sharp talons sank into his flesh with a tearing, wet sound. Blood spurted out with a whistling *hiss* when the claws punctured his windpipe. Thin, strong arms, scaly and brown, jerked him down into the hole at the bottom of the trench floor where in an instant, a dozen or more arms reached up out of the subterranean darkness and sank into his warm, quivering flesh. Mark's lifeless body twitched violently for a few seconds and then lay still.

"Mark . . .?" Janie called out, her voice trembling on the threshold of a scream. She had seen him fall—or jump—headfirst into the trench; she wanted desperately to believe that it hadn't looked as though he had been pulled in. Every muscle in her body was wire-tight as she eased herself up from the ground. The night closed in around her with a dead, muffling effect as she stared, horrified, at the trench.

"Mark—? That isn't very funny, Mark," she called, trying to find courage in the sound of her voice. In the fading light, the dust silently settled to the ground.

"Come *on*, Mark," she said, glancing quickly behind her, as if looking for the nearest escape route. "If this is one of your half-assed jokes—"

She stopped, freezing into position, crouched beside the fire. Something told her this was *not* one of Mark's half-assed jokes. Something bad had happened. He had fallen into the trench and might have hurt himself. Maybe he was unconscious underneath the pile of dirt and debris.

Slowly, Janie eased into a full standing position. Her lungs ached, but she was unable to take a deep breath. What finally forced her to breathe, at least enough so she could fill her lungs and try to scream, was the sudden burst of noise that issued from down inside the trench.

It was a loud chittering that reminded her of the sound insects make—hundreds of insects, beating futilely against a window screen. It filled the night. While she stood rooted to the spot, Janie watched in amazement and horror as a seething, tangled dark mass erupted out over the edge of the trench.

It certainly wasn't Mark!

The blur of motion resolved itself into a snarling pack of small, clawed creatures only after it was too late. With a final, wavering scream, Janie fell beneath the tearing claws and fangs of the creatures.

– 7 –

"Jesus Christ! I *told* them to get the hell out of here!" Officer Parkman said. He stood by the shredded tent, his lower lip trembling as he shook his head and stared at the mutilated remains of Jane Crawford.

Parkman's partner, Fielding, was standing several paces behind Parkman. His face was sheet white, and he looked like he was about to lose whatever he'd eaten for breakfast. What was left of Janie was barely identifiable as human. It looked as though someone had taken a chain saw to her. Splintered bones, tangled chunks of red meat, and purple-veined internal organs were scattered all around the campsite. Some looked as though huge bites had been taken out of them.

Taking a deep breath, Parkman walked over toward the excavation site where he saw a flashlight lying on the ground near the edge of the trench. As soon as he looked down into the trench, his stomach gave a violent squeeze. Sticking up into the air from the rubble was a single boot. Parkman lowered himself into the trench and bent to pick up the boot to inspect it. When he saw that the foot was still inside it, he screamed and dropped it to the ground. The boot landed sole down. A glistening knob of broken leg bone stuck up out of the torn flesh, pointed skyward. His stomach went horribly sour as he backed away from the trench.

"Jesus *Christ!* How could he . . . *do* something like this?" Fielding

217

sputtered from over by the campfire. After glancing skyward, he dropped to his knees and, with a loud retch, threw up onto the campfire.

Parkman walked quickly away from the trench. Every muscle in his body felt unstrung and ready to unravel. Trembling wildly, he put as much distance as he could between himself and the carnage spread over the campsite. He couldn't stop his hands from shaking as he took the walkie-talkie from his utility belt, snapped it on, and spoke into the microphone.

"Unit four to base. Unit four to base. Come in please. Over."

"Unit four, this is base. We copy. Over."

"Base, we're out at the place where those college kids were digging. We have—" Parkman's throat closed off with a strangling gag. For a moment, he thought he was about to join his rookie partner on his hands and knees, but he braced himself.

"Jesus Christ!" he shouted into the walkie-talkie. "Get someone out here! You should *see* what that madman LeFevbre's done to them!"

— A Micmac Indian tale told around the campfire —

Brother Wolf sat on the rock ledge in front of the den, looking out at the cold, still night. Overhead, the sky rippled with blue starlight which cast a subtle glow over the world. Silence reigned except for the distant hiss of wind-blown snow. Far off, winking like a single orange eye in the night, was Old One's campfire. Brother Wolf's heart grew heavy as he watched the flames, dancing merrily as they pushed aside the darkness.

Brother Wolf shivered and sighed, his breath a thick, moist cloud in the darkness. This was not the first night during this long winter that he had wished he had kept the sun hidden in his den after stealing it from the sky. Its warmth and light would have kept him comfortable throughout the winter. But Old One had known of his theft without Brother Wolf having to tell him of it. And he, unlike Old One, did not have the knowledge to make fire, so he could not have one in his den. Although he could appreciate the fire's warmth, in his cold animal heart, he also feared the flame.

"But I am lonely and cold up here in the mountains," Brother Wolf said to the wind. "I am worse off now because I no longer share the warmth of Old One's campfire on nights such as this."

In his heart was a deeper pain, the pain that he also no longer shared the company of Old One; but he would not admit this, even to the wind, who would whisper it all around the world.

219

Brother Wolf stared at the full-bellied moon, riding high in the sky. Unable to resist the urge any longer, he stretched back his neck, narrowed his eyes, and howled at the cold beauty of its light, as Old One had said he must. His voice echoed in the canyons and was carried away by the wind.

For a long time, he sat thus, baying loudly as his nose pointed up at the moon, following its slow, silent journey across the sky. But after a while, Brother Wolf became aware of another sound—a rough scratching noise coming from behind him, from the far corner of his den. His voice cut off abruptly as he stood, turned, and cautiously sniffed the air.

"Who dares to enter my den?" Brother Wolf asked. His voice rumbled gruffly in the depths of his chest as he tried to pierce the pressing darkness.

For an answer, there came again—louder this time—a scratching sound like that of Brother Mole, digging in the earth. Brother Wolf lowered his head. The muscles in his shoulders tensed as he bared his fangs, prepared to destroy whoever was invading his home.

The den filled with a rough scratching sound of dirt and loose stones being pushed aside. Then, faintly in the angled glow of moon-light filtering into the darkness, Brother Wolf saw the intruder crawl up through a hole in the den floor.

"Well, well, if it isn't Little Brother, my old friend," Brother Wolf said when he saw two rounded eyes glaring at him from the far corner of his den. "And why have you come to visit me?"

Little Brother made no reply as he hunched his shoulders and squatted flat on his feet, his bony knees nearly touching his ears. For a long moment, he just sat there, crouching on the den floor and staring at Brother Wolf.

"Ah-hah, that's right," Brother Wolf said, "I just remembered. When Old One created you, he did not give you the gift of speech."

Brother Wolf cast a wary glance out at the night, down to the winking orange campfire in the distance, and then said, "But I will do for you something even Old One would not do, Little Brother. I will give you the ability to speak. I, too, would like someone to talk to on these cold winter nights. Come—come here, and I will teach you."

As the moon made her slow journey across the sky, Brother Wolf instructed Little Brother in the gift of speech. It didn't take him long to realize that Little Brother would never master the art. No matter how many words Brother Wolf tried to teach him, Little Brother could only remember half of them, and time after time, he interrupted his lesson by saying to Brother Wolf, "Little Brother . . . hungry."

At first, Brother Wolf asked him to be patient, that after he had learned to speak he would have time to eat; but Little Brother grew insistent, and eventually Brother Wolf gave in to his demands.

"Fine, you may leave my den now and go eat," Brother Wolf said, "but before you go, tell me. What do you eat down there in the darkness where Old One has placed you?"

"Little Brother eats . . . many things," he replied in a shrill, chittering voice that sounded most like Brother Bat's high-pitched squeal. "Whatever I find . . . Some, large and furry . . . others, small and smooth."

"It's a pity that you can never enjoy the world as Old One created it," Brother Wolf said. His heart filled with hurt and envy that he, too, no longer enjoyed the world, not since Old One told him his company was not enough to satisfy him. A memory came to him of the night when Old One created Little Brother. He recalled that Old One had been about to say something to Little Brother but had been interrupted when he, Brother Wolf, had come to him after returning the sun to the sky.

"I know, Little Brother, that the sun hurts your eyes and burns your skin, but there is something Old One asked me to tell you the next time I saw you." He lowered his head, cringing at the lie he was about to speak. "On the day he created you, he intended to tell you that all of his creation has been made for you, Little Brother, to *devour*, as the night where you live devours the day that hurts you."

"Little Brother . . . *hungry*," was the shrieking reply.

In that instant, Brother Wolf realized his mistake. Hissing loudly as he bared his fangs, Little Brother reached out to him with his long, clawed hands.

With a frightened yelp, Brother Wolf turned and ran from his den just as Little Brother grabbed for him. A spark of pain, like a flying ember from Old One's campfire, hit the tip of his tail. Howling loudly, Brother Wolf raced down the mountainside and ran straight to where Old One sat, smoking his pipe in front of his wigwam.

"Brother Wolf," said Old One, letting a billow of smoke rise from his mouth until it hid the moon. "It's been a long time since I have seen you, but why are you running so fast and howling in pain? What has happened?"

Panting, Brother Wolf lowered his head to the ground, knowing that Old One need not have asked; he could see clearly into his heart and know what he had done.

"What you have done was not wise," Old One said solemnly.

Brother Wolf looked at him, silently pleading for mercy. He was surprised to see that Old One's face was creased with laughter, not anger; his eyes sparkled like sunlight reflecting off the river. A long, loud roll of laughter came like thunder from his chest as he looked at Brother Wolf in the light of his campfire.

"I know why you laugh at me," Brother Wolf said humbly. "I have been foolish, trying to do the work of creation that is only in your power to do."

"No, no," Old One said. His voice sounded like boulders, tumbling down the mountainside in the night. "That is not at all why I laugh. I can see that what you have told that poor, miserable creature has come back to haunt you no sooner than the words were out of your mouth. I cannot unsay those words, so from this night on, my creation and everything in it is indeed at the mercy of Little Brother. From now on, when he returns to the upper world every five years, he will devour whatever he meets."

"Then why do you laugh, Old One?" Brother Wolf asked, still trembling with fear.

"Why, just look at yourself," Old One said, shaking like an earthquake with laughter. "You are so frightened that your fur, once so sleek and black, has turned gray and wiry. It stands up as though you are in fear. And this is the mark you and your kind must bear from now on for what you have done."

— Summer, 1982 —

— 1 —

"Hey! You don't be doin' that!"

The gruff voice of Tyler Clay's grandfather, coming so suddenly from behind them in the dark barn, made both Tyler and Chuckie Harper, his best friend, nearly jump out of their skins.

What made Tyler's grandfather yell at them was not so much what they were *doing*, but what they were *thinking* of doing. It didn't take much for Old Man Clay, as everyone in the town of Thornton called him, to figure out what these two boys were up to. After all, he had been a rambunctious ten-year-old kid once himself; and on a hot, summer afternoon, what is *any* ten-year-old boy up to after his chores are done if it isn't a bit of trouble? If Old Man Clay had been ten years old right then, he most likely would have been there with them, too, trying to lift the iron grate and see what was down in that tunnel under the barn.

"Geeze, grampa, you scared the be-Jeezus . . . scared the *heck* out of us," Tyler said, looking at his grandfather with fear-widened eyes.

"Meant ta," Old Man Clay said. His scowl deepened as he made his way across the barn to where the two boys were standing. His bad left foot dragged behind him, leaving scalloped curlicue marks on the hard-packed dirt floor.

"Let's get the heck *outta* here," Chuckie whispered harshly to Tyler.

Twin lines of sweat ran from his armpits and down his sides, tickling his ribs. As much as Chuckie liked Tyler, he disliked Tyler's grandfather. The old man gave him a serious case of the heebie-jeebies. Beside that horrible limp of his, which reminded Chuckie of Long John Silver, the old man's left hand was missing two fingers at the knuckle joints. His pinkie and ring fingers ended in little knobs of white scar tissue that made his hand look more like a claw than a person's real hand. If he had lost much more of his hand, he might have had a hook like Captain Hook.

"We was just . . . just checking this thing out," Tyler said, trying his best to sound all innocence. He slipped his hands into his jeans pockets and bounced up and down on his sneakered toes.

"Well, I don't know how many times I have to tell yah, but I want you stayin' away from there," Old Man Clay said. He tilted his head toward the grate that covered the three foot square hole in the far corner of the barn, over behind the cow stalls. Thick iron bars were set in a heavy metal frame that was held in place by a large, rusted padlock and hasp on one side, and twin heavy duty hinges on the other.

Tyler had discovered this curiosity while playing in his grandfather's cow barn shortly after he and his folks first moved to the old family homestead about four years ago, back when Tyler's father lost his job at the National Paper Products mill in Hilton. Tyler remembered asking back then what the iron grate was for and where the stone-lined tunnel led. The answer his grandfather had given him then hadn't quite convinced him, and like all childhood questions that go unanswered, this one had festered until it was close to the most pressing question on his mind. So now, after weeks of talking and planning, he and Chuckie had decided—today—to try to lift up the iron grate so they could get inside the tunnel and see exactly what was down there.

"We were just checking it out. What is this thing, anyway?" Tyler asked. He stared at his grandfather, who was still eying the heavy barred grill.

"If I tole yah once, I tole you a dozen times," Old Man Clay said gruffly. "That there's the poop chute. Used to be used for cleanin' out the stalls. Easier to shovel cow shit down there n' clean it out from the bottom, I guess."

"But it doesn't really look like it would drain out all that good," Tyler said, staring at the grate with narrow-eyed suspicion. He and

224

Chuckie had also checked out where the tunnel came out behind the barn. It, too, was closed off with a similar iron grate.

"I mean, if this tunnel goes straight down here, wouldn't it have to be—"

"'N what d'yah be needin' that lengh of rope for?" Tyler's grandfather asked as if he hadn't even been listening to him. "I hope to Key-rist you wasn't thinkin' about tryin' to go *down* there!" He squinted as he looked from one boy to the other. Chuckie didn't like the way the old man's gaze lingered on him, as though he were sizing him up or something.

"We—uh, well, you remember that ring with the red stone I used to have?" Tyler asked with sudden inspiration. "I—uh, I dropped it down in there just now when me and Chuckie were looking in."

"Consider it gone, then," Old Man Clay snapped.

"Com'on," Chuckie said, taking a pinch of Tyler's shirt sleeve and jiggling it. "Let's get outta here."

"And *you*, boy," Old Man Clay said, pointing a shaky finger at Chuckie. The white nubs of his amputated fingers curled into the palm of his hand. "You don't be egging my grandson on to do nothin' stupid, you understand?"

"I—I didn't!" was all Chuckie could say before sputtering into silence.

"You boys may not've known it, but I was out here in the barn, 'n I overheard everythin' you was saying," Old Man Clay growled.

Flustered and unable to recall exactly what either of them had said, Chuckie took a few quick steps backward. He stumbled and almost fell when the back of his foot caught on the edge of the iron grate. The dirt he kicked up rained down into the dark hole with a soft, hissing sound. It might have been his imagination, but Tyler thought he heard a long, rasping echo sound from deep inside the tunnel.

"You think you're so damned curious to go down inta that tunnel there, huh?" Old Man Clay asked. His usual dark scowl deepened. "Well, maybe I've got a mind to open 'er up and lower you on in. Would'cha like that?"

"No—no, honestly, Mr. Clay," Chuckie stammered. "We didn't mean nothing by it. Honest! I'm sorry if I—"

"Well, then, you just stay away from my barn, understand? Both of yah! Stay the *hell* out of my barn!"

225

With that, Old Man Clay turned and started toward the barn door, dragging his gimpy leg behind him. The boys waited until he was gone before they dared to move.

– 2 –

"When we eatin'?" John Clay Jr., Tyler's father, asked. It was late in the afternoon when he got home from the lumber yard, entered the house, and dropped his lunchbox onto the counter.

Katie Clay looked up from the vegetables she was peeling, let her gaze shift past her husband, then looked back to her work. She hated the way her husband always walked into the house like that, without a single word of greeting, as if she were as much a fixture in the kitchen as the stove or refrigerator.

"Have you heard 'bout what happened?" she asked with a tight tremor in her voice. Using her paring knife as a pointer, she indicated the copy of the Portland *Evening Express* on the kitchen table.

"'Nother kid's gone missing, huh?" Junior asked after scanning the headline. He hooked the rung of a chair with his foot, pulled the chair out, and sat down heavily.

"That's right," Katie said as she wiped her hands on a dishtowel. She turned around and leaned back against the edge of the counter, fighting the impulse to go straight to the refrigerator and get her husband a beer. Let him fend for himself once in a while, she thought bitterly.

"This one disappeared outside of town, somewhere's up near Highland Pond."

"Don't see where that's any concern of ours," Junior said.

"That's three kids—" Katie said, holding up three parboiled fingers. "All boys between the ages of nine and twelve from 'round here—all gone missing within the space of a few weeks! I'd say it's our concern, 'specially considering what happened just north of here in Holland a few years back."

"What's *that* supposed to mean?" Junior snapped. He was starting

226

to feel edgy, wondering where in the hell his beer was. Maybe Katie had forgotten to buy some the last time she was at the store. He sure didn't feel like hauling ass down to Nicely's just for a cold one.

"Well, there was that fella—what's his name? I can't recall. Anyway, he was pickin' up kids from around town and killing them, sinkin' their bodies into the Bog up there." Katie's worried eyes shifted past her husband when she saw John's father limping up the walkway. "If we got some kind of whacko like that on the loose, I think you better talk to Tyler and make *sure* he doesn't talk to any strangers 'round town."

"Sure, sure," Junior said. He finally decided that Katie wasn't about to get him his beer, so he got up and sauntered over to the refrigerator himself. He grabbed a bottle of Budweiser and popped the top on the counter edge. "Hell, Tyler's smart enough to take care of hisself."

"What's this 'bout Tyler?" Old Man Clay asked as he slammed open the door. He dragged his bum leg over to the kitchen table and sat down heavily. Sweat-streaked dirt and hay chaff covered his face, hands, and clothes.

"Oh, nothin'... nothin' a'tall," Junior replied. He grabbed another bottle of beer without asking if his father wanted it and handed it to him. Old Man Clay opened it with his pocket knife and took a long, noisy gulp. Wiping his mouth with the back of his hand, he glanced at the headline in front of him. Dropping his fist down hard on the table, he flattened the folded newspaper.

"Kids!" he snarled, his voice no more than a low rumble. "Goddamned! Gotta be careful as hell 'round about this time o'year!"

— 3 —

"He only told us to stay out of the *barn*," Chuckie said, leaning close to Tyler's ear. They were both crouching on the ground out behind the barn where the back side bordered on the woods. "He never said nothing about us having to stay out of the *tunnel!*"

Built on the side of a steeply sloping hill, the foundation of Old

227

Man Clay's barn was constructed of huge blocks of granite. Out back, from ground level, it was nearly ten feet straight up to the ground floor. Several tall oak trees cast thick green shadows over the boys. Sunlight flickered through the leaves, making the foundation look alive with energy.

Tyler shivered as he studied the iron grating that filled the dark tunnel entrance at ground level on the back corner of the foundation. It was almost identical to the one on the barn floor, but the heavy iron bars of this one were embedded no more than four inches apart in a thick layer of cement that collared the top of the tunnel's mouth. The bottom half of the bars were sunk deeply into the ground. How deep, no one knew; but Tyler and Chuckie were trying to find out. They had dug down more than two feet and still had not found the bottom.

"Come on, Chuckie," Tyler said, frowning seriously. "You know darn right well he meant he didn't want us snooping around in there." He indicated the tunnel mouth with a tight nod of his head.

"Yeah," Chuckie said, laughing softly, "but you've gotta find that precious little ring of yours, remember?"

"You know I was lying about that!"

"Yeah, but were you lying about wanting to see where this tunnel goes?" Chuckie asked. His voice was sharp and taunting as he sat back on his heels and smugly placed his hands on his hips. His face and clothes were caked with dirt.

"Well," Tyler said, looking from his friend to the dark tunnel mouth. "We know there's some kind of tunnel inside there 'cause we've seen it."

"And as far as you 'n me know, this opening here and the opening in the floor up there in the barn are the only two ways to get in there, right?"

Tyler gnawed at his lower lip and nodded. "Yeah . . . unless they ain't even connected."

"'N who knows what might be in there, huh? I mean, what if there's a whole room inside there just around where the tunnel curves out of sight? What if there's a whole cellar under the entire barn, filled with all sorts of neat stuff?" Chuckie lowered his voice with mock awe and added, "This is a wicked old barn. What if there's like treasure or something buried under here?"

"My grandpa told me, the whole inside of the foundation is filled up solid with dirt and rocks," Tyler said. He snorted with laughter.

"And anyway, why would anyone want to bury treasure under my grandfather's barn?"

Chuckie shrugged and said, "Who knows? But don't you think we ought to get inside there and see for ourselves?"

Bringing his hand up to cover his mouth, Tyler shook his head. "I dunno . . . I think maybe we ought to leave well enough alone."

"You ain't going chicken shit on me, are you?"

"No way," Tyler said, shaking his head harder.

"Well, then — get digging. These bars sure as heck can't go all the way to China."

– 4 –

The sun was close to setting by the time Tyler and Chuckie got the hole dug down to the bottom of the frame holding the bars. Both boys were dripping with sweat as they sat back and wiped their faces with their shirts while they admired their work.

"We've either gotta get this thing out of the cement, or else dig down far enough so we can get underneath it," Chuckie said.

Tyler sighed with exasperation and shrugged, thinking either prospect seemed like much more work than he cared for.

"My mom's gonna kill me for tearing this shirt," he said, displaying the rip he'd gotten while leaning against the rough stones of the foundation and trying to get leverage to loosen the grate.

"Yeah, well, just don't tell her how you did it, okay?" Chuckie said. He looked from his friend back down to the hole they had dug. Nodding with satisfaction, he asked, "Think we ought to wait 'till tomorrow, or do you want to give it a try now?"

"No, I think we ought to wait," Tyler said, his frown deepening. Wiping the sweat from his forehead with the back of his arm left a thick streak of mud above his eyes that looked like Indian war paint. "It's gonna be dark soon, anyway."

Tyler didn't want to mention it, but several times while they had been digging, he had heard — or *thought* he had heard — a faint scuffing

229

sound echo from deep within the tunnel. He only mentioned it to Chuckie the first time he heard it. After Chuckie teased him about "going pussy," he decided it must just be the echoes of their work . . . if not his imagination.

"And anyway, it don't matter how dark it is," Chuckie said. "It's gonna be dark as West Hell in there, no matter *when* we go in. 'Sides, we've got flashlights with us. What do you say we do it—*now?*"

Tyler was ready to tell his friend *no* again, but just then he heard the harsh clanging of a cow bell—his mother's signal to let him know it was time to come home for supper. Trying hard not to show the relief he felt, he got up, hastily brushed his knees, and shouted that he was on his way.

"Gotta go. Catch you later," he called over his shoulder as he started up the slope toward the house. Before Chuckie could say anything, Tyler was around the corner and out of sight.

For a long while, Chuckie remained where he was, staring at where Tyler had disappeared. Then his gaze shifted back to the iron grate, the stone-lined tunnel, and the digging they had done so far. It was all well and good that they had gotten a start on this, he thought, but why wait until tomorrow to get in there? What if Tyler's grandfather came out behind the barn and saw what they had done? He'd know in an instant who had done it, and Chuckie knew that gimpy old pirate wouldn't hesitate a second to blame him for instigating the whole thing.

"What the hell!" Chuckie muttered.

Sucking in a deep breath, he gripped the shovel with both hands, leaned forward, and started digging again, throwing scoop after scoop of dirt over his shoulder. With the lessening of light, he found it increasingly difficult to see what he was doing. He considered using one of the flashlights but decided that he didn't want to chance drawing any undue attention to himself.

Darkness seeped in all around him, spreading like an ink stain from the woods behind the barn. Crickets trilled in the field, and the sudden squawk of a night bird sent shivers up his spine, but Chuckie kept working furiously. He wasn't about to quit now—not until he got that damned iron grating out of the way and he could see for himself what was inside that tunnel. He didn't realize there was someone standing behind him until a hand clamped down hard on his shoulder. For an instant, he thought it was Tyler, now finished with supper and come back to give him a scare. When he turned and saw that the hand was missing two fingers, a feeble little squeak sounded in the back of his throat. Tears filled his eyes as the white nubs of scar tissue dug painfully into the meat of his shoulder.

— 5 —

"So, you think you're some smart guy, huh?" Old Man Clay asked.

Before Chuckie could answer, the old man clamped his other hand over Chuckie's mouth. He leered close to him from out of the darkness, letting his hot, beer-sour breath wash over Chuckie. A cold prickling filled Chuckie's stomach.

"So you want to see what's down in this here tunnel, huh? Well, mista' smart guy, looks to me like you're gonna get your wish after all."

Chuckie's eyes were wide open with a fear so strong he wasn't even able to blink as he looked up at Tyler's grandfather. He tried to shake his head in vigorous denial, but the pain in his shoulder spread like fire up his neck. He wanted to speak, wanted to beg the man to let him go, wanted to tell him that he hadn't meant any harm; but the old man's other hand cupped his lower face like a vise, squeezing anything he might have said back into his chest.

"So now—" Old Man Clay said, his voice lowered to a growl. "Why don't you come along with me, 'n I'll show you something you won't *ever* forget!"

With a quick motion that caught Chuckie completely by surprise, the old man spun him around and gripped him tightly in a hammer lock with one arm. For an instant, he removed his hand from Chuckie's mouth, but as soon as Chuckie opened his mouth and sucked in a breath to try to scream, the old man stuffed a crusty handkerchief into his mouth. It tasted horrible. Something sickly and sour bubbled up from Chuckie's stomach into his throat, but the handkerchief forced it back down. Clasping both of Chuckie's arms behind him at the wrists, Old Man Clay pulled his hands up hard, as if he were working a stuck pump handle. A bright bolt of pain shot up Chuckie's spine, exploding in his brain like a fire cracker.

231

"Come along, then," the old man wheezed as he pushed and dragged the boy up the hill and around the side of the barn. With his arms pinned behind his back, his mouth gagged, and his vision blurred by tears of pain and terror, the boy stumbled several times, but the old man wrenched his arms back and forced him to keep on moving. They went around the side of the barn and in through the front door. The rich smell of fresh manure and hay chaff stung Chuckie's eyes, making it even harder for him to see in the lessening light.

"You know right where it is, don't 'cha, boy?" Old Man Clay hissed as they walked down the row of stalls. Several cows turned and looked at them, their sad, dumb eyes glistening in the evening gloom as their tails flicked at the flies swarming around their haunches.

Chuckie worked his tongue against the cloth blocking his mouth, but so much was stuffed inside, he couldn't apply enough pressure to expel it. He thought he was going to suffocate. Inside his mind, he was screaming . . . begging for Old Man Clay to let him go. When at last they reached the corner of the barn where Chuckie could see the dark square that was the iron grate, his knees went all rubbery. He stumbled and almost fell.

"You're gonna learn something not too many people alive today even know about," Old Man Clay said. Chuckling deeply in his chest, he hawked and spit off into the darkness. He released his grip on Chuckie's arm, but before the boy could make his body respond to his mental command to run, Old Man Clay shoved him into the corner of the barn where he blocked any possible retreat. There was a clinking of metal as the old man fished about in the pocket of his bib coveralls. Finally, he produced a ring of keys, which he held up to the fading light while he searched for the correct one.

Kneeling down, all the while keeping his eyes fixed on Chuckie, he felt blindly for the lock. Chuckie cowered in the corner on the verge of bawling like a baby. After a bit, Old Man Clay got the key into the lock, twisted it, and released the shackle. The sound of metal clanging against metal was magnified in the darkness as it echoed in the stone-lined tunnel; but even as the old man pulled the lock away, Chuckie heard something else — a faint rasping sound, coming from down inside the tunnel.

"That might be them comin' already," Old Man Clay said. "Gotta hurry." He sniffed softly with laughter.

Chuckie's entire body went numb as he stared in utter horror at the iron grating on the floor. Whatever was down there making that noise sure as hell sounded like it was getting closer!

"You see, boy, these here iron bars are necessary to make sure what's down there *stays* down there. Catch my drift?" Old Man Clay said. "But you know—I don't think that's the only thing that keeps 'em down there."

Paralyzed with terror and too stunned to cry out for help, Chuckie raised his hand to his mouth and slowly pulled out the cloth. The inside of his mouth was desert dry, so he had to lick his lips before speaking. His voice was tight and high, but he managed to say, "What—?" What's down there?"

Old Man Clay looked sharply at him but continued talking as if he hadn't even heard him. "For the longest damned time, you know, I was losing cows up here in the barn. Oh, not often, but every couple of years, some mornin' I'd come out here 'n find one of 'em all ripped up and half 'et. It took me quite a while to realize there was a pattern to it all, but I started noticin' that things like that was happening just about every five years. Usually in the summer, but sometimes in the spring or fall. 'N then one night, must've been—oh, twenty years or more back, I heard one helluva commotion out here. I came runnin' out 'n got here just in time to see—well, I ain't 'xactly sure *what* I seen, but I sure as Hell saw *somethin'*! Looked sorta like a dwarf, all gnarly and brown-like. It went scurryin' back down into that hole there. First thing next morning, I made myself a couple of grates out of iron. Fixed one into place here, 'n put the other one out back where you was just digging. This one, though, is a bit different, you see. It's got hinges."

Saying that, he stood up and stepped forward, being careful to keep his weight on the grate . . . almost as if—Chuckie thought—he was making sure to keep it down. A warm pressure was building in Chuckie's bladder as he stared at the old man, all the while listening to the faint scratching sound that was definitely getting louder.

"What the hell is *down* there?" he asked. His voice was raw and broken as the old man slowly approached him.

"I haven't the faintest Goddamned clue," Old Man Clay said, smiling broadly. Without warning, his hand darted out like a striking rattlesnake and snagged Chuckie's arm. "This tunnel or whatever the hell it is must've been here since back when my father built this barn," he said as he pulled Chuckie forward. "But you know—I have a theory. Wanna hear it?"

Faint with terror, Chuckie couldn't even nod as the old man dragged him over toward the grate.

"I think this here tunnel goes straight down to Hell," Old Man Clay said in a voice tinged with reverence. "'N I think what I saw out here that night—what's been comin' up into my barn every now and then to kill my cows—is a horde of devils! Demons! You hear me, boy?" His eyes widened and rolled ceilingward with excitement. "I said *demons!*"

A strangled squeak came out of Chuckie's mouth as he looked from the old man down to the iron grate at his feet. He was barely aware of it when his bladder released, spreading warm urine over his pants. The old man's grip on his arm tightened and pulled him relentlessly toward the opening. Once he was at the edge, he placed his toe under the lip of the grate and raised it. Reaching down with one hand, he took the edge and flung the grate open wide. The rusty hinges squeaked in protest as the door fell open and hit the dirt floor with a loud *clang.*

"You see," Old Man Clay said, "I made sort of a deal with these particular devils. Once I realized they only come around every five years or so, I figured when I know they're comin' around again, I could give 'em a little something so's they'd leave me 'n my cows alone. Seems reasonable, and I reckon they're satisfied 'cause I don't believe for a minute they couldn't rip this open if they really wanted to. Actually, one year one of 'em *did* come at me but—fortunately—I had the grate closed 'n he only got a couple of my fingers."

He raised his hand palm out to Chuckie and wiggled the stumps of his amputated fingers.

"But since then, they've been pretty much leavin' me be," Old Man Clay went on. "That's 'cause every five years I send 'em down a little treat. One year it was a sick calf that I didn't 'spect to live. Usually, though, I try to get 'em a person. I find someone who's been givin' me some trouble, and I bring him on out to the barn here."

Without warning, the old man gave a quick kick to the back of Chuckie's knees. The impact knocked him to the floor. All resistance left the boy as he felt himself being pushed relentlessly face-first toward the dark opening. He spread his arms and legs out wide, trying to grab onto anything to keep himself out of there, but it was no use. His hands and feet left deep furrows in the dirt floor; then he felt himself pitching forward into the hole. He reached out and grabbed the far edge of the opening, clinging on to the grate as if it were a

234

DEAL WITH THE DEVILS

life raft as his legs dropped down into the black maw below him.

"*Please,* Mr. Clay," he said as he looked up at the old man. "You can pull me up now."

He was hoping to find just a small trace of pity in the old man's face, but there was none. Chuckie's lower lip was trembling, and he could feel his eyes filling with tears.

"This is just a joke, right? You're just trying to scare me 'cause of what I was doing. Pull me up now . . . *please—?*"

"Please *nothin'!*" Old Man Clay snarled. "You were the one eggin' on my grandson to go down 'n see what's in there, right? So now—"

He cut himself short when they both heard a loud scraping sound echo from inside the tunnel. Chuckie's grip on the grate held, but his fingers were going numb, and he could feel himself starting to slip. His feet scrambled against the unyielding stone of the tunnel mouth, trying to find something to stand on. The effort was futile. Chuckie made a strange, almost animal-like sound when the old man placed his foot on his head and began to apply steady pressure.

"Yup," Old Man Clay said, smiling broadly. "I'd say they're definitely on their way." Standing back, he cocked his foot up and then brought it down hard onto Chuckie's hand. Yelping with pain, the boy reflexively let go and, with a short, raw shout, dropped out of sight.

Old Man Clay moved quickly. Bending down, he grabbed the hinged grate and swung it back over the opening. It clanged shut just as another, louder scream echoed from down below. This one was human. A loud scrambling sound was followed by a burst of angry chittering noise. Chuckie's scream rose shrilly and then cut off abruptly. As Old Man Clay held the grate down with his weight and fumbled the lock back into place, the only sound coming from down below was a smacking, wet chewing sound.

Old Man Clay stood up slowly and brushed his hands on the seat of his pants. A smile creased the corners of his mouth as he stared for a moment at the locked iron grate. Then, nodding with satisfaction, he quickly scuffed out the marks Chuckie had made in the dirt floor before heading back up to the house.

"Well," he said softly to himself, "he was a bit skinny, but I reckon that ought to keep them little devils satisfied for another five years."

— A Micmac Indian tale told around the campfire —

— 1 —

It was midsummer. Hot, heavy breezes blew lazily along the deep forest trails. Overhead, the leaves rippled like green water, turning up their undersides, presaging rain. Far off in the distance, thunder rolled like boulders tumbling downhill. Oppressed by the heat, Brother Wolf was trodding slowly along the path that led to Old One's campsite beside the river with no opposite shore. While still some distance from the camp, Brother Wolf's sensitive nose detected something new, something he had never smelled before. As he got closer to the Old One's camp, he also heard a steady *click-click-click* sound, which both puzzled him and filled him with apprehension.

At the edge of the forest, he halted and, dropping down onto his belly, stared in wonder at Old One, who sat cross-legged on the ground in front of his wigwam, and the strange-looking thing sitting beside him. This new creature was the one making the *click-click-click* sound. After watching them in silence, Brother Wolf guessed that this must be a Human Being, the creature Old One had created so there would be someone who could enjoy his creation as much as he did.

In form, the Human Being looked exactly like Old One, only much smaller. Brother Wolf guessed that he would barely measure up to Old One's knee if they were both standing. The creature's skin was the color of red clay and as polished as a smooth stone found on a river bed. Whereas Old One's hair was white, the Human Being had long, sleek black hair that reminded Brother Wolf of what his own coat used to look like before it turned gray and wiry. The longer Brother Wolf watched this Human Being, the stronger his spite became until, before very long, he was thinking how wonderful, how absolutely exhilarating it would be to feel his sharp claws and teeth tearing and shredding that smooth, red skin. But Brother Wolf knew that he could never destroy Old One's prized creation because Old One could see into his heart and would know that he had done it.

"Don't hide there in the forest like a culprit," Old One called out. "Come and join me and Redman."

Brother Wolf stood up slowly and, puffing out his chest proudly, strode into the circle of Old One's campsite. All the while, Redman sat hunched over, rapidly striking one piece of stone against another. Small sparks flew to the ground with each *click*, making Brother Wolf shy away.

"Do you have as powerful magic as Old One and can create stars to sprinkle in the sky?" he asked.

"Watch," Old One said, nodding his head.

Before long, one bright spark dropped into the small pile of dried leaves underneath the rock. Redman leaned forward and, puffing his cheeks in and out, blew on it gently until a tongue of flame leaped into the air.

Brother Wolf watched in amazement as flames rose higher. Here, indeed, was a wonder! Old One was teaching this creature how to bring down to earth the fire that lights the sky. Brother Wolf's heart was sour with envy as he looked from the fire to Old One and said, "Why do you do this? You never taught me how to make fire."

"You are afraid of fire, as any sensible creature should be," Old One replied after taking a long puff on his pipe. Redman sprinkled more dried leaves onto his fire, then gently placed small twigs in a wigwam shape over the blaze.

Brother Wolf's heart twisted with jealousy. "I have also heard from my brother animals that you have also taught Redman how to carve rocks into sharp points and fasten them to sticks that fly silently through the air and kill," he said. "Why do you do these things for him and not for me, who was your friend long before this Human Being was created?"

Old One leaned back on one elbow, looked up at the red glow

238

of the sunset, and solemnly shook his head.

"Your senses are keen, and your muscles are strong," he replied. "Your claws are sharper than any arrowhead, and your teeth can cut deeper. You have no need for any other weapons."

"But I am curious, Old One," Brother Wolf said, suspiciously eyeing Redman and his fire, which now blazed high into the sky. "Why do you teach him these things?"

"Just look at him. He is naked and weak, and he needs all the help I can give him," Old One said. He drew long on his pipe and blew out smoke until it filled the sky, covering the dark red of the sunset.

"Who is to say that I, too, do not need protection," Brother Wolf said, his voice barely above a low growl. Green jealousy filled his heart and glowed in his eyes. His strong shoulders tensed as he looked over at Redman whose long, black hair was as sleek as Brother Wolf's own fur once had been.

"In the wintertime, I too am cold," Brother Wolf continued. "If I did not fear fire, I would love to bask in its warmth in my den. And there are many creatures who want to kill me, some for my flesh and some for my fur. True, my senses are keen and I am a swift runner; my claws and teeth are strong and sharp, but have you wondered if I might also need more protection?"

Old One laughed so loud the trees around the campsite swayed and almost toppled to the ground. The water in the river rippled and rose high up on the riverbank. Trembling, Brother Wolf flattened himself to the ground, prepared to feel the crushing weight of Old One's anger fall upon him.

"Who—?" Old One shouted between rising gales of laughter. "Who in the world do you need protection from, Brother Wolf?"

"From Little Brother, for one," Brother Wolf said, still trembling with the fear of Old One's wrath. "Every five years, he and his children come out of the caves and feed on me and my children."

"This may be as much your fault as it is mine," Old One said. His eyes glowed brighter than the sunset as he leaned forward and glared at Brother Wolf.

"Be content with what you have," Old One said, "for I will give you nothing more."

Cowering, Brother Wolf backed away from Old One's campsite and without another word, disappeared into the night-drenched forest.

– 2 –

"There he is. That is a Human Being sitting there beside the fire."

"Fire . . . feel hot."

"His name is Redman. He is what you were supposed to look like, Little Brother, until Old One decided to punish you and send you down into the underground."

"He look . . . strong."

"But not as strong as you, Little Brother," Brother Wolf said. "Not half as strong as you!"

Brother Wolf snorted with anticipation as he glared at Redman, then swung his gaze over to Little Brother, who crouched beside him at the edge of the forest. Brother Wolf could smell the fresh blood of a recent kill still dripping from Little Brother's mouth onto his chest and arms.

"Imagine it," Brother Wolf whispered to the creature beside him. "You should be enjoying the warmth of that fire instead of crouching out here in the cold darkness with me."

"Imagine . . . No imagine," Little Brother said, shaking his head. "Hungry."

"He is under your power," Brother Wolf said with a tensed and taunting voice. "Old One made all of creation—except for me—for you to *devour*."

"Yes . . . *hungry* . . . Now!"

"But—"

Brother Wolf knew, deep in his heart, that he wanted Little Brother to kill Redman, but something deep within him also told him that Old One would see clearly into his heart and know that he had put Little Brother up to the deed. Finally, he admitted to himself that he could not withstand the wrath of Old One, so he said, "But we must leave now. Redman has weapons that can kill us before either you or I could get near him."

"*Hungry!*" Little Brother said with a sniffing growl that filled the night.

"No!" Brother Wolf said sternly. "You must leave the Human Being alone. He was made in Old One's image, and we cannot hurt him."

"Not hurt . . . eat!" Little Brother said.

Brother Wolf bared his teeth and let loose a wild bark that startled

Little Brother, who scuttled off into the darkness squealing. Brother Wolf contentedly watched him disappear into the night shadows, unaware that the sounds he had made had alerted the Human Being, who now stood up, notched an arrow on his bowstring, and was watching Brother Wolf steadily as he pulled the arrow back to his ear and took aim. When Brother Wolf turned and saw this, his heart went cold.

"No, don't kill me, Redman," he said. "I am here to protect you. Little Brother wanted to kill and eat you, but I have driven him off."

"You lie," said Redman. "You are jealous of me. I saw it today at Old One's campsite, and I see your envy even now, glowing bright green in your eyes."

"No, that is not true," Brother Wolf said.

"How can I trust you when you have such a lean, hungry look in your eyes," Redman said just before releasing the bowstring. In one instant, there came the slick whistle of feathers slicing the air; in the next, the stone-tipped arrow pierced Brother Wolf's left eye and buried nearly half of the arrow shaft deep inside his brain. Without a sound, he dropped to the ground, dead.

— 3 —

"You may come out of the shadows," Old One said late that night when a stirring of brush awoke him. He crawled out of his wigwam and sat by the door, straining to see in the lingering glow of his campfire.

"Come, come speak to me, Redman," Old One said more sternly. Although he could see into the Human Being's heart, he could only see imperfectly. He knew that Redman was trembling with fear in the dark, but he didn't know why.

There was another, louder rustle of brush, and something silvery slipped out of the forest and into the clearing of Old One's campsite. For a moment, Old One was startled. The earth trembled beneath him as he stirred, unable to believe the testimony of his own eyes.

"How can this be you, Brother Wolf?" he asked. Filling his lungs

241

with the night air, he blew a gust of breath onto his fire, making the flames roar back to life. In the sudden glare of light, he saw what had deceived him. Redman stood there with the bloody skin of Brother Wolf draped over his shoulders. Brother Wolf's lower jaw had been removed, and his face leered sightlessly at Old One from the top of Redman's head.

"This was not wise," Old One said, realizing immediately what Redman had done. "I gave you gifts so you could protect yourself, but Brother Wolf was never your enemy."

"He came to my campsite, sneaking up on me in the dark," Redman said. "When I saw him, he lied to me, telling me he had saved me from Little Brother, who wanted to eat my flesh."

Old One sighed heavily and shook his head.

"Come to me, Redman," Old One said, as he eased himself back into a sitting position. "That is the one thing about you that still amazes me, that I cannot see as clearly into your heart as I can into the hearts of others of my creation. I don't always know what you think and feel." He sighed heavily. "Perhaps it is because we are so alike, you and I."

Redman was silent as he stood at the edge of the firelight, watching Old One cautiously as he patted the ground beside him, beckoning Redman to come and sit.

"Or perhaps I cannot see clearly into your heart because I am getting old and tired," Old One said sadly. "Come and sit here with me. Now that you have Brother Wolf's skin, you have taken on his powers and abilities. You are Shaman." Old One sighed so deeply a moist wind blew over the land. Rain-laden clouds gathered in the night sky. "I had hoped that my gifts would make you kind and wise, but I realize now that I was wrong. Suspicion appears to be the stronger force in the heart of a Human Being."

He leaned forward and, smudging his forefinger with ashes from his fire, beckoned again to Redman, who lowered his gaze as he approached and sat cross-legged on the ground in front of Old One. He wrapped the heavy gray fur tightly around him as though he feared Old One would take it from him.

"This bothers me that I can't see clearly into your heart, Redman," he said as he poked his forefinger first into one of Redman's ears, then into the other. "Among my gifts, I gave you the gift of speech, but from today onward, you and your children will no longer be able to speak with your brother animals. You will hear them, but you will not understand what they say. And this is because you did not believe what Brother Wolf said to you when he spoke the truth."

After he said that, tears for his lost friend spilled from Old One's eyes and carved a new river into the land.

— Spring, 1987 —

— 1 —

As Eric and Patty Strasser guided their bright yellow canoe into Cooking Pot Cove on the Saco River, Eric noticed something swirling in the water ahead of them. At first, he thought it might just be mud, stirred up from the riverbed by the current; but as they got closer to it, the reddish-brown tint looked more like blood.

"Jesus Christ, will you take a look at that," he said glancing over his shoulder at his wife.

"At *what?*" Patty said. Her pale face was shadowed by the wide, straw hat she was wearing. She cocked one eyebrow and regarded him with a sad, sour expression. Eric instantly read her frustration and, not wanting to bother or worry her, indicated the shore with a wide sweep of his hand.

"Why—at how beautiful this place is," he said grandly. "It's even nicer than Carmine described, don't you think?"

"Umm—yeah," Patty said, forcing herself to smile as she stopped paddling and wiped sweat from her forehead with the back of her arm.

Straight ahead was a short expanse of clean, nearly white sand, no more than fifty or seventy-five feet long. Bordering both ends of the beach, like bookends on an empty shelf, were large piles of boulders. Some of the stones looked to be as big as Volkswagens. Beyond the beach, the forest, brooding deep and green, rose up a steep embankment. Inside the sheltering cove, the river was calm,

245

flat and black. It reflected the trees and cloudless sky like a polished mirror. Birdsong filled the clear, late afternoon air.

"I just want to stop *paddling*," Patty said, her voice nearly breaking from exhaustion. She sighed deeply and let her paddle drag in the water behind her. "I have blisters the size of silver dollars on both hands, sunburn on my shoulders, and my back and shoulders feel like hamburger."

Eric smiled sympathetically, then dipped his paddle into the water and gave it a solid stroke. The canoe glided smoothly toward the shore. As they passed though the swirling stain in the water, his eyes darted downward, but he kept his thoughts to himself—even when he lifted his paddle and saw it dripping with a thin, red wash.

"Full speed ahead," he called out as he leaned hard into the next stroke. He could tell by the drag at the stern that Patty wasn't with him on it; now that they were so close to where they were going to camp for the night, she was just too damned tired to do anything else. His paddle blade flashed golden in the lowering sun as he increased his pace, trying to gain more speed.

The bottom of the canoe hissed up onto the sand, and Eric shouted, "All right! We made it!" He shipped his paddle and stood up, bracing himself on the gunwales. Before Patty could even lift her paddle out of the water, he leaped onto the shore and started pulling the canoe further up onto the beach. The sand was warm, almost hot beneath his bare feet.

"There's enough daylight left," he said. "I think we can take a bit of a break before we pitch the tent." He held his hand out to assist Patty onto dry land. Once she had her feet under herself, he pulled her close to him and gave her a tight, passionate embrace. His mouth sought here, and they kissed there on the beach, their tongues darting playfully into each other's mouth. When Eric's hand started sliding down her back to the curve of her hips, she pulled away quickly.

"Let's not get anything started," Patty said. She clasped her arms tightly against herself as she scanned the surrounding woods. A slight shiver shook her shoulders.

Eric shrugged and slapped his thighs with the flats of his hands. "Hey, who's around to notice?" he asked, all innocence. His spirits dropped when he saw the cloud descend behind his wife's eyes. "Hey, come on, Patty," he said softly. "You can't let it get you down so much. It's been—what? More than four months, now. And the doctor said we can try again, real soon." He craned his neck back and rubbed his shoulder as he looked up at the clear vault of sky. "And what *better* place to make a baby than right here, in good ole' Mother Nature?"

"Speaking of Mother Nature, I think I hear her calling my name," Patty said. Just a hint of a smile crossed her lips, and Eric smiled back at her, telling himself—at least for now—that was enough.

"Lady's room is right over there on the left, I believe," he said, hitching his thumb at the pile of rock to his left. Keeping her eyes averted, Patty walked slowly away. Eric watched her until she disappeared behind the boulders.

"No fair peeking," she shouted once she was out of sight.

"Ahh, come *on!*" he said, laughing perhaps a bit too loud at her joke. But it made him feel good, knowing that, while she wasn't exactly swinging from the trees, this weekend away—just the two of them—was definitely what she needed to help her *finally* get over losing the baby. It might have been easier, he told himself, if the miscarriage had happened sooner, during the first trimester; but with only a month to go . . . *Christ!* It was like losing a real person, even though they had never gotten to know him.

While Patty was occupied, Eric figured he'd get busy unloading their camping gear from the canoe and choose a tent site. He went back to the beached canoe, but just as he was reaching in for the canvas bags holding their weekend supplies, a shrill scream echoed in the hollow of the cove.

Eric kicked up fans of sand as he dashed around behind the boulder. He felt an immediate rush of relief when he saw Patty standing there, apparently unharmed; but as soon as he saw what she had found, a cold terror tightened around his heart. He wanted to go over to her, to hug and reassure her, but for some reason, he didn't dare take his eyes off the twisted, black . . . *thing* lying on the ground in front of her. He knew it was dead—that much was obvious—but something about it gave him a queasy feeling of danger.

"You know what that looks like!" Patty shrieked. "What it looks like almost *exactly?*"

She was nearly hysterical as she stood there, looking pathetic with her pants unsnapped and halfway down. The call of Mother Nature was all but forgotten. Splayed fingers of one hand covered her mouth. Her face was chalk white, and her eyes were near-perfect circles as she pointed with the other hand at the dark object lying face-down on the sand at the river's edge.

247

"I don't know *what* the hell it is," Eric said as a tight dryness gripped the back of his throat. "It looks to me like some kind of . . . of animal or something. It's dead, whatever it is."

Walking quickly to the fringe of woods, he picked up a long stick and, crouching low, cautiously approached the dead thing. Patty cowered back against the rock. As soon as he touched it, blackened skin flaked off and dropped like sprinkled pepper onto the sand.

"Looks to me like it's been burned or something," Eric said.

Patty's breath came in sharp, loud sips. Tears filled her eyes, blurring her vision as she watched Eric prod the dead thing. But even as she forced herself to look at it and try to figure out with him what it was, she couldn't stop seeing it as anything other than the shriveled, purple *dead* thing her own body had expelled a little over four months ago.

"That's no *animal!*" she said, her voice rasping like metal against metal. "Look at the arms . . . and those *hands!*"

Eric tried to wedge the stick under one of the arms so he could lift it, but it kept sliding off the stick and hitting against the sand with a soft crinkling sound, like tissue paper being crumpled into a ball. At last he got the right angle, lifted the arm, and held it suspended in the air for a moment while he studied it. The arm was surprisingly heavy for its size. Lean, almost stick-like, it ended in a hand that was broad and flat, like a shovel tipped with curved, black claws. Eric's first impression was of a mole's forelegs, but this thing was the size of no mole *he* had ever heard of. Its entire body was caked with cracked, leathery black skin that looked like the charred remains of a burned log. If it was any kind of animal, it looked like a mutated monkey or something.

Sighing deeply and shaking his head, Eric let the arm drop back onto the sand. Then, bracing his foot in the sand, he wiggled the stick under the creature's neck. After a bit of effort, he managed to prop it up and then roll it over onto its back. The thin arm flopped onto the sand, exposing a thin, compact chest, narrow hips, and long, knobby-jointed legs that ended in wide, flat feet that looked almost frog-like.

But it was the head—the head and the face that riveted Eric's attention. He had never seen anything like it; it was narrow and pointed at the snout, like a rat's with a sloping forehead and flared, pointed ears. Its eyes were closed, but Eric could tell by the bulges under both eyelids that they were large orbs—certainly not the narrow slits of an overgrown mole or shrew that he had been expecting. Beneath the wide, lipless mouth, a row of long, pointed white teeth protruded, again reinforcing the impression of a rat's face. All in all, the creature looked to be about three feet tall. Eric knew *damned* well there were no rats *that* big in Maine—or anywhere!

"It beats the shit out of me," he said as he stood up and backed away from the creature. When he looked over at Patty and saw how close she was to breaking down completely, he tossed the stick aside and went over to her. With a low whimper, she collapsed into his arms, her whole body stiffening.

"*It looks like my baby!*" she wailed, shaking violently as she buried her face in his chest and poured out her grief. "*It looks just like my little boy . . . my little baby who didn't live!*"

– 2 –

"I think we should do something about it," Eric said. "We *have* to!"

He and Patty had worked for nearly an hour, unloading the canoe, setting up the tent, spreading out their sleeping bags, and establishing a fireplace between the tent and the water's edge. They were both too exhausted to get started right away on preparing supper, so they were sitting side-by-side in front of the tent. Eric was sipping on a beer, and Patty was nursing a wine cooler as they held hands and watched the sun touch the lowering clouds on the horizon with vermilion fire.

Patty's grip on his hand tightened painfully, and she was silent as she kept her gaze fixed out across the rippling river. The next breath she took shuddered like faulty bellows and, as much as she tried not to let it happen, tears stung her eyes.

"I mean, we can't just *leave* it here," Eric went on, pressing his point. "We don't even know what it *is*! We've got to do *something* about it! At least bring it to someone who can identify what it is."

"I told you what I want you to do," Patty said, her voice low, no more than a whisper. "I want you to bury it. I never want to see it again because of what it reminds—" She fell silent and noisily sniffed back her tears.

"But it's not like *anything* I've ever seen," Eric said. He was trying to be sensitive to Patty, knowing that, in some twisted way, the dead thing *did* look a bit like an aborted or miscarried fetus, but whatever that creature was, it intrigued him.

"It's clearly some type of animal. As impossible as it may seem, I think it might be something scientists may not even know exists. What if it's never even been discovered . . . until now?"

When Patty eased her head around and looked at him, there was a cold, flat distance in her gaze that disturbed him. He knew damned right well that as much as she might be sitting here talking to him, a good part of her mind was dwelling on when she had lost her baby four months ago.

"And anyway, what difference is it going to make?" Eric asked, suddenly rankled with anger. "I mean, for Christ's sake—I'll wrap the damned thing up in a blanket or something. You won't have to look at it ever again, I promise!"

Patty's mouth opened, but no sound came out.

"I just think *someone* ought to take a look at it, is all" Eric went on. "I know it's all burned and deformed and all. It probably is just some dog or something—but . . . Hey! What if it's, like, one of those U.F.O. aliens? Maybe one of their flying saucers crashed nearby or something."

Patty looked at him, her eyes betraying not even a trace of humor. "I said it before, and I'll say it again." Her voice was steady and measured. "I want you to take the spade and bury the damned thing." She shivered before wrapping her arms around herself. "God! I never want to see that thing—I don't even want to *think* about it! I just *know* it's going to give me nightmares!"

"Well—" Eric said, stiffening his shoulders. "I'm sorry, honey, but I'm *not* going to do that." He heaved himself to his feet, pausing to brush the sand off the seat of his pants. "I'm not about to leave something like this behind. It's too unusual." Looking down at her, he was stunned by the cold distance in her eyes. He turned and went down to the canoe to get the square of canvas ground cloth he had been careful not to put under the tent when he pitched it. "I'll wrap it up and stow it in the bow of the canoe. You can forget all about it. You won't even know it's there."

– 3 –

Firelight flickered bright orange against the pressing night and underlit the draping branches of the nearby trees. A half moon rode low in a sky dusted with faint starlight. Blue light rippled on the water. The sheltered cove resounded with the snap and crackle of the camp-fire while, far off, the sounds of night birds, frogs, and crickets filled the darkness. Huddled in a sweater against the chill, Patty sat on the sand with her arms wrapped tightly around her legs.

"The trick of this," Eric said, "is to get the bark to slide easily." He was sitting cross-legged in the sand, a near empty bottle of beer between his legs. He had a thin birch twig pressed between the palms of his hands and was rolling it vigorously back and forth. He paused repeatedly to check it and then, once he was satisfied, took his jack knife, cut a circle around one end of the twig, and slid the coat of bark down. Then, after cutting an angled notch at one end of the twig, he held it between his thumb and forefinger and placed it on the edge of his lower lip.

"The other trick is that you have to blow v-e-r-y gently," he said. After taking a shallow breath, he blew into the notched end. At first, there was just the hissing of his breath through his pursed lips, but as he worked the bark collar up and down, he eventually found the correct position and produced a high, shrill whistle. As he adjusted the bark collar slightly, the sound went up the register until it disap-peared. Smiling with satisfaction, he held out the birch whistle and inspected it by the firelight.

"God *damn*, I haven't made one of these in *years*," he said. "Not one that actually worked, anyway."

"Boy did that hurt my ears!" Patty said, rubbing the side of her head with the flat of her hand.

"Yeah, that was the thing about these birch whistles," Eric said with a laugh. "When I was a kid, I always thought—you know, like those silent dog whistles they sell, that I could use this to call my dog. But with every damned one of these I ever made, whenever I'd blow into it, my dog would start whining and yipping, and then she'd run away from me." He sighed softly as he took a swig of beer, stared into the flames of the campfire, and sadly shook his head with the memory. "Yeah, good old Trixie. I'll tell you, she was one hell of a good ole' dog."

Leaning forward, he held the birch whistle out to Patty. "Here. Give it a try."

Patty took the whistle from him and raised it to her mouth. While Eric coached her, she positioned the notched tip on her lower lip, slid the bark collar up and down, but after several tries was still unable to produce any sound.

"It makes me dizzy," she said, shaking her head.

"You're blowing too hard into it. Just the tiniest little breath will make the sound. You must've whistled using a blade of grass or piece of paper between your thumbs, right? It's just like that. You have to control your breath."

Patty tried it a few more times but still couldn't get any sound out of the thing. Eric watched her as she worked at it, her face bright orange in the firelight. She seemed actually to be concentrating on it, giving it her best; but there was still a distant darkness, like a glazing of deep ice, in the depths of her brown eyes—a darkness he had never seen there before . . . at least not until four months ago. He also hadn't missed how, when they sat down around the campfire, she had positioned herself so she was looking away from the river, as though just knowing that burned, shriveled, dead *thing* was wrapped up in the canoe was too much of a reminder of other things—things she'd just as soon forget but couldn't.

Finally, in frustration, she handed the birch whistle back to Eric. He slipped it into his shirt pocket before leaning his head back and draining his beer. Glancing at his watch, he said, "Well, it's almost nine-thirty. What do you say we tuck in for the night?"

"Isn't it funny how it seems so much later," Patty said. She twisted around where she sat, letting her gaze shift past the dark silhouette of the beached canoe to the silvery river beyond.

"That's how it is when you get back to a more natural sense of time. And speaking of time, we've got nothing but time, so maybe we could—you know, fool around a little." Eric arched his eyebrows in a wicked Jack Nicholson leer.

Patty scowled. Biting her lower lip, she shook her head and said, "Not tonight—" She hugged her shoulders and shivered. "I dunno . . . I just don't feel—" Her voice dropped away as she looked back at her husband and saw the genuine concern in his eyes. She stood up, went over to him, and, bending down, kissed him firmly on the mouth. His hands reached up for her, grasped her by the waist, and pulled her down on top of him as he keeled backward onto the sand.

They undressed each other slowly and made love on the sand with the campfire warming their skin with its soft, orange glow. Half an hour later, they slipped into their sleeping bags and, contented, drifted off to sleep.

– 4 –

"What was that?"

Patty's voice hissed like tearing cloth in the dark confines of the tent as she reached out blindly and jiggled Eric's shoulder.

"What was *what*—?"

"I heard something," she whispered. She kicked aside her sleeping bag and, on hands and knees, leaned over the dark lump that was her husband. "Something's down by the river, near the canoe."

Eric groaned and tried to sit up as his wife crawled over him toward the tent door. As quietly as possible, she started unzipping the fly screen.

"That zipper sounds like a mosquito farting," Eric said, snorting with suppressed laughter as he rolled onto his belly and army-crawled up to the tent opening beside his wife.

"Shush! Look . . . Down by the river."

Side by side, they lay on their stomachs, staring out at the night. The moon had set hours ago, and the campfire was nothing more than a small pile of glowing red coals. Above the jagged black of the tree line, the sky practically vibrated with dusty blue starlight. The beach sand glowed with an eerie phosphorescence. A light breeze and the faint murmur of the river were all they could hear.

"Maybe you were having a dream," Eric said. He cut himself off when he caught a shifting of motion beside the black hulk of the canoe. At first, he thought it was nothing more than a moving shadow, but his mind instantly asked him what could make a shadow shift in pitch darkness. A shiver danced lightly up his back between his shoulder blades as he peered toward the river. After a few seconds, he noticed more dark shapes moving around the canoe. Then something scratched lightly against the metal side of the canoe.

"What the—"

"I told you," Patty whispered. Her breath was hot against his ear. "Something's trying to get into the canoe."

"Probably just a couple of raccoons or something," Eric whispered as he pulled himself up into a crouch. "They can smell the body of that thing we found and think it's some kind of food."

He looked at Patty but in the darkness couldn't make out the expression on her face. When he looked back out at the canoe, though, he saw another one of the visitors move from the fringe of the woods over to the canoe. As he tracked it, Eric could have sworn it looked like a small, deformed person. The chill tingling up his back got stronger.

"Wait a sec.," he whispered. "I've got an idea." He crawled to the back of the tent, rustled about in the darkness for a moment, and then, grunting with satisfaction, rejoined Patty at the front tent flap. Lying flat on his belly, he propped himself on his elbows and raised his hands to his mouth.

"You might wanna block your ears," he said, and then, very gently, started to blow into the birch whistle.

With the first, high-pitched note, the effect was instantaneous and surprising. The canoe seemed to explode with activity as loud, squealing sounds filled the night. Several animals leaped out of the canoe, hit the beach sand running, and disappeared into the shadows under the trees and behind the boulders. They moved too fast for Eric to see clearly what they were; but within seconds, the night was silent, and the beach was deserted.

"There, you see—? I told you this thing was good for scaring away animals."

"Yeah, sure," Patty said, her voice a trembling whisper, "but what the hell *were* they?"

"I have no idea," Eric said, shrugging even though he knew the motion was wasted in the darkness of the tent. "Must have been raccoons, but they sounded more like foxes, judging by the way they yelped. It's too dark; I couldn't see squat." He decided not to mention the one fleeting impression he'd had that at least one of them had looked—well, almost like a monkey or a dwarf as it shambled across the beach. "I'd better check out the canoe, though, just to make sure they didn't—you know, ruin anything." He didn't specifically mention

254

the twisted black thing they had found, knowing how much it might upset her.

He handed the slim whistle to her and then felt around in the darkness until he found the flashlight. Without bothering to put on his jeans, he ran the fly screen zipper up the rest of the way and crawled out of the tent. The night air was cool on his skin, almost cold. His breath made tiny puffs of steam that instantly dissolved into the darkness as he swung the light around the perimeter of the beach.

"What the *fuck?*" he muttered as he started slowly toward the canoe. In the circled beam of light, he could see dozens—hundreds of tiny footprints criss-crossing the sand. Even to his untrained eye, they didn't look anything like raccoon or fox tracks. Hell! They looked almost like human footprints . . . *tiny* human footprints, as if a whole pack of kids had been out here playing after dark.

"Wha—what is it?" Patty called. Her voice sounded even higher, tighter.

"Oh—nothing," Eric replied. "Everything's cool."

He directed his flashlight into the bow of the canoe, shining it full on the canvas wrapped body of whatever the hell that thing was. To his relief, he saw that the animals hadn't gotten to it; the canvas was still intact. When he trained the flashlight downward, he grunted with surprise to see dozens of scratches on the side of the canoe. And these weren't little digs and dings from paddling too close to the shore. Some of the marks were a foot long and longer—deep furrows that had removed the yellow paint right down to and actually scarring the shiny metal surface.

"What the shit *is* this?" Eric whispered.

He was concentrating so intently on the damage to his canoe that he didn't hear the creatures' approaching from behind. In an instant of blinding panic, once it was too late, he sensed something—*many* things, rushing at him from the surrounding darkness. He heard Patty's shrill scream rip the night as he grabbed a canoe paddle and, crouching low, spun around just as small, compact bodies slammed into him from every direction at once. Low-throated, chittering noises mingled with the sound of clicking claws. The sound reminded Eric crazily of swarming insects. With a strangled cry, he swung the paddle once, smiling grimly when he felt it crack solidly against one of the creature's heads. Before he could swing again, he fell to the ground, crushed beneath their massed weight as long, curved talons sank into him and tore him to bloody shreds. The last sound he made was a long, wavering, bubbly howl.

255

– 5 –

Patty crouched inside the tent, trembling with terror as she watched the seething dark mass of creatures overwhelm her husband. A small corner of her mind was trying to convince her that this wasn't happening—that this *couldn't* be happening; it all had to be in her imagination, a dream or something. But she couldn't ignore for long the testimony of her own eyes and ears. Even after Eric's scream had been cut off, she could hear raw, wet ripping sounds and a stomach-churning crunching that could only be—

"Oh, God! No!"

—teeth crushing bone.

She tried not to think it but knew that those creatures out there were *eating* Eric. She didn't realize she was making a low, whimpering sound in the back of her throat until she saw—first one, then several of the creatures look up and turn their attention toward the tent.

They know I'm in here! she thought, as her blood turned to ice water. *And I'm next!*

She backed out of the doorway, her eyes flicking back and forth in the darkness, wondering frantically if there was something—*anything* she could use as a weapon. Eric always brought along an axe and a mallet on camping trips, but he had stored them away in the canoe after they had made their campsite and chopped their firewood for the night. Suddenly, she was aware that she was still holding onto the birch whistle, gripping it so tightly the palm of her hand ached. It was her only hope. If she could only make a sound with it—just enough to scare those things away—she might be able to keep them at bay at least long enough to get to the canoe and out onto the river.

It was her only hope.

Tears stung her eyes, blurring her vision as she crawled to the front of the tent. Her heart stopped beating for a frozen instant when, through the fly screen, she saw that the beach was deserted. Her hands were shaking wildly as she raised the whistle to her mouth, placed the notched end on the edge of her lower lip, and gripped the sliding bark collar with her thumb and forefinger. She was just inhaling to blow into it when both sides of the tent bulged inward. Loud, frenzied squeals filled the night as razored claws ripped down through the fabric, splitting the tent wide open. The creatures poured into the tent, slashing and scrambling wildly. Before they could snag her and press her down, Patty kicked free of the tangles and propelled herself out into the night.

Still clutching the birch whistle, she ran down the beach toward the canoe. The sand dragged at her feet. With every other step, she stumbled and almost fell, but she forced herself to keep going, knowing that the canoe was her only hope as long as those damned creatures couldn't swim!

Her ears filled with the sounds of the creatures, shredding the tent. She knew it was a matter of seconds before they came after her, caught her, dragged her down and ate her, too. As she ran, lurching toward the canoe, her eyes were fixed on the dark motionless lump lying in the sand next to the broken canoe paddle. Through her stark terror, she tried to convince herself that this wasn't Eric. It *couldn't* be! It looked as though large pieces of him were . . . missing. She wanted to scream, but the night air filled her lungs like flames, searing off any sound she might have made.

She reached the canoe, stumbled, and banged her knees hard against the side. The impact made a resounding *gong*. She shouted as pain lanced like a bolt of electricity up to her stomach. When she glanced down and saw the twisted tangle of black, glistening meat that had seconds before been her husband, she nearly fainted. The sudden barking yelp of one of the creatures snapped her back to attention. They were coming after her.

Digging her feet into the sand, she grunted loudly as she leaned against the bow of the canoe and frantically pushed to get it off the shore. For a terrifying instant, the canoe felt like it was stuck there; then, grating loudly on the sand, it started sliding into the water. Her teeth chattered wildly as she waded into the river, guiding the boat away from the shore. Once she was knee-deep, she glanced back and saw that the creatures had drawn to an abrupt halt at the water's edge. She almost laughed out loud as she dove face-first into the canoe and grabbed the one remaining paddle.

"*There* you *bastards!*" she shrieked. Nearly hysterical, she tossed her head back and let loose a burst of shrill laughter. "Now, you can't get *me!*"

She got down on one knee and began furiously chopping the water with the flat side of the paddle. Fans of silvery spray flew high into the night sky, but lost in her fear, she didn't realize what little distance she was actually putting between herself and the shore. The full impact of what had happened still hadn't hit her. All she knew, all she could admit at this point was, Eric was dead! Killed by those *things!* Whatever the hell they were!

Massing on the shore, the creatures barked and gibbered in a frenzied pack as Patty's wild paddling brought her further away from the shore. One or two approached the water's edge, but as soon as they touched it, they howled and pulled back onto the beach. With just the faint glow of starlight to see by, it was impossible for Patty to see clearly what these creatures were as they howled their anger.

"Yeah, well *fuck* you!" she cried. *"Fuck* you *all!"* Tears coursed down her face, and strong, electric tremors rippled through her body.

She kept slapping the water, unmindful of her progress as the canoe darted wildly back and forth until it finally drifted out of the cove and into the open river. Relief flooded through her, but she didn't dare to stop paddling. Once she knew she was safe, floating along with the sluggish current close to shore, she noticed to her surprise that, in spite of everything, she was still holding onto Eric's birch whistle. She sat forward and slid it into her jeans pocket, then continued paddling wildly. She didn't notice the drifting log in the darkness and was surprised when she slammed it with the paddle. The sudden shock sent the paddle flying from her hands. It landed with a loud smack far out in the water where it was caught up and swept away by the faster current.

"No! *No!"* Patty screamed as she watched in horror as the distance between her and the paddle widened. Fear, cold and bright, gripped her when she looked around and saw that she was drifting toward the shore. Cupping her hands, she leaned forward from the stern and paddled furiously. The water was cold; it numbed her arms right up to the shoulders. She realized the true extent of her danger when she saw several dark, slouched forms moving silently through the woods, tracking her agonizingly slow progress down the river as she got closer and closer to the shore.

This can't be happening! her mind screamed as the canoe glided nearer to the wooded river bank. She couldn't hear the creatures above the splashing sounds she was making, but her eyes were riveted to the woods, where black shadows mingled with the twisted shadows of low-hanging branches. Even redoubling her efforts didn't seem to help. The canoe glided steadily closer to the shore as if in the grip

THE BIRCH WHISTLE

of some powerful, relentless magnet.

Before long, the dark shoreline was seething with the creatures as they followed along beside her. She was crying hysterically, slapping the water with her hands and expecting, at any moment, to hear the canoe grinding on the river bottom. She knew, when that happened, in the next instant she would feel the stinging slash of their claws and teeth.

In a total panic, she brought the birch whistle up to her mouth and blew hard into it. The only sound she made was the shrill hissing of her own breath. Eric's words echoed in her mind: *You're blowing too hard into it. Just the tiniest little breathh will make the sound.*

But Patty was so panicked now she was close to fainting. There was no way she could stop the raw panting of her breath or the trembling that gripped her body. No matter how hard she tried, she couldn't produce the sound that would hold these damned things at bay!

"Please . . . *please*," she whispered, fighting to control her shaking hands.

"Just one little note . . . *please*, just *one!*"

But it was no good. The canoe came closer to the wooded shore, and the creatures were waiting for her. When she was no more than six feet from the shore, a sudden inspiration hit her. The motion almost flipped the canoe over as she lurched to the bow of the canoe and grabbed the canvas-wrapped figure. Struggling to stand up and not lose her balance, she faced the mass of dark creatures lining the shore.

"Here! Is *this* what you want?" Patty shouted. Nausea and fear filled her stomach with acid as she wondered how in the hell she *ever* could have thought that her baby—her poor, lost baby boy—had looked even a tiny bit like this . . . this *horror*. She dropped into a low crouch and began swinging the canvas-wrapped body back and forth to gain momentum.

"One . . . two . . . *three!*" She picked up speed with each swing, and then let go on three. Tumbling end over end, the package and its horrible contents flew through the air. She didn't see where it landed in the woods, but she heard it hit the ground with a sickening *thump*.

"*Take it!*" Patty shrieked. "*Are you satisfied?*"

In answer came a rising chorus of ghastly shrieks and squeals that made her think of a pack of rabid dogs. But she knew these things weren't even close to dogs. Even if the one she and Eric had found washed upon the shore *had* been damaged or burned somehow, these creatures had to be some terrible abomination of nature.

As the canoe drifted under the overhanging branches of a large pine tree, Patty was just beginning to think that her plan had worked; all they had wanted was the body of their companion. But a rustling sound in the trees overhead drew her attention. She looked up into the dark net of branches just in time to see several dark shapes appear out of the night. With low, terrifying growls, they dropped down onto her. Within seconds, their claws sliced her to bloody tatters and then threw her lifeless body onto the shore, where dozens more of the hideous creatures piled down on top of her and began to feed.

Moments later, angling out into the middle of the river, a canoe with blood streaking its sleek, yellow sides got caught up in the swift current and was swept downstream under the moonless, starry sky. Trailing behind it in the swirling water was a small slip of a birch branch with a tiny notch cut into one end.